True Nature

by

Neely Powell

True Nature

Cover Art by *Debbie Taylor*

The Wild Rose Press, Inc.
PO Box 708
Adams Basin, NY 14410-0708
Visit us at www.thewildrosepress.com

Publishing History
First Black Rose Edition, 2013
Print ISBN 978-1-62830-199-1
Digital ISBN 978-1-62830-200-4

Published in the United States of America

Maybe the peace of the church was what did it.
Because that's when I tapped into Hunter.

I felt him moving through the forest. I saw him, his body sleek and black, golden-green eyes glowing. He wasn't running as he had last night, but prowling through the undergrowth, twining around trees, huddling at the base of rocks. Often, he stopped to sniff the air. A low growl rumbled in his throat. The forest was deeply shadowed and growing darker by the moment.

Was this happening now or was it a future event? I had no idea. My mind was spinning, hundreds of miles from the quiet church. But my spirit was with Hunter, and he was stalking something.

Chymera.

I concentrated on the scene in my head. I heard voices in the distance. I saw Shamus. Fraser's loyal bodyguard with other men, close on Hunter's trail. I saw the high-powered rifles they carried. At least Hunter wasn't alone and unprotected. But what was he thinking? He was an alley cat who used his shifting abilities for fun. Did he really think he could battle the monster that killed Fraser?

Praise for Neely Powell

"I'm delighted that Jan Powell has returned to fiction and joined forces with Leigh Neely. Their first paranormal novel *TRUE NATURE* is sure to be a true hit. Bravo, Neely Powell!"

~Erica Spindler, NYT bestselling author

~*~

"Neely Powell writes stories we never want to end."

~Linda Wisdom, national bestselling author

~*~

"I'm excited that a favorite category romance author, Jan Powell, has partnered with Leigh Neely for tales of shapeshifters, ancient feuds and modern-day mysteries. *TRUE NATURE* marks the powerful paranormal fiction debut of Neely Powell."

~Janice Maynard, USA Today bestselling author

Dedication

Though her name is on the book,
this book is also dedicated to Leigh Neely.
Thanks for always believing
we would and could do it.

~Jan Hamilton Powell

~~*~~

Dedicated to my lovely daughters-in-law,
Stacie Hall Neely and Tina King Neely,
and to my treasures: Sam, Jack, Myla, and Caleb
—with love and appreciation,
for all you've brought to my life.

~Leigh Neely

Acknowledgments

We are deeply grateful to Lisa René Smith and the late Linda Houle of L&L Dreamspell for their belief in our work and their faith in us.

Thanks also to Callie Lynn Wolfe, Senior Editor, and the team at Wild Rose Press for unending patience and seeing the potential in an unconventional story.

Chapter 1

I was wet, so cold, I was shaking and furious when I saw the office was dark and it wasn't even five o'clock. Damn Hunter and Darla. I'd been running around in freezing rain tailing a soccer mom to prove her infidelity, and my partner and our girl Friday had left work early…again.

Rain in January in Wayne, New Jersey was damn cold. I stomped to the door and struggled to unlock it with numb hands. I wasn't prepared for the client's wife to sit in the freezing rain for three hours selling candy bars for her daughter's school. She'd been dressed in a lovely designer raincoat and duck boots while I'd been wearing my wool coat and trying to fade into the background in a strip mall with a small parking lot.

I dumped my backpack on my desk as another car stopped out front. Glancing out the window, I realized it wasn't a familiar one and hurried to get my wet coat off and straighten my suit jacket. I ran a hand through my short dark hair, wishing the damp didn't make it curl so much.

The front door opened and a blond woman about my age hesitated, took a deep breath, and stepped inside. She looked around tentatively and finally settled on me.

"Can I help you?" I asked, pressing my gun closer to my side. God, I was jumpy after an afternoon with a

1

soccer mom and her offspring.

"I hope I'm in the right place." Her voice was soft. "I'm looking for Zoe Buchanan, a private investigator."

I relaxed and extended my hand to shake hers. "I'm Zoe, what can I do for you?"

She introduced herself as Elizabeth Baines Howerton. The name rang a bell, but I wasn't sure why. I guided her to the leather chair in front of my desk. She gingerly sat on the edge of it. She clutched her— ironically—clutch purse until her knuckles were white and pulled her legs tightly together. This woman was one taut nerve.

"My sister's missing and I'd like you to find her," she blurted. "I've heard you do well finding missing persons."

I rubbed my hands together for warmth as another chill ran over my body.

"I have had some success," I said. "Have the police exhausted all their efforts?"

She chewed on her lower lip. "No one thinks she's missing but me."

"Why do you think she is?" I asked and wondered if I was dealing with someone a former Southern housekeeper of ours would have referred to as "tetched in the head" or in medical terminology, just plain crazy.

She looked down at her hands and then met my eyes directly. "My family doesn't think she ever existed. I believe I have a sister somewhere who's waiting for me to find her, and my family says it's absolutely not true."

I didn't say anything for a moment, and her gaze never left mine. Her eyes were the purest blue I had ever seen, and she radiated honesty. There was no body language to indicate deceit.

"Where do you think your sister is, Ms. Howerton?"

"Please call me Lizzie." She released the breath I hadn't realized she was holding. Putting her purse in her lap, she raised her hands as if to pray and pressed her fingers against her lips. Tears drifted down her white cheeks when she closed her eyes. She fought against very strong emotions.

"I think," Lizzie said in a trembling voice. "That my sister is somewhere not too far away, waiting for me. I have felt her missing since I was three years old, and I need to find her. Will you help me?"

I like to think I'm a practical person, but more often than not, I solve cases on gut instinct. Something about this woman's simple plea touched me in a way I couldn't explain. Cases like this were why I'd become a private investigator. I like the jobs that don't fit the usual police investigation. This just might be one of those.

"Have you ever seen 'Unsolved Mysteries?'" she asked.

"Sure." Where was she going with her story now?

"I saw an episode of this program recently and it helped me see I'm not crazy for believing I have a sister."

"Tell me about it."

"There was a woman on the show who had discovered she had psychic ability. She kept asking her mother about her sister and her mother kept insisting she didn't have a sister. One day the psychic woman was going through some papers that belonged to her parents and she found a picture of a girl she didn't know. She confronted her mother, and it turned out it was her half-sister, her father's daughter from a long-ago relationship."

"I remember that," I said, knowing I'd seen the show in reruns on Spike network.

The woman became certain that she would meet her half-sister, and the half-sister would soon die. And surprisingly, everything happened as predicted.

"When I saw that episode I thought it was a sign that my feelings could be more than imagination, too."

Anything that involved psychic influences intrigued me, too, for reasons I didn't like admitting to myself. I often thought I just had a PI's good instincts, not psychic abilities. I wasn't like one of those black-clad women who they call in when a child or a spouse goes missing. You would never find me on the cover of a tabloid magazine or on a low-rent talk show. Of course, I knew there were things stranger than psychics—much stranger, believe me—but I resisted the "psychic" label all the same.

Nevertheless, I opened my legal pad and got a pen. Even crazy people deserved an audience sometimes.

The darkness settled outside as Lizzie explained why she thought she had a sister. In spite of my natural skepticism, I was impressed by her absolute belief in this fact. She had been raised an only child, but she was sure she had a missing twin. She had never told anyone until now how often she sensed the sister's presence.

"There have been times when I felt her so close, I thought I could look up and meet her eyes," she said. "I have this scene that is burned in my mind. It's my sister and me, standing on the stairway in our house in London, posing in our white Easter dresses. She's standing right beside me, and we're holding hands."

Lizzie was quiet for a moment. "My father says it never happened, but I can't erase the picture. I believe it did happen, and I believe I have a sister."

With a sudden change in mood, she wiped away her tears and gave a little laugh. "That's why I want you to take this job for me. Becky Miller told me how you helped her find her biological mother. Now I want you to help me."

"Becky Miller's case was a little easier. We just had to get her sealed adoption files opened. My partner, Hunter MacRae, is a family law attorney, and he helped with that."

"I know, but I believe you can help me, too."

We looked at each other, and I realized she spoke the truth. My hesitation evaporated.

"I'll admit I'm interested, but let's start at the beginning? Where were you born?"

Her smile was fleeting but she moved back in the chair and relaxed. "I was born in New Jersey, but soon after that we moved to London, where I lived for three years. My parents lived there for almost fifteen years after they married. My father was the son of a diplomat, and my mother's family has been in English politics for years. They met at a state function. "

"Why were you born in New Jersey?"

"My mother desperately wanted a child. She kept trying to get pregnant without success until she was almost forty. They came to New York frequently and she learned of a friend who had conceived with help from Dr. Charles Hayden. Mommy went to see him as soon as she could get an appointment. It was the early stages of in vitro fertilization and it worked. Mommy stayed until after I was born, then returned to London and—"

I stopped her again. "How did your mother get pregnant over here if your father was in London?"

"She brought it with her. The doctor sent her a container," she said with a shrug.

I was still suspicious. "When were you born?"

"In 1985. My mother told me it was a difficult birth. She wanted more children, but was unable to have any more. Dr. Hayden said at her age it was just too risky to try again."

She looked much younger than her age. Her eyes were animated now and her body pulsed with new energy. She explained that she and her parents had moved to New York City when she was three. As she talked, she was no longer the tense, reticent young woman who had entered the office. Her mousy brown hair even seemed livelier now and her clear blue eyes sparkled with intensity.

"You mentioned that your father dismissed the idea that you have a sister," I said. "What did your mother say?"

"I never found the courage to ask her. My mother loved me but she was a private woman. It was her family's way." She sighed. "I never felt comfortable asking her if we had family secrets. She died recently. Losing her made me realize I had to find my sister. All I have left is my dad."

I cocked my head. Grief did strange things to people. Maybe that's all this was.

"I have complete faith in you," Lizzie said again, her gaze once more steady on mine. "To prove it, I'll pay double your usual fee."

My interest became more intensified. After all, I hadn't billed what I usually did for this month. I'm very practical when it comes to money. It's better to have it than not have it. Besides, a search like this would probably just be going through electronic files and old records, so it wouldn't take much time.

Lizzie leaned forward in her chair. "I'm so sure I have a sister that I'd like to give you a challenge. Instead of looking to find her, find everything you can to prove I'm wrong." She sat back a smug smile brightening her features.

I would probably live to regret thinking "how much trouble could it be?" But I could never pass up a dare. Accepting the challenge, I agreed to work for her. She wrote a check for my retainer and the first week of work. I tried not to feel guilty as I accepted it. After all, I had the option of proving her wrong.

I promised to stay in touch but warned her that my progress might be slow. As I led her out the front door, I felt sure we'd talk often.

I was once again unlocking my desk when I heard a noise from the back. When Hunter and I opened up our practice, we purchased this small, older home and had it renovated. What had been three bedrooms off a side hallway were now offices. The noise came from there.

I listened and went down the hall, pausing at the closed door to Hunter's office. No light showed at the bottom of the door, but again, I heard a light thump.

I drew my gun, then opened the door and flipped on the light. "Don't move!" I stepped into the room.

My eyes met the emerald eyes of the black panther behind Hunter's desk. He looked at me with an expression that can only be described as regal disdain.

Oh yeah, there is an aspect of my partnership with Hunter MacRae that's very interesting and a bit of a secret—he's a shapeshifter, with the uncanny ability to change into any kind of feline form he wishes. I know you're chuckling—what's funnier than a lawyer who can change his form and metabolic make-up at will? Not much.

The black panther was Hunter's preferred form, and he primarily used it to escape a husband who came home earlier than expected. There's the element of speed, of course, and the fact that even an angry husband won't pursue a wild animal if he happened across it in a chase through the backyard. This form served Hunter well.

As I holstered my gun, the air sizzled with electricity and movement, and Hunter became a man— dark-haired, green-eyed and handsome.

When he stood before me in his stunning naked male splendor, I noticed his hands were smeared with blood.

What had he done this time?

"Call the police," he said. "There's a body in the woods."

Chapter 2

A sharp January wind cut through the area behind the office. Hunter thrust his hands in his coat pockets. Thank God he had extra clothes here or he would have been forced to shift back to panther form. Zoe would have to deal with the police on her own. He'd ended up at the office because he'd forgotten to restock the clothes he kept in his trunk. Someday soon, he was going to have to master the magic of keeping his clothes on when he changed.

In the distance, voices called through the woods. It was lit up like midday, with security lights so bright they created a glare. In the darkness at the edge of the woods, beams from flashlights shone through the trees as the police fanned out from the body.

The body. In his head, Hunter pictured the hideous mass of blood and twisted flesh. He had been running toward the office when the smell of fresh blood caught his attention. After years of feline prowling, he had seen his share of dead animals. But never a dead person. Never such a vicious killing.

Zoe had insisted on seeing it herself, of course. She had handled it, although Hunter suspected she'd thrown up when she went back into the office and waited for the police. Hunter was oddly fascinated. There had been a smell near the body. A mark of some sort. It called to his second nature in a way that was new.

Before his mind could stray too far in that direction, he snapped his attention back to his surroundings. He needed to focus. He strode through the yard to where Zoe hovered on the well-lit back porch.

"I hate lying," Zoe muttered. "I'm not good at it. I think the lead detective suspects something's off about our story."

Hunter shrugged. "There are no lies, Zoe. I found a body in the woods."

"While you were in the form of a panther."

"That's not important. We found the body and phoned it in." Together, they had created a story before the police arrived.

"It sounds simple enough," Zoe agreed. "So why did the detectives separate us for questioning?"

One detective had talked to Zoe out here while his partner chatted with Hunter in the front yard. Almost two hours had passed since the police arrived.

"It's standard to split up witnesses," Hunter began, and then turned as footsteps approached.

Detective Michael Scala, homicide cop for the Wayne Police Department, came up the shallow flight of stairs. He had questioned Zoe earlier.

"You guys doing all right?" the cop asked.

"Oh, heck yes, we love spending Friday nights out in the cold with cops everywhere," Hunter quipped.

The detective didn't smile, and Zoe glared at Hunter. He sobered and added, "At least the rain stopped."

Scala squinted up to the sky. "Snow's coming, though. Going to make the crime scene hell to finish processing."

Cheerful guy, Hunter thought.

"Can you tell me again what you were doing in the woods?" Scala asked in an offhand way.

Hunter avoided looking at Zoe. Just like back in seventh grade after being caught smoking behind the dumpster at school, she was probably looking at him like Oh, shit, what do we do now? Good God, even when neither of them had done a thing, Zoe had a guilty look in her big brown eyes. It shouldn't appear that the two of them were telegraphing signals to each other, so he looked away.

"Miss Buchanan?" the detective asked again.

"It's Zoe, please," she reminded him.

Hunter's attention snapped to Zoe. He recognized the note in her voice. She found this guy attractive. He glanced at the detective. Tall. Dark hair. Appeared to be well built. Hunter supposed this cop was acceptable for Zoe in a strong, silent Clark Kent way. He was sharper than he let on, too. It wasn't difficult to imagine suspects and witnesses being fooled into thinking he was all good looks. There could be a quick, intelligent trap behind those eyes.

Taking a deep breath, Zoe said, "I'm sorry, Detective—"

"Call me Mike," the detective said with a smile.

Zoe's expression was glazed, the same look she'd had when she confessed to cheating on her boyfriend in college. This was ridiculous because the louse had first cheated on her repeatedly. But Zoe was a compulsive confessor. Her need to tell what she'd done was well known. Hunter needed to stop her before the handsome cop got her to say too much.

"It was upsetting," Hunter cut in. "Finding a body

in that kind of condition was pretty upsetting to both of us."

The detective turned to him again. "Tell me again why you and Mr. Buchanan were out in the woods."

"We came out of our office and heard a racket in the woods," Hunter replied. "Dogs were barking up a storm."

Scala frowned and flipped through the notes on his pad. "No one else in the neighborhood seems to have heard anything."

"Who else was around?" Hunter asked. This block was all houses converted into small businesses and offices. Most of them are shut up tight by 7:30, which was about when he and Zoe went in the woods, located the body, and called it in.

"A couple of people were working late in the realtor's office across the street. They didn't hear any dogs barking," Scala explained.

Hunter's shrug was deliberately casual. "We did. Zoe and I thought it was strange."

Apparently having gathered her wits a bit more, Zoe added, "We went out to investigate. The dogs ran off. Hunter tripped and fell into the…" She swallowed.

"That's how Mr. MacRae got blood on his hands?"

Hunter nodded. He'd had blood on his paws, and blood remained on his hands even after he shifted to human form. They had needed an explanation for the police.

"Kind of gruesome," Scala noted.

"Very," Zoe agreed.

"You run across much like this in your work?"

Zoe flashed a smile. "I spend most of my time following cheating spouses and checking out disability claims for insurance companies. We don't get many bodies. How about you?"

"Not many like this," Scala retorted as he flipped his notebook shut. "The coroner's crew is taking over now."

"Does that mean we can leave?" Hunter asked.

"Yes. We'll be finished up in another hour or so," Scala said. "We'll be back in the morning at first light."

"I hope you find something that helps," Hunter said. "Do you think this was a homeless person who died out there and the animals got at him?"

"We're not sure what we've got yet."

Hunter nodded. "You have our phone numbers. Let us know if there's more we can do."

"Will do." The detective looked back at Zoe. "I'm sure we'll talk again."

Scala walked away, stopping to talk to an officer who was stringing yellow police tape at the edge of the small yard.

Hunter bent and whispered to Zoe, "I think he likes you."

She punched him in the arm.

"And you like him," Hunter continued.

"Get in the freaking house." Zoe opened the door and pushed him inside.

"Sure you don't want to stay out here and admire the detective?"

"Damn you," she grumbled.

They went through what had once been a utility room, wiped their feet on a sturdy rug, and hung their coats. Zoe groaned as they moved into the kitchen that was now breakroom. "God, what a mess. Why in the hell were you out in the woods, anyway?"

"We kitties will roam," he said, deliberately purring.

"One of these days you're going to get yourself killed running from husbands."

Hunter's grin faded. "Somebody did get themselves killed. In a bloody awful way. I had a hard time backing away from it."

Zoe cringed. Most of the time she was a good sport about his special "abilities." But she didn't like being reminded that Hunter's animal nature meant he loved doing some really nasty things.

A look of horror crossed her face. "It wasn't somebody's husband, was it?"

"I haven't killed any humans. Although I have been tempted to rip out the throats of some of the lowlifes we've dealt with in the last three years."

Zoe moaned. "Please don't say that, Hunter."

"What I felt tonight wasn't pleasant," Hunter said, his expression still serious. "There was something about finding that body. Something completely new to me."

Zoe leaned forward to touch his forearm. "Are you okay?"

He shook his head, trying to clear the disturbing thoughts. He needed to talk to his grandfather about this. Another shifter might be able to tell him why he had reacted so strangely to the scents and the blood.

"It's nothing," he told Zoe. "Let's chill out. Put it out of our minds." He held up his hands. "Even though I washed up after the police got here, I still feel gross. I think I'll grab a quick shower."

One of the advantages of working in a remodeled house was a full-size bath. But Zoe wasn't ready to let him off the hook yet. "One day you're going to end up flayed by a jealous husband or put in a zoo by animal handlers."

"Probably," he agreed, turning toward the bath. "Would you mind making some coffee?"

She was still grumbling when he shut the bathroom door. No doubt, she would continue to curse his activities with married women. If they argued long enough, she'd call him an alley cat, and he'd call her a prude. And on and on. They would never agree.

As Hunter ran the shower and stripped, he considered his proclivity for uncommitted relationships. Was it because he was a shifter? His grandparents had been married for a long time, but maybe most supernaturals had problems with commitment. Other creatures existed, but he wasn't acquainted with any of them.

According to the lore about mythical creatures, the vampire represented the sexual natures and the risk of obsession. Zombies came to be when independence was lost and identity taken. He'd heard that the werewolf was the worst because the monster dwelt within the human and the battle of wills was the fiercest of all.

The shapeshifter was considered milder by nature and could change shapes anytime, while werewolves needed the full moon. Hunter's flexibility made it easier for him to live on the edge.

So maybe he took too many chances. That was his way.

When Hunter returned to the break room, Zoe was drinking coffee, eating cookies, and leafing through a copy of *Out There*, the tabloid Hunter loved because it was devoted entirely to UFOs, shapeshifters, weres, vampires, skin walkers, demons and other things humans found frightening.

"I thought you hated that rag." Hunter poured a mug of coffee.

"I do. But I figured I'd better read up on the current perception of the supernatural world since you are in imminent danger of discovery."

Hunter rolled his eyes and took an appreciative gulp of coffee. Zoe never changed. She always expected him to be outed or eaten or both. She was sure a simple Neighborhood Watch sighting of an "escaped" panther would bring the villagers out with their lanterns and farm implements.

He and Zoe had been best friends since they were thirteen. He had been a skinny, lonely kid, all arms and legs and awkwardness. She had been a tomboy and pretty much an object of scorn to the snotty girls and boys in their private school. But together, they had defeated a band of middle-school bullies. From the beginning, it was like they had an almost mythical bond. Neither of their families provided much affection or closeness, so they had found that with each other. She was still the only person outside his family to know he was a shifter.

People often asked Hunter why he and Zoe weren't together as a couple. There was one time, years ago, when they had explored being sexual together. The "incident," as they called it, ended with laughter rather than consummation.

Hunter smiled at the memory.

Zoe slapped the magazine down in irritation. "I'm glad you think all of this is funny. Are you even the least bit worried?"

"What are you doing here on a Friday night?

Shouldn't you be out dancing in some club or trawling for warm bodies?"

"I don't trawl bars," Zoe said through gritted teeth. "That's Darla's gig, not mine."

Hunter grinned. He was teasing her, as usual. He knew the most exciting thing Zoe had done on a Friday night of late was go to a book signing at the Doubleday Book Store in New York City. If she wasn't reading, she was watching movies. "Spending your nights with the DVR is not healthy. How many times have you watched all the seasons of "True Blood?" Real men are a lot warmer in bed than a movie or a book."

Zoe snorted. "At least I don't see men whose wives chase me through dark streets."

"No one was chasing me tonight. I just needed a quick getaway." Hunter gave a low growl, remembering the freedom of his run. "There's no way any of those old farts could catch a black panther. Seriously, what were you doing here so late? I left at three and I'm sure Darla left shortly after. She always has a date on Friday night."

Zoe sniffed in disapproval, got up and refilled her coffee mug. "I was adding my data to the Corbin file when a new client came in."

Hunter sat while she told him Lizzie's story.

He was slightly confused. "How do you know she has a sister?"

"I just know," Zoe replied.

He nodded. He was used to these feelings from Zoe. It was how she solved most of her cases.

"Plus," she added, "she's paying me double the customary fee."

"Not a bad deal." He reached over and took one of

her cookies. God, it tasted awful, but he was starving. "What about the Corbin case? Did you find out anything we can use?"

"Nope," Zoe said derisively. "If today was a typical day, that woman doesn't have time for an affair. I didn't see her glance at another man."

He stood, threw the half-eaten cookie in the trash, and drained his mug. "Maybe some days are better for her than others, and she only meets her lover on alternate Thursdays or something."

Zoe rolled her eyes.

"I know you don't like Walter Corbin, but he's expecting us to deliver so he can get a divorce on his terms." Hunter rinsed out his mug before Zoe could gripe at him about it. "He's firmly convinced his wife is having an affair. Just do what you gotta do to get proof. If she's not doing anything there'll be no proof. I know Walter's a soulless bastard, but he helps pay the bills."

"And it's not like he's the first soulless bastard we've dealt with. You seem to attract them."

"That's what happens when you're the best divorce lawyer around, baby." Hunter headed back down the hall to his office. "Let's get out of here. How about Pizza 46?"

"Sounds good."

Together, they checked locks and lights and got their coats.

Zoe frowned at him again. "You think the clothes you had on today will eventually get back to you this time?"

"Oh, yeah, Mandy's old man is the dry cleaning king in Newark. He has six stores, including one about two blocks from where they live. They'll be delivered to the office within a couple of days."

Zoe's eyes widened. "You're sleeping with Mandy Morris?"

Hunter laughed as he set the alarm and closed and locked the door.

Zoe didn't say anything more as they made their way to her car. The police presence in the street was down to a couple of patrol cars. Hunter didn't see either of the detectives, but waved to a couple of officers as he got into the passenger seat and pushed it back as far as it would go.

"We're gonna need to get my car after we eat," he said. "It's parked two blocks away from Mandy's place in Eagle Rock. I'll give you directions."

"I remember from the last time we went back to get your car," she said.

"Hey, can I help that her old man is a hundred years old and can't fulfill her sexual needs?" he asked, his face a picture of innocence in the overhead light in the car.

"He's sixty-three and connected to the mob. Maybe you should at least try to time your visits so he doesn't catch you in the act."

"He was supposed to be gone until almost midnight."

She backed out of her parking spot. "Maybe it's time to go out with women who aren't married."

"Where's the challenge?" He patted her thigh. "Even you like a good challenge. Why else did you take on Lizzie Howerton's case?"

Zoe conceded the point.

"While we're back on that subject. Did you know Lizzie's mother left all her money to her daughter? Her husband, who is Lizzie's father, didn't get a dime, and he's contesting the will."

"Damn," Zoe muttered. "That's why her name seemed familiar. It's been in the papers. I knew this case was going to be trouble."

"Yeah." Hunter laughed. "Looks like you've got your own troubles and should just leave mine to me."

****

Hunter loved eating at Pizza 46, which oddly enough was just off Highway 46 in a strip mall. It was always hopping on Friday nights. Zoe and Hunter ordered at the counter and watched for the next table to empty. But it turned out they didn't need the table. Zoe's cell phone rang. Her expression turned grim as she said, "We'll be right there."

The odor of hot pizza filled Zoe's car as they headed toward West Paterson. Kinley Russo was a pro-bono client who was seeking to divorce an abusive husband. Zoe and Hunter took two or three cases a year like this to help them feel more charitable and less cynical.

Even though Kinley had an order of protection and had called the police many times, Eric kept popping up, leaving his young wife frightened and disillusioned about ever being rid of him. Of course, sharing two children with him meant he'd never truly be out of the picture.

Zoe pulled into Kinley's driveway and Hunter noted that all the outdoor lights were on. He shed his coat and yanked his sweater over his head. "Leave the car unlocked, so I can get back into my clothes. I'm going to have a look around and give 'ole Eric a big scare if he's still here."

Zoe headed for the front door with her gun drawn. Hunter kicked off his shoes and scrambled to the shadows of the boxwoods that separated Kinley's house from her neighbor. He shucked his pants and shivered in the cold wind. Almost immediately, his bones began to shift. In his familiar black panther form, he prowled the perimeter of the yard, sniffing for signs of Kinley's husband, but found nothing.

Shifting back to human, he ducked behind the boxwoods when lights from a passing car spanned the driveway. He retrieved his pants from the bushes along with the rest of his clothes and the pizza from the car. He tapped on the front door to the house. Zoe met him, still carrying her gun.

"He's not out here," Hunter murmured as he slipped inside.

"Not in the house, either."

"I told you he was gone," a voice called from behind Zoe. Hunter followed Zoe into the living room to the left of the foyer.

Kinley sat in the center of the sofa, her pretty face smeared with tears, her hands twisting a tissue in her lap. Hunter set the pizza box on the coffee table and spied the bruises on Kinley's neck. Eric was usually more careful to hide the telltale marks of his anger. The bastard was escalating, losing his control.

"Where are the kids?" Hunter asked. "Are they all right?"

"They're at my sister's," Kinley replied. "What the hell was Eric doing here? Didn't you get the locks changed?" Hunter took the chair opposite the sofa.

"Yeah," she said wearily, tears sliding down her cheeks. "But I gave an extra key to my neighbor Wanda in case the kids got locked out. Eric went to see her and cried about how I was treating him, and she gave him the key."

Hunter exchanged a look with Zoe. They had heard about Wanda, who didn't believe in divorce and kept trying to convince Kinley to stay with Eric. "Why in the world did you give Wanda a key?" Zoe said as she sat beside Kinley.

"She is so close. I thought it would be easier for her to get here if the kids got home before I did." Kinley dropped her face into her hands. "He said he was going to kill me if I don't let him come back."

Zoe patted her on the back. "He's trying to intimidate you. Don't let him get to you. We'll change the locks again tomorrow, and I'll take the extra key. You'll give your kids my cell phone number, and I'll come whenever they need me."

Hunter's anger simmered as he saw the outlines of Eric's big hands on Kinley's wrists. Bright red marks were already purpling into bruises.

"Did you call the police?" Hunter knew the answer even as he spoke.

"I couldn't do anything. I came around the corner from the hallway, and he grabbed my arms. He held them down so I couldn't move while he was talking to me."

Her words were choppy, as if sobs weren't far away. Hunter felt like part of the Spanish Inquisition, throwing questions at her before she had time to think, but they were necessary. "Do we need to take you to the hospital?"

"No." Kinley wiped her damp face. "I'm sorry, guys. I hated calling you, but I was really scared this time. You'd think I'd be able to take care of myself by now."

Hunter slipped over to flank her on the sofa and took both of her hands in his. "This is not about you taking care of yourself. You'll be able to do that once you get your new home established. Right now, this is about you letting us protect you while we convince Eric that you're serious. You want him out of your life, and you want to live your life on your own terms."

She nodded in agreement. "Thank you. I don't know what I'd do without you."

He gave her a squeeze. "Take a couple of deep breaths and calm down."

Zoe pulled out her cell phone and took some photos of the bruises. "Just for our records," she said and headed for the kitchen.

She fixed tea and Hunter heated the pizza in Kinley's immaculate kitchen. They devoured the pie, only able to coax their client into choking down half a slice. Hunter and Zoe took several tours of the house, checking closets and under beds, glancing out the windows to see if they could spot anyone lurking nearby.

Both of them talked to Kinley gently, reinforcing what they had been telling her since she started divorce proceedings.

"You're right to do this," Zoe said. "It's going to be difficult, but we'll help you through it."

Gradually, she calmed down.

"I don't know about you, but I don't think I would be comfortable staying alone after an experience like this," Zoe said. "Can you stay with your sister or someone tonight?"

"I don't know… I'll be fine here," Kinley said. "The girls haven't stayed away from me in three months. I was so happy they wanted to go to Lydia's overnight. If I go there this late, I'll just upset them."

"How about a friend?" Hunter suggested. "Is there someone I can call for you?"

"No," Kinley said with a disgusted sigh. "To tell the truth, I've lost all my friends because of Eric. The ones he didn't run off with his nasty mouth got fed up with me letting him hurt me and said they just couldn't be around me anymore."

Zoe jumped in quickly. "I'll stay here tonight." She pitched her car keys to Hunter. "Stop by my place and bring me some clothes on your way in tomorrow."

Kinley protested, but Hunter and Zoe insisted.

"Just grab me a pillow and a blanket," Zoe said, "I'll sleep down here."

"You can sleep in the girls' room," Kinley offered.

Hunter saw the look of dismay on Zoe's face. He knew that Kinley's daughters' room was a vision of pink, ruffles and lace. Worse, dolls and stuffed animals lined every surface. Hunter almost laughed, thinking of Zoe trapped in that room. She hated pink, and thought all dolls were like Chuckie.

He struggled not to snicker as Zoe said to Kinley, "I'd rather stay down here to keep an eye on things."

Hunter left the two women to work out the sleeping arrangements. He halfway hoped Zoe would end up in the ruffled nightmare upstairs. He could tell by her disgusted look that she knew exactly what he was thinking.

"Don't be afraid of the dolls," he muttered as she let him out the front door.

"Go chase your tail or something." She closed the door with a snap.

He laughed out loud and decided chasing something wasn't a bad idea.

As he folded his six-feet-four-inches into Zoe's compact BMW, Hunter's mind and body raced. Maybe it was all the shifting he had done today, but he was revved with energy and excitement. Heading toward the office, he worked out his plans to retrieve his own car and spend the night at Zoe's house. It was too late to go to his apartment in Jersey City.

Was part of the hum he felt from finding the body in the woods? He still couldn't wrap his brain around that idea. He pulled to the rear of the driveway behind the office. The street was now clear of police vehicles and officers. He glanced toward the woods, again feeling a tug of exhilaration.

He'd taken that same route home from Mandy's house three times now when the old man had come home unexpectedly. Her husband was most likely getting suspicious, and that was why he kept popping in early. Probably time to end it with Mandy. He'd sure miss those sweet breasts and long, silky legs.

Going to his office, he quickly undressed and grabbed a bag out of a file cabinet drawer. The flat square with two straps was a small backpack. He could slip it on as a human and it would remain in place while he was a panther. Made from heavy black cotton, it couldn't be seen in the dark. It ensured he'd have clothes and car keys when he needed them.

Hunter had been roaming these woods off and on since he and Zoe opened the practice. He had never seen or heard anything untoward until tonight. Now he felt an uncertainty that was alien to his confident nature. These were his woods, dammit. A low growl escaped his throat.

He needed to go back through the trees and release some of this jittery energy he felt. He could cover the miles at a dead run and get there almost as quickly as he could by car.

Hunter let his body flow into its animal form. What was once so difficult was now as easy as taking a deep breath. Letting out a low growl, he stretched his lithe cat body and bounded out the open window. He stopped to watch the window slowly close, enjoying that he could take care of these little details with his intense mind control. He'd worked hard to learn this element of his powers. His grandfather promised, as he grew stronger he'd be able to do more. Hunter streaked through the night, sticking to back roads and heavily forested areas. He paused at Lookout Point, a park not far from Mandy's house. He padded across the parking area and jumped up on top of the marble memorial that honored victims of the 9/11 attack on the World Trade Center. He looked out over the leafless trees and sleeping communities that led to the Hudson River in front of the majestic skyscraper forest of Manhattan.

The mournful howl of a coyote echoed through the woods. He jumped down, hugging the shadows of the monument, peering into the bare January trees. Was it just a coyote, or something more? Unease prickled his fur. But he wouldn't back down or hide. He skirted the darkened monument and surged into the night, once again feeling powerful and in control.

Almost thirty minutes after leaving the office, he reached Mandy's exclusive neighborhood. His car was in the parking lot of the strip mall where her husband had the first of his chain of dry cleaners.

Keeping an eye out for traffic, he shifted into human form again, removed his small backpack, pulling out the jeans and T-shirt. Near the building and well out of sight of any passing car lights, he dressed quickly, then headed back to the car, shivering. He'd definitely remember to put another jacket in the car.

On the way to Zoe's, he turned up the radio as Neon Trees sang "Animal." He stopped long enough to grab a gallon of milk and three sub sandwiches at a grocery store. Changing twice in one night left him hungry. As he drove, he ate the first sandwich and remembered the day he'd learned his family's genetic secret.

He was sixteen at the time. Summoned to the Manhattan office of his father, Stirling MacRae, he was surprised to find Fraser, his grandfather, there too. The two men had looked very tall and stern, standing together in front of the windows. Though over eighty, Fraser was still fit of form, his hair only sprinkled with silver, his intense green eyes alive with the vitality of a man many years younger. Stirling was striking, as well, but later, when he knew the truth, Hunter had realized that the father and son gave off two very different vibes.

On that day nearly thirteen years ago, the two men looked so grim that Hunter was sure his grandmother was dead. He reacted accordingly.

"Is something wrong with Nana Isobel?" Hunter rushed to his grandfather's side. "Is she sick?"

With uncharacteristic gentleness, the older man placed a hand on Hunter's shoulder and squeezed. "No, lad," he said, his Scottish accent as strong as ever. "Your grandmother is well and happy. I've come to take to you to our home for a while. There are things you need to learn about your family."

Hunter turned to his father for the first time. "What's this all about?"

"Your grandfather will give you all the information you need," Stirling MacRae said. "I've had your things packed so you can leave with him now. You'll take the company helicopter back to the estate."

"What if I don't want to go?"

"That doesna matter, boy, you have to go with me," Fraser said. "Now, come on, I want to get back to the estate before it gets dark."

The "estate" was a house as big as a small town in the Adirondack Mountains. The family owned another estate in Scotland, a ski lodge in Canada, a beach house in Hawaii, and a villa in France. But the Adirondack estate was Fraser's pride and joy. He had it built once he established himself in New York City. As soon as Stirling started taking over the law firm, Fraser and Hunter's grandmother spent as much time there as possible. Hunter had visited for at least a month every summer until he'd become a teenager and found life in the city more interesting. Since then his visits had been brief, usually with the rest of his family for holidays and his grandfather's huge birthday celebrations.

Birthdays were big events in the MacRae family— often with several celebrations. While Fraser and Isobel brought family and close friends to the mountains for birthdays, Stirling took advantage of the occasions to host tax-write-off galas filled with clients and business associates. These were must-have invitations for a certain group in the city. You weren't officially a part of New York society unless your name was on a guest list for a MacRae-hosted event.

Hunter's sixteenth birthday party had been held at the Marriott in Times Square with Cold Play and the Beastie Boys providing entertainment. Even though his father had filled the club with lots of people Hunter didn't know, he and Zoe and their friends had enjoyed an evening of unlimited food, music, and games. Hunter smiled, remembering he'd gotten to third base with Lindsey, his new girlfriend. The brand new Porsche his father gave him certainly aided that conquest. Now he was supposed to leave Lindsey and his great car behind to visit grandparents?

"No way," he muttered angrily. He wasn't leaving the city right now.

"You have no choice." Stirling's face was set in the uncompromising lines that Hunter recognized well.

"It's time for you to learn about your heritage," Fraser added, "and for that, you'll need to be with me."

"But for how long?" Hunter protested. What was this, anyway? An abduction?

Not answering, Stirling moved around his desk and gestured toward the door. "Go on, the pilot is waiting."

It was late evening by the time they arrived at the estate. Isobel was at the door and enveloped Hunter in a breath-stopping hug as soon as he stepped inside. He felt comforted by the scent of fresh roses that surrounded his grandmother. She was the only person in his family who seemed at ease in expressing her affection. His father and mother, even his grandfather, had always felt distant to Hunter.

"Ciamar a tha thu?" Isobel placed her hand on his

cheek, as she asked him how he was in Gaelic.

"I'm fine, Nana," Hunter muttered.

Isobel Ferguson MacRae always spoke to her grandchildren in Gaelic, hoping to keep the language alive with the younger generation. Hunter had learned it to please her.

"I'm so glad you're here." Isobel gave him a firm kiss on the cheek. "I've missed you."

Fraser conferred quietly at the door with Shamus, the aide who was never far from his side. Isobel took Hunter's hand and led him through the vast foyer to the living room. The glass front of the mansion made it feel like the forest that surrounded the estate was indoors. The landscaping had been carefully designed to present an array of plants and bushes with intricate paths throughout so guests could enjoy walking among the blooms and greenery.

"I need to call Zoe." Hunter disengaged himself from his grandmother's grip. "I need to tell her I'm going to be away for the rest of the summer."

Fraser walked in, for once without Shamus, and said quietly, "Tell her you'll be here about six months."

"What the hell will I do for six months?" Hunter shouted. "What about school?"

Fraser grabbed his grandson's shoulders and gave them a strong shake. "You watch your language in my home. You tell your friend you'll be here six months, and you'll write to her. Your schooling will be taken here. That's all she needs to know."

"Write her? You mean, like a letter?"

"Of course," Fraser said.

"What about email?"

"There are no computers available," Fraser said.

"You'll have plenty of paper and postage." He placed an arm around his wife's shoulders. "Go ahead, call. Tell her you'll see her in six months."

Realizing that arguments were fruitless at this point, Hunter snatched up the phone and turned his back on his grandparents. Zoe kept asking questions, and he kept repeating himself. When she asked him what he was going to do about school for tenth time, he'd yelled, "I don't know what's going on, Zoe. I gotta go. I'll send you a letter soon."

She cried then. He felt a pang of guilt and a growing depression.

"I'm sorry, but there's nothing I can do. Tell Brad to stay away from Lindsey. I'll be back before school is out."

She was still crying when she hung up. Hell, he felt like crying himself. With him out of the picture, Brad, his rival for Lindsey, had a perfect opportunity. He had no idea what his father and grandfather had cooked up, but he was pretty sure it wouldn't be fun for him. He went upstairs to his bedroom without speaking to his grandparents. Shamus brought him dinner, but he didn't eat.

The next day he and his grandfather hiked through the forest and up the mountain, pausing long enough to eat sandwiches and drink coffee. For the first time in his life, Hunter knew fear. His grandfather wouldn't talk to him, and he couldn't imagine what they were going to do in the woods. He couldn't have talked much anyway; it took all his strength to keep up with the old man.

He adjusted the straps on his backpack, and felt its weight grow heavier. He wondered briefly if they would spend the night in the damp woods with no sleeping bags and shuddered at the thought.

Around sundown he thought the terrain looked familiar. Soon they reached a cabin he recognized from his childhood.

"We could have driven up here, couldn't we?" he asked. "You'll sleep well because of the walk. You need to sleep well tonight." With no further explanation for that mysterious statement, Fraser went to the side of the cabin and turned on a generator. He came back across the front porch, unlocked the door and led Hunter inside.

Hunter was relieved to find the cabin had been modernized since his last visit, with a nice bathroom, a full kitchen and comfortable furnishings. At his grandfather's direction he stowed his backpack in one of the two bedrooms. The two of them heated canned soup and ate it with crackers, topped off by peanut butter and jelly for dessert. Without being told, Hunter cleaned up. He sensed his grandfather wouldn't tolerate him trying to get out of chores while they were here.

Fraser stood. "Shamus will be up here tomorrow with fresh food. He'll deliver once a week while we're here. Good night, boy."

"Are we going to bed? It's only eight o'clock," Hunter said, astonished.

"There's no TV or games here. If you need something to do there's a good selection of books in the shelves. You might want to take a look at some of the ones about Scottish lore to get yourself ready."

"Ready for what?" Hunter asked dumbly, but his grandfather had said all he intended.

After doing the dishes and taking a hot shower,

Hunter took his grandfather's advice and selected a book from the shelves in the living room. Though he wasn't particularly interested in Scottish lore, there were few other choices. He fell asleep with the book propped in his hands. He dreamed of walking through dark, never-ending woods. He kept seeing the bright eyes of predators in the darkness but they never approached.

He awoke to rain pouring on the roof and the smell of pancakes and bacon. Shamus must have arrived with the food. His grandfather had a plate piled high for him when he got into the kitchen. He sat and drowned his pancakes in maple syrup.

Fraser poured himself another cup of coffee and sat across from his grandson.

"It's time to give you your explanation, boy. I want to you to listen to what I have to say before you make any comments."

Hunter poured more syrup on a new stack of pancakes and shrugged. What were his choices?

Fraser leaned back in his chair. He sipped his coffee one more time before he spoke.

"My great-great-grandfather Thomas MacRae lived in Nairn on the Moray Firth and made his living with the tavern and inn his father had established. Even though he was approaching his fortieth birthday, Thomas was not married. His reputation as a lover was well-known in the small town, but he had never settled down," Fraser said, his lips barely curving in a half smile.

"He loved the sea and was walking along the shore one day when a young woman came toward him. She had the red hair and fair skin of a Scot and the beauty of an ancient siren. She looked distressed, and he immediately wanted to help her.

"She said her name was Deirdre Killin, and she was a widow. She had run away from her brother-in-law, who planned to marry her after his brother's death. She'd never liked him, but was now afraid of him because she'd learned he'd been complicit in her husband's death. Everyone thought it was an accident, but it turned out the ogre brother-in-law had helped things along."

Fraser paused to drink more coffee and take a breath. Hunter continued to enjoy his food, interested despite himself. His grandfather had always been a wonderful storyteller.

"Thomas gave Deirdre a job at the tavern. She could cook like an angel, and her good food brought in more guests. Eventually the two of them fell in love, and they were making plans to marry when her brother and her brother-in-law showed up. Thomas told the men that Deidre would not be going back with them, and it made them a bit angry."

Fraser stood to pour more coffee and milk in his mug, and Hunter put his empty plate and silverware in the sink. As Hunter washed his dishes, Fraser continued his story. "Deidre had told Thomas they were a cowardly bunch and that they'd probably try to catch him unawares. That night he watched from a stool in his liquor closet while the two men sneaked into the back room where Thomas slept. When they walked to the bed to stab him, Thomas crept from his hiding place and stabbed the brother-in-law instead. He turned to stab the brother, but what he faced was not a man. It was an animal, a cat larger than anything he'd ever seen."

"Wait a minute, Grandda," Hunter interrupted, as he set his cup in the drain. "Are you saying—?"

"Just let me finish my story, boy," Fraser said. "The cat growled and pounced. Responding without thinking, Thomas threw his bloody sword in front of him, hoping to deflect the cat's body. Because the cat was almost upright before it jumped, the sword impaled it. Thomas pulled up as the cat slumped and twisted the sword with all his might. The cat fell to the floor in the throes of death."

Fraser emptied his cup again and rose to wash it.

"What happened then, Grandda?"

Turning his cup upside down in the drainer, Fraser grabbed a paper towel and dried his hands, leaning against the edge of the sink.

"The cat fell to the floor and began changing, its body slowly turning back into the body of Deidre's brother. As Thomas stood over it, wondering if he could believe what his eyes were seeing, Deidre came in the door. She went to her knees beside her brother and cradled his head in her lap.

"As she rocked him there, she looked up at Thomas and said, 'I knew my brother's greed would finally be the end of him. He was so sweet, but he was always looking to get rich without working. I'm sure he brought that odious bastard here because he was promised gold. My husband's family had plenty of it.'"

Fraser sat back down and leaned his forearms on the table. "Thomas' greatest fear was that his beloved Deidre could not forgive him for killing her brother. He knelt in front of her and put his hands on her shoulders. 'I'm sorry,' was all he could say, but he said it over and

35

over.

"Finally, she put her brother's head on the floor and went into Thomas' arms. 'It doesna matter, my love,' she told Thomas. 'It doesna matter. He would have me live with that monster.'"

"But what about the big cat, Grandda, didn't Thomas ask her about the big cat?"

"Of course. Her family lived in the Highlands in a remote village. They were raided one night, and most of the men were killed. The women were captured and raped repeatedly. Eventually the warriors left the town and the women and children worked hard to rebuild it without their men. The only men who were left were so badly injured it was months before they could work. The women did all the work to repair their homes.

"Soon it was discovered that many of the women were pregnant. Most of the babies were boys. Everything continued normally until two months after the boys turned sixteen. They all fell into a raging fever and writhed in pain. The local woman who provided what medical care they had was at a loss. Boys were ill throughout the village and no one could help them. Their mothers suffered unbearable agony because they couldn't stop the sickness of their sons and feared they were all going to die.

"On the third night, the boys became restless and fought with their mothers and caregivers, finally escaping to the woods. The women followed, but were stopped when the woods came alive with growls and screeches." Fraser spoke calmly, never taking his gaze from Hunter.

"Soon Scottish wild cats began creeping out of the forest, and the women hurried to their homes to lock themselves and their other children inside. They were terrified the big cats would find a way to get into the houses. Instead, the cats each wandered to a house and lay down on the doorstep, quietly cleaning their bodies and bothering no one.

"No one came into the streets, not being sure what the cat would do. Then one by one, the cats turned back into the young sons of the women who'd been raped. As they entered their homes, once again human, they found their families terrified of them and afraid to let them live with the women and children.

"The boys went to the church, the largest structure in the town, to decide what to do. They knew their lives were changed forever by what had happened to them, and they had to gain control or they'd be run off like wild animals. They appointed a leader and built their own residence. All the boys lived together and visited their families for meals and fellowship. They took care of the town and protected the women from attackers and marauders."

Fraser paused, looking intently at Hunter. After a few silent moments, he spoke, "Are you with me so far, Hunter?"

Hunter couldn't stop his grin. He sure didn't know what the point of this story was, but his grandfather has always appreciated honesty. So he said, "Frankly, Grandda, this sounds like a fairy tale or a video game. It's a nice story for a dark, stormy night."

Fraser took a deep breath. When he spoke, his voice was quiet but firm. "Listen to what I'm saying with an open mind. That's all I ask."

Though a disrespectful retort rose to his lips, Hunter took heed of the older man's serious tone. He didn't have any idea why he had been ripped from his life in the city to walk through the woods and sit in a cabin listening to his grandfather's Scottish lore. But he had a feeling the man wouldn't tolerate any further interruptions. He nodded.

"When the boys became old enough to want mates," Fraser continued,

"they fought the urges, not wanting to inflict on anyone else what had been inflicted on them. Still, the need to mate and procreate would not be dismissed so easily."

Hunter noticed his grandfather's accent became more pronounced as he told the story. He wondered how his grandfather could feel so connected to such a fanciful tale.

"They eventually began to marry and start their own families. With the birth of each girl, there was much rejoicing, but the birth of boys was always shadowed with sadness."

"Did Thomas still marry Deidre?" Hunter asked suddenly.

"Yes," Fraser said. "They were married for more than thirty years and had six children. Two of them were boys."

"Did they—" Hunter stopped, not sure how to go on.

"Their sons were both shapeshifters, just as their uncle had been. When they turned sixteen, Thomas and Deidre took them away and stayed with them until the change had passed. They kept the secret, never letting anyone outside the family know what happened. When the boys married, they waited to see whether they had boys or girls before telling their wives. It occasionally meant they raised a boy on their own, without benefit of a wife," Fraser said. "The birth of a boy didn't always mean he would be a shifter, but it was more likely." He stood and motioned for Hunter to join him. "Let's walk outside for a while."

The woods around the cabin were dark. Though the rain had stopped, it was a cloudy, dismal day, the air heavy with moisture that dampened their clothes. They walked in silence for a few moments, and then Fraser turned to Hunter and placed a hand on the teenager's shoulder.

"Do you understand what I've been telling you, Hunter?"

"Our family has some real skeletons in the closet?" Hunter said with a chuckle.

When his grandfather's face didn't lose its serious expression, Hunter felt a nagging fear begin to grow.

"Our family was forever altered when Thomas and Deidre met," Fraser said. "It wasn't just her genes. It was also what happened when Thomas killed Daniel Killin, Deidre's brother-in-law."

"So he died from the stabbing? Thomas killed both men that night?"

"Yes, and Daniel Killin was a mutant shifter. When he changed, he remained half-human. Apparently, this afflicted many in the Killin family. For some reason, this turned them cruel and cold. Most became vicious criminals who took what they wanted, be it money, land or women. Some, like Daniel, even killed their own kind to get what they wanted. Daniel had wanted Deidre, and he killed his brother for her. "

"But how did that affect our family?" Hunter asked, caught up in the tale despite his wariness.

"Thomas saved Deidre by killing Daniel and her brother."

"The Killins swore a blood oath against our family. It continues until this day."

"A blood oath?" Hunter repeated. He couldn't—wouldn't—believe what he was hearing. He laughed again. "It's a great story, Grandda, but that's all it is, right?"

Fraser looked away from Hunter, gazing through the forest as if trying to choose his words. He squeezed Hunter's shoulder again and looked down, his face a mask of regret and sadness. Hunter was astonished to see tears in his grandfather's eyes.

"Did you understand I was telling you a true story about our family?"

"How could it be true? It was about shapeshifters and things from fairy tales," Hunter argued.

"The stories that survive always have a grain of truth to them," Fraser said quietly. "*A bheil thug am thuigsinn?*"

Hunter froze, starring at his grandfather in horror. "Do you understand me?" the old man had asked in the ancient language.

"Are you saying—" Hunter stopped, unable to go on.

Fraser looked at him levelly and slid his arm across Hunter's shoulders to pull him close for a brisk, tight hug. "It's time to add your story to the tale."

With that, Fraser walked away. He turned back and quietly said, "*Tha thid.*"

Hunter stood in the damp forest, trying to catch his breath, longing to be anywhere but where he was, and frightened by his grandfather's parting words.

"It's time."

Remembering that night left Hunter chilled as he pulled his car to a stop in front of Zoe's cozy house. Snow had been falling steadily for the last few miles. But he'd been lost in memories of that summer night in the mountains, the day of his first change when his grandfather introduced him to the ways of the shifter. Fraser taught him to hunt and to fight. He had encouraged him to run free, to enjoy himself and to pursue his own dreams.

Hunter wondered, however, if there wasn't something more he now needed to know.

He sat in the silence of the car a moment longer. The back of his neck prickled. If he was being watched, would he know it? He got out of the car and sniffed the air. Yes, it was there again, the same scent that had surrounded the body in the woods. Who—or what—was there?

Hunter stood in the cold, listening and waiting, until snowfall began in earnest. Since his first change, he had never felt as human or as vulnerable as he did tonight. He went into the house and locked the doors and checked all the windows.

He didn't like this feeling. Was it fear?

Chapter 3

I jerked awake and sat up. "Hunter?" I looked around for him. Hunter was afraid. I felt his fear. What was wrong?

It took a few seconds to remember I was sleeping on Kinley's couch. Hunter wasn't here. As for him being afraid, I didn't think such a thing had happened since the summer he learned he was a shifter.

"Get hold of yourself." I flopped over on my side but listened intently. The house was silent. Something else had awakened me. Something about Hunter.

He and I shared a deep connection from the start, but lately I had been jolted on numerous occasions by a sharp awareness of him. The time or place seemed to have no rhyme or reason. But it was damned inconvenient right now. I could call him to make sure he was all right, but he would no doubt growl and hang up on me.

I tried to go back to sleep, but it was no use. Being sleepless in Jersey wasn't nearly as romantic as being "Sleepless in Seattle." Because of course, there's no Tom Hanks. After I'd turned over about forty times and switched ends of the couch several times, I decided to quit trying to sleep.

I tried to focus my thoughts on the Corbin case, the rich bastard who wanted me to catch his wife cheating so he could get out of alimony even though he was cheating on her. That seemed to be a running theme in my cases these days. Searching for Lizzie Howerton's lost sister was a nice relief from the usual nonsense I suffered.

In my head I outlined what I would need to get started—a copy of Lizzie's birth certificate, medical records from the clinic, and maybe even records from her pediatrician. I'd call Lizzie in the morning and arrange for her help with as much as possible.

After I completed some legwork and research, I'd see if I could discover something more concrete to support her feeling of having a sibling. Of course, she could simply be crazy. She wouldn't be the first client who wasn't playing with a full deck. I once had a woman who paid me five thousand dollars to search for a poodle I discovered had been dead for three years. My client was ninety-three so I couldn't really hold it against her. I returned her money, too.

But my instincts about this case, which seldom steered me wrong, said something else.

I tried to plan some more, but I'm useless without a pen and paper in my hand or a keyboard at my disposal. Too tired to get up and retrieve what I needed from my purse, I turned my thoughts to Hunter and our earlier activities with the police.

Who was the body in the woods? And why did it feel like a portent of some sort?

Portent? I almost laughed out loud. True, my gut instincts were sharp, but I was imagining things. This was just another adventure courtesy of Hunter's shapeshifting. If he hadn't been prowling through the woods, someone else would have found that body. And I wouldn't have lied to the police.

That still made me uncomfortable.

I tried to empty my mind, but it wouldn't settle down. Getting up, I checked all the windows downstairs.

If houses had personalities, this one's was grim. I felt heaviness in the air, like the house was grieving for its family. I thought Kinley should leave here. Obviously she wasn't thinking that way. It was the only home her girls had known and that made it important to her.

Returning to the couch, I wondered if Hunter would ever settle down with just one woman. It wasn't likely. It's a little easier to tell a potential mate that large noses run in the family rather than "a panther is my favorite form, but I can become any kind of cat you like." In spite of my practicality, I had a romantic side. I was sure there was a woman somewhere who would accept Hunter as a shapeshifter. He was a good and loving man. Of course, it had taken him almost a year to tell me about it. I knew he didn't believe he would find a woman who would accept him.

He'd once told me, "Debutantes don't knowingly date wild animals."

As final exams neared in our senior year of high school, Hunter and I sneaked away for a long weekend in Washington, D.C. The school thought my stepmother was having surgery and Hunter said his aunt had died. We'd both gotten adept at forging parent notes, so we weren't worried about getting caught. His father's administrative assistant adored Hunter and made the arrangements for us.

We went to the wonderful Hay Adams Hotel, and as we watched rain run in rivulets down the window looking over The White House, Hunter said, "Puberty has hit me hard, Zo."

"Yeah, I know the feeling," I said with a grimace. "I have to shave my legs now. I've already got three scars on my ankles."

He reached into the mini bar and got each of us a Coke. "Hair's a big problem for me, too, especially when I get angry."

"At least you have enough to shave." I laughed. "Your buddy, Damon Morgan, still has blonde peach fuzz that nobody but him can see."

Hunter kept looking out the window, his expression somber and sad. I realized he was very serious.

"What's going on? Is it something with your parents?" I couldn't keep the fear out of my voice. "Was that why they sent you away?"

Hunter was good-humored. More often than not, he was the one trying to get me out of a blue mood. He was obviously dealing with something weighing heavy on him.

"They didn't really send me away. I was with my grandfather, learning about the dark secret in my family."

I was frightened. He stood at the window watching the rain.

"What's going on? What dark secret? Do you have a malevolent twin hidden in the attic?"

My attempt at humor fell flat. When he turned, the expression in his eyes chilled me. I wrapped my arms around myself and shivered.

"Zoe, go sit on the bed. When I come out of the bathroom, don't move. You've got to promise me you won't scream or run."

"You're scaring me, Hunter," I whispered. "Whatever it is, you can tell me."

He put his hands on my shoulders. "You're my best friend, and that's why I know I can tell you anything. Please, just sit on the bed and wait for me."

Scared from my head to my toes, I nodded. He headed for the bathroom, and I propped a couple of pillows against the wooden headboard.

When the bathroom door made a slight squeak, I squeezed my eyes shut to delay looking at Hunter. What if he had a terrible tumor or an awful scar I couldn't bear seeing?

He padded around the bed and bumped against the side of it. Taking a deep breath, I opened my eyes and felt them grow wider and wider as my shock reached epic proportions.

A tiger cub stood beside the bed.

True to my promise, I didn't move or scream. I didn't even breathe. However, the thing that mystified me was that I was still looking into Hunter's sad eyes. It was him. I could see him in the cat's face.

He bumped his head against the side of the bed, and I gasped. I struggled for control and my breath was shallow. Reaching out, I carefully touched the top of the cub's head. He blinked but didn't move.

I stroked him and scratched behind his ears like I would a house cat. The tiger's eyes closed and he purred so I continued to pet him. What a pair we made—a frightened teenage girl and a sad little tiger in a luxurious suite of a five-star hotel in Washington, D.C. It was weird but the city had witnessed stranger things.

I smiled, remembering that day. Maybe it was strange that I accepted what Hunter was without hesitation. Or maybe I had already known, somewhere down deep, that he was unique.

Sighing, I punched the lumpy pillow Kinley had given me and stretched out on the couch and fell asleep.

The next morning I heard Kinley in the kitchen and stumbled to the bathroom to wash my face and clear my head. I found a towel and bathrobe waiting for me. I made some order out of my wavy hair and pinched a little color in my cheeks. I came out thirty minutes later ready to face the day. All I needed now was the strong black coffee I smelled as I slipped my gun in my robe pocket.

"Good morning," Kinley said as she set a plate on the round wooden table in the kitchen. "I hope you like your eggs scrambled."

"They're always fixed my favorite way when someone else cooks them." I looked at the small jar she'd placed by my plate. "Are these homemade strawberry preserves?"

"Yeah, the girls and I put them up this summer. They're very easy to make. I could give you the recipe," she said with enthusiasm.

"I think I'm missing the first ingredient," I said with a dramatic pause, "the desire to make them."

I smeared lots of butter and preserves on my toast and sighed with contentment. Here was more proof Eric Russo was an ass with no idea what a true jewel he had in his wife.

"How are you this morning?" I asked.

"Not too much worse for the wear." Kinley showed me the bruises on her arms and neck.

The purple and pink marks would mean she'd be wearing long sleeves and turtlenecks for a few days.

"Are you sure you don't want us to put you and the girls in a place he doesn't know about until the divorce is final?"

"No, I want this to continue to be our home, and he's going to have to accept that."

She moved her food around her plate, but never took a bite. There was a soft knock at the front door. Kinley jumped, and I went to see who was there.

Hunter peeked at me through the lace curtains and held up a bag. I was relieved to see he was fine. My fear last night meant nothing. I unlocked the door and he came in with a whoosh of cold air.

"Man, it's freezing out there this morning. Any chance a guy could get some coffee with cream?"

"Since you brought my clothes, definitely." I dropped the bag on the sofa.

Kinley handed him his coffee and pushed her plate toward him. "I hadn't started on this. Why don't you eat it and I'll fix myself a bowl of cereal. I don't have much of an appetite."

We ate and talked. Hunter told Kinley she'd be getting new locks today—at his expense. When Kinley protested, he promised it would come out of Eric's divorce settlement.

Hunter was slathering preserves on his fourth piece of toast when Kinley and I stacked the dishes in the sink. She wiped her hands with a towel and headed toward the living room. "I'm glad I've got you both here. I have to discuss something with you."

Hunter raised his eyebrows at me as she left the room, but I shrugged. I had no idea what she wanted.

Kinley came back with a legal-sized manila envelope. She pulled the contents out and laid them on the table. "Before I started this whole process, I took some steps to ensure my girls could have a good future—with or without me."

"Don't worry, Kinley," Hunter said. "If we need to, we'll hire around-the-clock security."

"I know, and I appreciate that, but I knew from the beginning that this wasn't going to be easy, so I did what was needed for my girls to get the best care." She handed me one document and passed the other to Hunter. He had to get up and wash his hands so he wouldn't get preserves on it.

"I did this on the Internet. I kept seeing those commercials about getting legal help and I decided to be brave and try it," she said. "Does it look legal?"

I read the details of a life insurance policy that named both girls as beneficiaries and Kinley's sister, Lydia, to oversee the disbursement of the funds. Lydia was the sister closest to Kinley in age, and that was where the girls had spent the night. Lydia had no children of her own so she doted on them.

When I finished looking over the policy, Hunter passed me what turned out to be Kinley's will, which outlined her wishes to have Lydia named as the girls' legal guardian in the event of Kinley's death. "I know you could have done this for me," Kinley said. "But you've already done enough."

"Well, it's legal," Hunter said. "But Eric is still their father. If something did happen to you, he could contest your sister having custody."

Kinley nodded. "I was afraid of that. But she could use this document to state my wishes, couldn't she?"

"Of course," Hunter agreed, but he couldn't lie to her. "But he might get custody anyway."

Kinley held his gaze. "I just didn't want any doubt about what I wanted for my daughters." Sitting quietly, she gazed out the window of her sweet little suburban kitchen and fought tears. "Eric loves the girls. He just isn't very patient. Maybe I bring out the worst in him."

"Don't say that," I was furious she blamed herself. "He's a bully and an abuser."

"You're right. He's just following his mother's example of what a family should be. She was a tyrant, totally overshadowing his father when Eric was a child. Her advice to Eric on our wedding day was to 'make sure she knows who's in charge.' He took it to heart."

I grimaced at the sweet honesty in her words. It was her world, and she had come to grips with it and realized she could take control of it. I looked up at Hunter. I was sure he was thinking the same thing.

He confirmed that when he said, "We'll do everything we can to make sure your wishes are carried out exactly as you want." He took Kinley's hand into both of his. "Right now, we're going to make sure you're safe."

She gave him a sad smile. "Thanks, but you can't be with me twenty-four hours a day. I also know a lot of this depends on my own determination, and, by God, I'm as determined as hell to be strong and independent. I want to rescue myself."

She was such a little thing, and she had such aspirations. Would we be able to help her achieve them?

I shivered as another one of those feelings—another portent?—moved over me.

Chapter 4

A locksmith and his assistant made quick work of Kinley's front, back, and garage doors. Then Hunter and Zoe talked Kinley into joining her daughters at her sister's house. If Eric decided to return, she'd be gone, safely stowed for the weekend.

About eleven-thirty, Hunter pulled to a stop beside Zoe's car. Crime scene tape was plainly visible in the woods, bright yellow against the snow and the bare winter trees. It wasn't difficult for Hunter to relive the scene he had happened upon last night.

"Something wrong?" Zoe asked as she reached for the passenger door handle.

Hunter forced last night's carnage from his mind and teased her, "I wonder if the handsome Detective Scala will be showing up to interview you again. Maybe you'll get lucky."

"No." She was emphatic. "I want him to stay the hell away. I don't like lying to anyone, much less the police."

"So you'd turn him down if he called?"

She started to speak, then gave a reluctant laugh. "Well, it's against my better judgment, but I'd probably go out with him."

"Why don't you call him?"

Not bothering to answer, she opened the car door. "I'm going to spend the afternoon tailing our hospital

CEO's lovely wife. I'd like to put this case to bed."

Hunter's cell phone rang. He chuckled as he recognized Mandy's number. "Speaking of bed."

Predictably, Zoe got out and slammed the door. Hunter laughed. "Hey, beautiful lady."

Mandy's sweet voice purred, "Just wanted to make sure you're okay, you naughty boy."

"I made a clean getaway."

"Without your clothes?"

"I'm a man of many talents."

"Don't I know it," Mandy replied.

Hunter laughed again. "You're very talented yourself. I'm thinking we need an encore performance. I'm free now." The thoughts he'd had last night of breaking it off with Mandy didn't seem so compelling today.

"Sorry, young stud, but Charlie is due in from golf any minute. He doesn't have another late-night meeting until next Wednesday."

"You can come to my place later. I'll make my famous grilled-chicken salad and homemade Russian dressing."

"You do know how to tempt me." Mandy gave a low chuckle. "But whatever would I tell my dear husband?"

"What time does he turn in for the night?"

"Usually around ten o'clock. What do you have in mind?"

"Dessert with lots of whipped cream in my apartment at ten-thirty?"

"How can a girl resist an offer like that? See you later."

Hunter slipped his phone back into his pocket,

content to anticipate the coming attractions. He shifted his car into reverse and pulled out of the office drive. He imagined Zoe glaring out a window at him.

He knew Zoe thought he just jumped from one bed to another to satisfy his own whims. The truth was he loved women, all of them. He'd once had a fling with a voluptuous client whose husband was divorcing her because she had gained weight. To Hunter, she was a gorgeous woman with soft curves and lush, natural breasts. All and all, a wonderful experience, enjoyed by both of them. Remembering, he gave a low growl and hit the CD button. Matthew Sweets' "The Big Cats of Shambala" blasted through the car.

It was cold but beautiful outside. Perfect for a run. He headed through Wayne to Hamburg Turnpike and Wayne Paterson University. Just outside the campus was the High Mountain Park Preserve. He knew there would be some hikers today, but with the cold weather and wind, maybe he'd be able to run unnoticed. The area protected a great many wildlife species, so no one would be surprised to see a bobcat streaking through the trees.

But first he needed to fuel up. Despite the meal at Kinley's, he was still hungry. It happened that way after changing as he had last night. He needed a quick hit of sugar and caffeine. At the doughnut shop on Valley Road, he slid into a parking slot. He stopped here several times a week. Already salivating at the thought of a quick half dozen of glazed and filled heaven, he grunted as his phone beeped. He checked the read-out and was surprised to see it was his grandfather.

"Grandda?" he answered.

"I'll never get used to everyone knowing who's

calling," the older man replied. "Time was you could surprise someone on the phone."

"It's a new world."

"Aye, but not necessarily better."

They chatted for a few moments. Hunter was tempted to tell Fraser about the body in the woods and the strange feeling of being watched. He knew, however, that Fraser would not discuss such things over the telephone because he didn't believe phones were secure enough for some types of conversations.

In fact, his grandfather didn't call very often. After the summer Hunter had changed for the first time, Fraser gave him a lot of training in the ways of shifting. But as Hunter became an adult, his grandfather had let him lead his own life. Fraser never placed any pressure on Hunter to join the family firm. As arguments raged between Hunter and his parents, Fraser had always been on Hunter's side. Since the two of them were the family shapeshifters, Hunter felt his grandfather understood the need for freedom and making his own way.

"I'd like to see you," Fraser said.

"I can come up to see you and Nana in a few weeks. Maybe bring Zoe—"

"I need to see you soon." Fraser's tone had shifted. "It's important."

"What's wrong?"

There was a heavy sigh. "There are things we need to discuss."

Hunter frowned. "What is it?"

"I'm not ready to talk now. I'm coming to the city on Tuesday. I'll see you at the offices for lunch."

"I can check my schedule."

"You will be there." Fraser hadn't talked this way

to Hunter in a long time.

So Hunter agreed, although he remained puzzled. "Is this business or family?"

"We'll talk Tuesday." Fraser cleared his throat. "I hope you're being careful."

"What do you mean?"

"With your abilities," Fraser said, his tone guarded. "You must respect who we are."

"Grandda, I really need to know what this is about, but—"

"Just be careful." Fraser clicked off the line.

Hunter stared down at the phone. The body and what he'd been feeling were connected to this, he was sure. It wasn't like his grandfather to warn him that way. Fraser had taught Hunter how to protect the secret they shared and how to protect himself. Why the sudden concern?

He pushed through the door of the doughnut shop. Instantly, his senses went to full alert. His nostrils flared as he caught a scent. Of her.

The red-haired woman sat at a table facing the door, sipping coffee and working at a laptop. It wasn't the first time he had seen her here. Several times over the past weeks, he had detected her scent despite the overhanging aromas of deep-fried sugar and rich coffee. She smelled like herbal soap and body lotion, undercut by the outdoors, and a trace of something wild.

Today, she was dressed in her usual jeans, with sturdy hiking boots tucked under the table. They were scuffed but in good shape, the mark of a regular hiker. She wore a flannel shirt over a thermal undershirt. Her heavy fall of vibrant hair was scooped back in a long ponytail. A thick curl just brushed her shoulder. She shouldn't appeal to him. This outfit was pretty much her standard uniform. And he usually liked his women expertly made up and wearing sleek, sexy clothes. But there was something about her.

She glanced up. A tiny smile curved her lips. Their gazes met, and she didn't look away.

Hunter's body responded immediately. He grinned, then went to the counter for coffee and doughnuts. Once he had his order, he headed straight to her table. She watched him approach with an amused expression.

"Good hike?" he asked.

She cocked an eyebrow at him.

"Your boots give you away," he replied by way of explanation. "I've seen you in here before. I hike nearby, too."

Her dark brown eyes crinkled at the corners as she returned his smile. "Yes, I've seen you before, too."

He waved his coffee cup toward the empty seat at her table. "Can I join you?"

"Sure." She clicked a few keys on her computer before closing the screen. "Are you headed into the woods today?" she asked.

"Depends…" Hunter bit into a cream-filled confection.

"On what?"

He swallowed. "You mostly."

"I really don't see how I could possibly figure into your plans," she drawled.

"You just need to use a little imagination." It was a short stretch for Hunter to imagine what he wanted to do with this nature-loving redhead. "We could head into the woods. Together."

She laughed, a throaty sound. "I've read 'Little

Red Riding Hood.' I don't mess around with wolves."

Hunter enjoyed her honesty. "I'm just a big pussy cat. I would never try to take away your goodies like the wolf did."

"That's great, because I take care of my goodies."

He laughed again. "You can trust me. Look, no fangs or nasty claws." He wiggled his fingers for her.

"My mamma taught me never to go in the woods with a strange man."

"Then let's not be strangers." Hunter brushed sugar off his fingers with a napkin, extended his hand and introduced himself. "I live in Jersey City but my law office is in Wayne, so I like to come up here and take a break occasionally."

She eyed him skeptically, then took his hand. "I'm Cynthia Donelson. My friends call me Cyn."

"Sin," he said with a low laugh. "I definitely want to be one of your friends."

"That's spelled C-Y-N," she said, her eyes darkening as she looked into his.

"Still, a good name."

She pulled her hand from his, but he sensed her reluctance. However, he scented the slight tang of pheromones.

"I think I've seen your law firm advertised," she said.

"We do some ads in the local paper. What do you do?"

"I'm a writer, working on a new book."

"Truth or fiction?"

"Depends on who you ask. I'm doing research on the New Jersey Devil."

Hunter couldn't have been more surprised. The

New Jersey Devil had been a creature of legend in this state for more than 250 years. Supposedly, he had been born cruelly deformed and hidden by his parents until the day he sprouted wings and flew away. Since then, there had been frequent sightings of the demonic creature with the pointed ears, hoofed feet, and a long tail. As much as Hunter had roamed the woods, he had never happened upon the Devil. But who was he to disbelieve the existence of a fellow mythical beast?

He didn't blink at Cyn. "Are you finding much evidence?"

"There's plenty in the public record," she replied.

"Lately?"

"Some odd reports of activity in the forest."

He shifted in his chair, thinking of his grandfather's warning. He studied Cyn a bit closer, but her expression was bland. It was rare to hear someone admit so freely to a belief in the supernatural, but he certainly wouldn't argue the point.

"Animals have been stirred up as of late. Surely you've heard reports of bears and coyotes attacking people in the open. It's like something is up that humans don't know about."

"Do you think that's a sign that the Devil is visiting the area?"

She returned his gaze steadily. "Possibly."

"And you write about this kind of thing for a living?"

"Before coming up here I spent two years studying the Bell Witch legend in Nashville."

"Sounds familiar," Hunter said.

"The Bells lived near Nashville in the 1700's. They were haunted, terrorized really, by an unknown entity.

Their property has been the site of well-documented paranormal activity ever since. I wrote my dissertation on the subject and turned it into a book published this past summer."

"That's cool. A bestseller?"

Again a smile curved her lips. "Not really, but I have high hopes for the Devil. In the meantime, I'm guest lecturing in folklore at Wayne Paterson University." She hesitated, then added, "I also write for a couple of publications. Ever heard of *Out There?*"

"I read it all the time," Hunter said with enthusiasm. "You're awfully pretty to be running around looking for monsters."

"And you're awfully smart to use such a stupid line on a woman who has two PhDs," she retorted.

Hunter had the grace to blush. It had been a while since he'd been in a battle of wits and lost. "Can I make up for that by taking you out for dinner in the city?"

"Maybe another time," she said, then checked her watch and slipped the computer into her backpack.

"Have to get home to someone?" Hunter was surprised to feel a spark of jealousy. No matter that he already had a hot date with Mandy, he was used to women being very interested in what he offered.

"No one at home." Cyn's smile was easy. "But I'm busy tonight. And I'd prefer we stay around here when we go out. I put in long days and usually like to grab a meal late."

"When" they went out, not "if." Slightly mollified, Hunter rose and followed her to the door. "That works for me. I'll give you a call...if you'll give me your number."

She handed him a business card. "You can reach

me at this number. Leave a message and I'll get back to you when I can."

She left him with a dazzling smile and her strong and alluring scent. Hunter noticed that she looked around, surveying the parking lot before she got in a dark green Jeep Grand Cherokee. She drove away without looking back, which irked a little. But mainly he felt a tug of sexual curiosity he hadn't felt in a long time.

With a woman who hunted legends for a living.

"Shit, this is crazy," he said, but grinned as he headed to his car.

He went home instead of the wildlife preserve, thinking of what Cyn had said about the local animals being stirred up. His frequent runs of late might be the cause, not the New Jersey Devil. He could work out his physical frustrations with the punching bag in his home gym. He had learned that part of being a shifter was exercising control.

Then there was Mandy to consider.

Funny, an evening of whipped cream and Mandy just didn't seem as appealing now. He was almost relieved when she cancelled. Seems her husband stayed up late and didn't want her to go out "to tend to a sick friend."

On Sunday, Zoe had a break in the hospital CEO case. The wife really was cheating. Zoe was bummed, and Hunter ended up spending much of the day with her.

He thought about calling Cyn. However, all thoughts of the redhead fled when Mandy showed up at his office on Monday morning.

He, Zoe, and Darla were in the front office when

Mandy walked in wearing a black, belted trench coat and black leather boots with stiletto heels. Her dark, glossy hair hung loose around her shoulders. Her blue eyes sparkled when she took off her sunglasses.

"Mr. MacRae, I was hoping for a moment of your time." Mandy looked at him and only him.

Zoe sucked in her breath. Darla giggled. Hunter gestured toward his office. As Mandy disappeared down the hall, clearly familiar with the layout, he turned to the two other women, grinned and opened his arms wide. "What's a guy to do?"

He turned his back on his colleagues, went into his office and locked the door.

Mandy had already dropped her coat on the floor and leaned on the edge of his desk. She wore only a black silk teddy and panties with a black garter belt and fishnet hose that dipped into her black boots. A silk rose rested just above her soft mound like a cherry on a sundae.

Hunter growled and was already shedding his pants as he pulled her toward the plush sofa against the wall.

Somewhere, faintly, he heard Zoe cursing.

Chapter 5

"Well, hell," I muttered as I walked back to my office cubicle. Darla and I were aware of the entertainment Hunter sometimes provided for his female acquaintances and clients while we worked nearby. But this was pretty brazen. Mandy Morris's husband was well known in the business community.

No doubt she and Hunter would have a slick answer if caught.

"I sure hope so," I muttered as I sat at my desk. If Charlie Morris was as connected as he was purported to be, even Hunter's ability to run and claw his way out of trouble might not keep him from getting whacked.

My belief in happily-ever-afters was taking it on the chin these days. First, another sad chapter unfolds with Eric and Kinley. Then, on Sunday, Walter Corbin's wife ends up at a beach house where she spent the afternoon with the 20-year-old son of a family friend. She wasn't tutoring the young man in French. Turns out the cheating bastard was right about his cheating wife.

Now Hunter was down the hall screwing another man's wife.

What I needed to do was change my focus. I had an appointment to see Lizzie Howerton this afternoon, so I went to the Internet to learn everything I could about the Howertons.

Lizzie and her mother, Camilla Baines Howerton, ran the charitable foundation of the Howerton family. There were countless pictures of them hosting thousand-dollar-a-table luncheons and speaking at various civic clubs on behalf of their favorite charity, St. Jude's Children's Hospital in Memphis, Tennessee.

A feature article explained that a child of a sorority sister of Camilla had large-cell lymphoma, a rare cancer, at age eleven. The girl was treated at St. Jude's and survived. She was now 22, cancer free, finishing her nursing degree and planning to work in pediatrics. Camilla had devoted her time and money to the cause.

I read the gossip in the New York Post and found Camilla mentioned frequently, but never a hint of marital problems or scandal. Camilla and Douglas Ray Howerton were photographed together during fashion week and other big events around town. He was at her side in public along with their daughter, but in the end, Camilla had cut him out of her will, leaving everything to Lizzie.

Maybe the Howerton marriage was for the society columns only. Hunter's parents had maintained such a marriage for nearly thirty-five years. My own parents had been terribly unhappy but still together when my mother was murdered. Maybe the mystery of the morning should be why I even still believed in marriage.

Forging ahead in my research, I found Douglas's name in some financial articles. He had been one of Bernie Madoff's victims, and had taken a few more hits in the Great Recession. But according to how their financials looked on the surface, it shouldn't have made a difference. Camilla's family really held the purse strings. She died a billionaire.

But why had Camilla cut Douglas out of the will? Why hadn't sweet Lizzie mentioned it to me when we were talking? She acted as if the only problem she had in the world was finding the sister everyone else said she didn't have. It was time to go find some answers.

Darla was printing a stack of paperwork when I emerged from my cubicle with my briefcase in hand. She looked up and smiled. "You've been quiet this morning."

I explained about our new client who had walked in on Friday afternoon.

Darla seemed unperturbed as she put various copies into folders. "Who in the world would come in here to do business that late?"

"People who think we're open until six o'clock like the sign on the door says," I said, waiting for her to acknowledge her absence.

She shrugged. "Usually it's dead here on Friday afternoons." She picked up the stacks of paper and began putting them in folders.

I started to admonish her but decided it would fall on deaf ears. Hunter wouldn't back me, and it wasn't worth the trouble it would cause.

"I'm working on the Howerton case this afternoon and won't be back until late."

Darla gave me a wave, but still I hesitated. I asked, "I know Hunter has court this afternoon. You're not nervous to be here alone, are you? After the body in the woods?"

Hunter and I had updated Darla on the events of Friday night as soon as she came in this morning.

The pretty blonde paused. "Do you think I have

reason to worry? I'm just not sure someone interested in him would be interested in me," Darla said with her usual supreme confidence.

I nodded, not sure why it hadn't crossed my mind that Darla could pretty much handle anything. "All right." I turned toward the door.

"Don't worry about me," Darla called. "You know I'll be leaving well before dark."

I resisted the urge to respond to that tiny dig and went to my car. I hit Highway 23 and went to the New Jersey Transit stop to grab a bus into the city. Occasionally I enjoy driving into Manhattan, but most days I just hop on a bus.

It's a pleasant ride to cruise through the Meadowlands past Giants Stadium and the IZOD Center and whiz by Secaucus to enter New York City through the Lincoln Tunnel.

Though I love the view of the Manhattan skyline, I also get a little squeamish as we head through the tunnel. I have a real fear of being stranded and having to stay there for hours without seeing the sky. If that ever happens, I'll be the idiot screaming and climbing the walls. Just peel me off and take me outside; I'll be fine.

At the Port Authority Terminal, I get caught up in the beat of the city. People are everywhere, and they all have places they need to be with great urgency. I have just enough time to grab a hot pretzel for lunch before taking a cab to the Howerton residence on Park Avenue.

This was one of the family's many homes, where Lizzie and her mother stayed most often when in the city. Douglas usually set up camp in the family's suite at the Helmsley Carlton House. The separate living spaces were yet another indication that Baines/Howerton was more corporate than matrimonial.

At the Howerton mansion, a sour-looking woman in a black skirt and heavily starched white blouse answered the door when I rang the bell. "Yes?" she asked, frowning. "May I help you?"

"I'm Zoe Buchanan. I have an appointment with Ms. Howerton."

From behind the imposing woman Lizzie squealed my name. Yes, she actually squealed. It was hard to believe this woman was several years older than me. "It's so good to see you. Mary, would you please bring some coffee and snacks to the study?"

"Yes, Miss Lizzie," the woman said brusquely and left us.

I'm accustomed to wealth, but even I was impressed. The antique desk against the wall in the foyer held a beautiful Baccarat vase filled with fresh flowers. The smell was heavenly. I'm not much on antiques but I was pretty sure I'd seen that desk in a Sotheby's catalog a few months ago. One of my aspirations is to go to one of those auctions and buy something grand.

Lizzie led me down a hallway to a dark paneled room. I almost lost consciousness as I gazed at floor-to-ceiling bookcases filled with leather volumes. How wonderful it would be to have a library like this. As I spied Jane Austen, Edgar Allen Poe, and F. Scott Fitzgerald, I wondered if they'd let me move my office here. Of course, I probably wouldn't get much work done. My idea of a perfect day was one filled with reading and eating. Good times.

"Do you have news?" Lizzie asked, taking a seat on the leather sofa in front of a fireplace.

"I've been doing research, and I want to double-check some facts," I said.

Sour Lady Mary entered the room with a teacart complete with silver coffeepot and china cups and saucers. I'm always amazed people actually use these lavish sets. I am accustomed to coffee in sturdy mugs at my kitchen table.

Over coffee and cookies, I asked Lizzie for other details she could give me about her birth at The Hayden Clinic in Secaucus, New Jersey. According to my research, the center had closed after Dr. Hayden's death.

She shrugged. "No, I guess it was a special place that catered to women like my mother."

"What was your mother like?"

"Oh, you know, wealthy and wanting to birth children without the pain. I think she was given drugs from the time labor started until after I was born. She didn't even see me until the day after she gave birth because she was so out of it. She spoke of Dr. Hayden and his wife, Elaine, like they were saints. Mommy always said Dr. Hayden cared about his mothers. Each nurse had only two mothers and their babies to care for. Mommy talked about it when she was so sick. I stayed with her almost constantly and we talked more than we ever had."

"And yet you couldn't bring yourself to ask about your sister?" I asked.

"I wish I had," Lizzie replied. "But I couldn't bear to upset her." A single tear rolled down her cheek, which she wiped away with her dainty napkin.

"Yet you know your sister exists." I stated this as fact.

Gratitude replaced Lizzie's tears. "Yes, my sister does exist."

"Then let's get down to work. Tell me about your life."

Most of Lizzie's younger years were spent in the care of a parade of nannies. Most left or were fired because they couldn't get along with Daddy.

It all sounded familiar. Even before my mother was murdered, I was left to the care of housekeepers and nannies. I had one nanny who stayed five years. I adored her, but she left to marry and raise her own children.

"Do you think anyone on your family's staff knew your sister?" I asked Lizzie.

"If they do, they're not telling me. Most are too respectful to tell me I'm crazy, but they don't believe me." She pursed her lips. "Something happened in that house in London."

"No one ever said anything about it?"

She shook her head. "I think we left because something happened. My mother always missed living in England."

"Can you get me a list of all the staff from that house? Who was your nanny then?"

"I don't remember. Daddy won't talk about it. Those household account records have been difficult to find. I've put in a call to my mother's old assistant, who is now retired, but she's off somewhere in South America." She gave me the woman's contact information, as well.

"Maybe someone in your mother's family might

know."

Lizzie's sigh was rueful. "Mother was an only child and the dutiful daughter. She married my father because my grandfathers wanted their business merger to have a little more stability."

She looked at her hands for a moment and then said, "Daddy had his young men and Mommy went to the 'spa' several times a year."

Her tone was matter of fact. The business of marriage.

"I knew what was going on, but couldn't actually do anything about it," she said, smoothing her skirt. "Like many of my friends, I've just accepted it."

I asked some more questions about her mother's closest friends. There weren't many. Camilla had spent most of her time on her charities and her daughter.

Lizzie laid her napkin on the tray and stood, clasping her hands. "I hope some of this information will help you find my sister."

"There's one more thing I need to ask you about." I also got to my feet.

"I want you to have all the information you need."

"Why is your father contesting your mother's will?"

"Oh." Lizzie's face reddened with embarrassment. "You heard about that. But then, I guess you would. Mommy left all her money to charities and me with the condition I continue her work. She was furious with Daddy for losing so much money and getting in the news about it. Daddy was hoping to use some of Mommy's money to bounce back."

"Hoping?" I said, incredulous. "He was hoping your mother would die so he could recoup his losses?"

"She had always rescued him before. This time she wouldn't. They argued. I begged him not to upset her. Mommy was very sick, and there seemed no point. The doctors had said she had only weeks. So Daddy backed off. Then, a week before she died, without any of us knowing, Mommy changed her entire will."

"Your father wasn't happy about that, right?"

"Daddy still isn't happy."

She took a deep breath. "But you don't have to worry. My allowance comes from a trust fund, so I'll be able to pay you what we agreed to."

"I wasn't worried about that," I said, though it had crossed my mind. "But things could get messy."

"Oh, don't worry about that." She waved her hand in dismissal. "Mommy's lawyers—"

She stopped. "My lawyers will meet with his lawyers and they'll hash it out. I don't intend to go to court with Daddy. It'll get settled one way or another."

I thought she believed what she was saying, and I hoped she was right. But I felt there was one more thing I should say. "I hope your pursuit of your sister doesn't come into play with your father's suit."

"What do you mean?"

I tried to speak kindly but with frankness. "Everyone who knows your family is saying your sister never existed. Your father may try to use this search to show you shouldn't have control of the family money."

"Just let him try." A gleam of determination replaced Lizzie's spacey demeanor. I had to wonder if her giddy young woman act was just that—an act.

We made arrangements for her to get me some additional phone numbers and addresses of employees, families, and friends. Then I headed for the bus and home to New Jersey.

I was back in the office before five. Darla was already gone, of course. Hunter was nowhere to be found.

I ran through some messages and put in a quick call to check on Kinley. She hadn't seen Eric since Friday night. Every other Monday, Eric's mother picked the girls up from school and kept them overnight where he could see them. Kinley was not happy with the arrangement, but it was the best compromise we could reach while the divorce was being finalized. I advised her to check the new locks and get some rest.

Then I wrote up my notes in the Howerton case file, including people to interview. Daddy Douglas topped the list.

Going to the Internet, I put Dr. Charles Hayden in Dogpile. Though there were ten pages of results, most of it was in obituaries from people who had been involved with the Hayden Clinic. I added his widow, Elaine Hayden, to my list.

By then, my stomach was rumbling. I sent a text message to Hunter to let him know I'd be fixing his favorite chicken casserole for dinner if he wanted to come by and eat. It was a recipe from Delores, one of our family cooks. She used to fix it often for Hunter and me. Delores always said that when you can fix a great meal with a cut-up rotisserie chicken and canned soup, you feel like a domestic goddess.

At home, as I prepared our meal, I remembered the wonderful food Hunter and I had once shared in Scotland. We went there together the summer after he learned about his second nature. Most Scottish fare was all about meat, potatoes and gravies—hearty, delicious, and comforting. I liked it, though I did have to diet some when we returned home.

My thoughts went back to the little kitchen in the cottage where Hunter and I stayed. We were there for two months, in the countryside between Glasgow and Edinburgh. It was close enough to town to have fun and had enough land attached to give Hunter a place to roam free and work out the kinks of shapeshifting.

We were looked after that summer by two of the MacRae family's devoted employees. Tall, spare Robert McPhee had once been the right hand man of Hunter's grandfather and great-grandfather. Though his face was seamed with age, he didn't miss a beat. He knew where Hunter and I were at all times, and had even shown up a time or two unexpectedly, both in the city and out in the countryside.

It was eerie, I remembered. It was as if he had a special ability where Hunter was concerned.

Robert's wife, Molly, was as short and round he was tall and thin. Though as ancient as he was, she kept the cottage sparkling and the scent of delicious savories and sweets coming from the kitchen.

That trip was one of my best summer vacations. I was nostalgic as I pulled the bubbling casserole out of the oven.

Hunter's car was in the driveway and he gave a quick knock on the front door before unlocking it and yelling, "Hi, honey, I'm ho-o-ome."

"In the kitchen, sweet cheeks," I said with a laugh. "How was your day?"

"The usual. Great sex in the office. A nasty battle in the courtroom." He gave me a kiss on the cheek.

"You're playing with fire with Mandy."

"I could lie and say that I'm sorry, but I'm just a randy tom cat." Hunter grabbed plates from the cabinet. "God, that smells good. I'm starving."

"Want a salad to go with it?" I asked, though I knew what his answer would be.

"Nope, just give me some hot food."

I fixed a small salad for myself and heated some Texas toast with garlic butter. We ate in companionable silence for a while, and then I said, "I was thinking about our time in Scotland. Do you ever think about it?"

"A lot." He took another bite. After swallowing he continued, "I remember how great it was to run for miles with no worry about people coming after me."

"Are you going to visit this summer?" I carried my empty plate to the sink. "You haven't been back in a while. Do you think you have more to learn?"

He was digging in for another helping of the casserole. "I don't like to go as much since Robert and Molly are dead. They made the visits appealing. The only thing I work on now is trying to make my clothes disappear as I change, so I have them on when I change back. I still haven't mastered that."

"That particular trick would be very beneficial," I replied, thinking of finding him in his office naked on Friday night.

"I'm seeing Grandda tomorrow," Hunter said suddenly. "He'll be in the city."

I was surprised. The older man had always preferred the mountains in winter. He told me often enough he hated the piles of dirty city snow.

"Something's up." Hunter relayed his grandfather's phone call on Saturday.

"You think he's going to try to talk you into joining the family business." As usual, I was able to express what Hunter felt.

He nodded. "Grandda may have decided to join the dark side of the family."

Unexpected fear coiled in my belly, but I turned away, instinctively hiding it from Hunter. "You knew it could happen."

"Don't worry." Hunter always read me well. "I have no intention of leaving our firm."

That wasn't what I was worried about, but since I couldn't explain my feelings, I said nothing.

"Do you like what you do, Zoe?" Hunter continued.

I turned back to him, puzzled. "What do you mean?"

"It feels like enough? It satisfies you?"

I decided to be completely honest. "You know I'm not always thrilled with cases like the Corbins. It's better when I feel like I'm really helping someone, you know, like Kinley and her girls or even my new case, which we'll get paid for."

"You don't think I'm helping people who just want a divorce?"

I sighed and turned his initial questions back on him. "Does it satisfy you? Does it feel like enough?"

I expected a quick retort about the fringe benefits of distraught divorcees and rich clients. Instead Hunter regarded me for a long moment. "I'm not sure," he said finally. "I'm feeling kind of unsettled."

This pensiveness wasn't usual for Hunter, but before I could pursue the subject, he shook off the mood. He told me about the reporter for *Out There* that he had met on Saturday. By the time he had finished describing her and talking about the New Jersey Devil, he had dug a half a cheesecake out of the refrigerator and insisted I share it with him.

He left in a rush, no doubt eager to change and run off his pent-up energy from the day. I prepared for bed and tried to dismiss the nagging thoughts that were skirting the edge of my brain. They made me nervous. I had noticed lately that my "intuition" had grown stronger; something was happening to make my perceptions of events more focused.

As I crawled into bed and pulled the sheet across my legs, I felt an immediate and strong sense of alarm. Closing my eyes, I focused on that and struggled to identify why I should be alarmed and Kinley's face popped into my mind.

Kinley was in danger. I knew it as surely as I knew if I didn't act now it would be fatal for her. I called her, but there was no answer.

Without pausing to consider what I was doing, I scrambled out of bed and dressed. In less than five minutes, I was headed out the door. I telephoned Hunter but cats don't usually carry phones, I reminded myself.

I left a message telling him where I was going and why and told him to call the police if he didn't hear from me soon.

Though lights were on everywhere, there was no sign of life at Kinley's place. When I got no response to the doorbell, I headed to the back of the house. I crept forward until I could see the back stoop.

What I saw made me to fight to keep my dinner down. There was blood everywhere. A long spray covered the wall. Kinley lay in a crumpled heap at the bottom of the steps. When she moaned, I ran to her. Her face was a mangled mess, and her body was varying shades of blues and purples. She had been beaten relentlessly, and was barely breathing. What I couldn't understand was how she was still alive.

I reached for my cell phone and heard something behind me. Before I could turn, I felt a horrible pain in the back of my head. I fell forward.

Chapter 6

"Wake up, lass."

I tried to open my eyes, but my eyelids felt like lead. I could smell the outdoors; the air was cool and damp. Where was I?

I struggled to remember. Images flashed quickly. Fear. Had to get to Kinley. I felt like I was in the woods, but there were no woods around Kinley's house. She lived in a subdivision. Need to help Kinley. Where is Kinley?

"That's a girl. Come on now, wake up," a deep voice urged.

The voice had a familiar Scottish burr, and as I finally forced my eyes open, I looked into the green eyes of Fraser MacRae, Hunter's grandfather. Why was he with Kinley?

"Mr. MacRae?" My words came out as a hoarse whisper. I tried to clear my throat, but it made my head hurt too much.

"Come on, lass, let's sit you up here." His big arm came around my back and raised me to a sitting position. "I've only go' a wee bit of time, and I need to tell you something, something very important."

I leaned against him and concentrated on not passing out again.

"Listen, Zoe. Hunter's very life depends on your ability to know what's coming," he said, his eyes boring into mine.

"I don't understand."

He picked up my hand. "You've got the sight, girl. You have to use it to help Hunter. It's a gift, and it's time for you to learn to work with it in a better manner."

"The sight?"

"You call it your 'women's intuition' or 'gut instinct,' but it's the sight, the ability to see what's coming, and it's the one thing that will give Hunter an edge and keep him alive." His voice filled with urgency. "Just as Hunter is strapped with the curse that hangs over our family, you've got the responsibility that came down through yours."

I struggled to make sense of what he was saying, but it wasn't easy. His voice softened. "Why did you go to Kinley's house tonight?"

"She was in trouble and needed help." My memory returned in a rush. In Kinley's backyard, somebody had hit me and knocked me out.

I tried to look around again, but Mr. MacRae held me firm. "You can't help Kinley now, but you can help Hunter. When you feel compelled to do something, you must listen to your inner voice. It's a guide for you and Hunter. It will keep both of you alive. Do you understand?"

"Yes," I said, thinking clearly at last. "Lately it has gotten stronger. I am able to focus on something once it enters my mind, and that makes it stronger."

"That's exactly what I mean, lass. You're the key." His voice thickened with anger. "Chymera, that's what the goddamn monster Michael Killin calls himself now. He's like us but not like us. You'll learn soon enough."

I recalled something about chimera from Greek mythology, about an animal that was more than one species, with a lion's body and a dragon's head or something like that.

"Killin is the other side of the coin in our history." Mr. McRae never took his eyes from mine. "His mission is to destroy us, to wipe out entire families if possible."

I focused hard on his words, knowing his message was vital.

"His family has a genetic problem and cannot shift properly. They're a band of mutants, dedicated to eradicating shifters who live normally in our abnormal world. Every time we think we've got them under control, another one shows up."

"They're coming for Hunter." I struggled with dizziness as the full impact of his words penetrated the fog.

He gripped my hand. "Promise you'll keep him safe. Promise."

"I promise. I promise." I descended into another black hole. When I woke, I was cold and damp. I moved my head and moaned. Pain shot down my neck like searing heat.

"That's it. Wake up, Sleeping Beauty." The deep voice had no Scottish burr.

"Let me in here, Detective," another voice chimed in.

My eyes opened. I jerked as a bright light sent a brief but violent burst of pain through my brain. I blinked and started to push up with my hands.

"Uh-huh, ma'am," said the voice on my left. "I need you to stay put while I check things out."

I assumed he was a paramedic as he deftly wrapped a blood pressure cuff around my arm and asked, "What's your name?"

"Zoe Buchanan."

"Good girl. Do you know what day it is, Zoe?"

I looked up at the starlit sky above me. "It's night."

"That's true," he said with a chuckle, "but what night is it?"

I struggled to remember. All I could think about was Hunter's grandfather. I had talked to him. So strange for him to be here. But first there was Kinley.

"Kinley, where's Kinley?" I asked, once again trying to get up. "What about the girls? Where are the girls?"

Both men held me down. I recognized Detective Mike Scala, who had questioned me about the body in the woods.

"There are people helping Kinley. We didn't find any children here. The house is empty. You've got to stay down and let Joe here take care of you."

I looked into intense blue eyes in a chiseled face framed by dark hair. The eyes were kind, but filled with determination. If I tried to get up, he would have no trouble stopping me.

"There was so much blood." I closed my eyes as the scene flashed into my mind. "Oh, God, is Kinley dead?" When he didn't answer, I groaned. I turned my head. "Oh my God," I whispered.

Mike sighed. "She is. Why are you here?"

Joe removed the blood pressure cuff and examined my head. When he touched the tender place on the back, I flinched.

"I'm sorry, but I had to look at it. We're going to

get you on a stretcher and have you checked out at the hospital. Looks like you might need a couple of stitches too. Just stay right here for a minute." He moved away and walked to the ambulance.

"Feel like talking to me, Zoe?" Mike said.

"I think so."

"What did you see?"

I thought of Kinley's legs bent at an odd angle, her face almost obliterated. "She was laying there like a little rag doll."

Eric. Goddam bastard. He finally killed her.

This time when I tried to sit up, Detective Scala helped. I leaned into his shoulder and closed my eyes as my stomach rolled with nausea. He tightened his hold.

"It was her husband. Kinley's husband—"

"You saw him?" Mike replied. "He hit you?"

"No, but—"

"Zoe! Zoe!"

I opened one eye and saw Hunter arguing with two uniformed officers. His features looked stark in the glowing red and blue lights of the police and emergency vehicles.

"Hunter is Kinley's divorce attorney. Please let him through."

Mike motioned to the cops. Hunter hurried over to kneel beside me.

"What happened?" He reached for me, but Mike wouldn't let Hunter move me. I groaned and wished I didn't feel so sick.

"Hold on, man," Mike said. "We're waiting for the paramedic to get back. Just take it easy."

Hunter took my chin in his hand and turned my face to his. "What the hell happened?"

Against my best efforts, tears filled my eyes. "Kinley's dead."

"Ah, God." Hunter winced. "I should have protected her."

"Why?" Mike asked.

"Her asshole husband, Eric Russo." Hunter put his hands on his knees. "She thought he was accepting the divorce, but he kept dropping in to remind her she was his wife until death. I guess he took care of that option."

Mike started to say something but was interrupted by the paramedics and their stretcher. As they lifted me onto it, I felt sick again, and to my horror actually threw up. The paramedics cleaned me as well as they could with Mike and Hunter watching. How humiliating.

I'd seen lot of tough private eyes on TV come back from being hit in the head with no problem. I guess I need to work on my quick-recovery-from-being-knocked-out skills.

"We're going to need her clothes," Mike told the paramedics. "I'll send somebody to the hospital or pick them up myself."

"I'll follow the ambulance," Hunter said.

Mike grabbed his arm. "After I talk with you," he told Hunter. "We need to discuss a murder. Again."

"I'll be there soon," Hunter yelled as the doors to the ambulance slammed.

I wanted the luxury of unconsciousness. Between the nausea and the pain, I was sure this was going to be a bumpy ride.

Where's Bette Davis when you need her?

For a moment I was afraid I was badly injured. Kinley was dead and the best I could do was come up with a line from an old movie.

Chapter 7

Hunter strode across the crowded ER waiting room toward the information desk. Family members and patients were creating chaos. When someone yelled his name, he saw his golfing buddy, Taylor Bradford, an ER physician, coming his way.

Taylor grasped Hunter's hand for a hearty shake. "Zoe told me you were coming."

"The damn detective kept me in a patrol car asking questions forever. I thought he was going to arrest me, but I finally escaped." Hunter walked with Taylor back into the patient area. "Is Zoe all right?"

"She has a concussion, but she'll be fine in a few days. I wanted to keep her overnight, but she said you'd stay with her," Taylor said.

"Sure, sure, whatever she needs." Hunter ran his hand through his already-disheveled hair. "I think we're pretty lucky she wasn't hurt any worse. She could have been killed too."

"Zoe told me about Kinley," the doctor said, shaking his head. "I treated Kinley a couple of times when Eric banged her up. He's nothing but a damned bully. I begged her to go to a domestic violence group. She always said it was too embarrassing. I reported it, and they picked up Eric, but she never pressed charges."

Hunter caught the eye of a nurse he'd gone out

with a couple of times. She smiled and gave him a signal to call her. He smiled back and hoped he could remember her name after watching the police cart away the body of a client.

"I'm sure Eric killed Kinley," Hunter said. "I told the detective as much."

"No doubt." Taylor pulled back a curtain to reveal Zoe with an ice pack on her head.

"Hey, gorgeous." Hunter stooped to kiss Zoe's cheek. "How are you?"

She gripped Hunter's arm, her eyes filled with sorrow.

"I know," he murmured, reading her mind. "There's nothing you could have done. Kinley was gone before you got there."

"Damn Eric," Zoe muttered.

Taylor cleared his throat. "Hunter says he'll stay with you tonight, Zoe. Otherwise, you're not going home."

"I promise to take care of her," Hunter said. "Do I need to wake her up periodically?"

Taylor handed Hunter a sheet of instructions. "Just keep an eye on her. Give her Tylenol if she has a headache and use cold packs to reduce the swelling. If she seems worse, call me right away. Fortunately, she didn't need stitches."

Zoe pouted. "Hello, I'm right here and well enough to take my own instructions. I don't need a babysitter."

"Actually, you do," Taylor said. "You got hit pretty hard. Let Hunter keep an eye on you. Stay home and rest tomorrow. You might want to stay away from work for a couple of days."

Zoe made a noncommittal sound. Hunter could tell

she was going to be a very bad patient.

"I'm glad you were here tonight," she told Taylor.

He leaned down and gave her a quick peck on her cheek. "I'll always be on call for you. Call me at home if you need me. I'll get your papers processed so you can leave. I'm really sorry about Kinley, about all of this."

"Thanks, man," Hunter said as Taylor left.

Zoe removed the cold pack and sat up. "I feel like I was hit by a train."

"Not exactly." Hunter helped her sit up straighter. "Detective Scala thinks you were hit with a flashlight they found in the grass. It's one of those big black ones like the cops—and most crooks—carry."

"No wonder I've got a headache the size of Giants' stadium."

"Let's hope that flashlight will have Eric's fingerprints all over it."

"Have they got him yet?"

Hunter grunted in disgust. "From what little the police let slip in front of me, the jack-ass was found at his mother's house. The girls were spending the night over there with him."

"Oh, my God." Zoe jerked up and cringed. "Are they safe?"

"They were with Eric and his mother. The police have notified Kinley's sister, Lydia. I made sure they understood that Kinley had designated Lydia as their guardian should anything happen."

"But will that hold up? I mean, Eric's mother—"

"Won't put up a fight if she wants to have any relationship with those kids," Hunter said. "Remember, it was Lydia who finally convinced Kinley to hire us in the first place. I bet she has those little girls in her arms right now. And I'm going to make sure Kinley's wishes are honored."

"I hope so," Zoe murmured as a nurse came in. Hunter stepped out while the woman helped Zoe get ready to leave.

Hunter got his car and met Zoe, in a wheelchair now, at the front of the ER. Soon they were zipping through the dark, cold night.

"This is a nightmare," Zoe murmured. "I should have had someone watching the house."

"We didn't know," Hunter said. "We didn't expect this to happen. We've never had one of our clients, even in domestic abuse cases, get murdered. Damn Eric."

"Hopefully he's damning himself to the police right now," Hunter retorted.

"Is Mike questioning him?"

"I believe your Detective Scala was headed that way after he assured himself that I wasn't involved in the murder."

"He didn't suspect you."

Hunter smirked, remembering the detective's intent gaze and whip-like questions. "The good cop doesn't like me very much. He was questioning how we showed up at two murder scenes in four days."

"They're completely unrelated."

Hunter frowned. Scala said they were still working to identify the man found in the woods, but something about that scene still gnawed at Hunter. And now, more violence. He didn't like it. His thoughts centered on that, he took the corner a little faster than he intended.

Zoe winced. "Hey! Injured passenger on board."

"I'm sorry." Hunter reached across the seat to take her hand. "I'm just so damn mad that I let this happen."

"How did you let it happen? I'm the one who should have known. According to your grandfather, I've got the sight, and I should be able to discern when trouble is ahead."

"What are you talking about?" Hunter glanced at her with genuine concern. "I guess you really did get a hard hit."

"I talked to your grandfather tonight," Zoe said. "He came to me in a vision while I was unconscious."

Hunter stopped at a red light and looked hard at her. He reached up to touch her forehead. "You don't feel feverish, but you're sure talking like you're out of your head. There's no way you could have seen my grandfather. He's supposed to fly into town in the morning. I have to meet him for lunch."

Zoe pushed her hair back and met his gaze. "You can turn into Fluffy but I can't have a vision?" she deadpanned.

Hearing horns behind them, Hunter jerked forward. It was best that he just humored Zoe. "What did Grandda have to say?"

"He says I need to work on my special skill so I can help you." Zoe rested her head on her hands. "Apparently I have 'the sight,' or the ability to know when trouble is coming down the pike."

"So you're perceptive."

"We both know I depend on my gut feelings a lot when I'm working on a case, and more times than not, I'm right. Your grandfather said that my ability is growing and will continue to get better."

Hunter turned off Hamburg onto Ratzer, heading

toward Zoe's house. "What does that mean?"

"When he was talking to me, your grandfather said something about someone called chimera and called him a mutant."

Hunter jerked to look at her and Zoe screamed, "Red light!"

Slamming on the brakes, Hunter yanked the car into a side road and pulled to a stop.

"Have you heard of that before?" she asked. "Do you know what a chimera is?"

Feeling his anger drain leaving fatigue in its wake, Hunter rubbed a hand down his face.

"It's spelled C-H-Y-M-E-R-A. He's a bad guy, the leader of another family that has the same curse our family does, but something about their genetic make-up keeps them from fully transforming. Only their heads and upper body change, which is why the guy took the name Chymera."

He looked both ways and slowly pulled away from the curb. "I thought he was part of Scottish folklore, and Grandda used him to scare me. Come on, it's the twenty-first century. I never put much stock in those stories. After all, are we going to have to battle to see who is king of the mountain?"

"I hate to remind you again, but you do become a full-blown cat on occasion. It doesn't seem weird when you put it in context with that."

"Neither does Transformers, but we both know that's just a movie."

"Your grandfather said my gift is my family's curse just like your little species swap is a curse for yours." Zoe groaned suddenly and put her arms across her stomach. "God, Hunter, can we get home? I feel sick."

Hunter hurried through the quiet streets to Zoe's little house.

She was almost asleep on her feet by the time he walked her in the front door and up the stairs to her bedroom. He decided to forego pajamas, but dug in her dresser until he found the thick white socks she always wore to bed. He pulled them on and carefully tucked her in. She was so pale and still, he got scared and woke her.

"Zoe, what day is it?"

"Leave me the hell alone, Hunter," she said, slapping at him. "When I'm awake my head's hurting like it has a jackhammer in it."

"Just tell me who's president then." He rubbed her arm to keep her awake.

"It should be Michelle Obama, but it's Barack. Are you happy now?"

"Yeah, I think you're fine," he said, backing away.

Zoe mumbled something into her pillow and pulled the covers up. Hunter clicked the lamp beside her bed to low and leaned down to kiss the top of her head, the only spot without covers or a bandage.

Downstairs, he grabbed a can of beer from the fridge and pulled open a bag of nacho chips. He needed fuel to mull over what Zoe's conversation about his grandfather. He had barely begun when his cell phone rang.

His father.

At one o'clock in the morning.

This couldn't be good.

"Dad?" he said.

"I'm afraid I've got some bad news, Hunter."

"Is it Mom or Meagan?" Hunter said, worrying about his mother and sister.

"They're fine. It's your grandfather. I'm afraid he's dead," Stirling's voice broke, a rare sign of emotion. "The police believe he was attacked by a wild animal at the estate. We'll know more later, but we've got to get up there before they do an autopsy."

Of course, protect the family secret at all costs.

"I've talked to Shamus," Stirling continued, "and he's staying with the body until we arrive. I've ordered the chopper to be ready in a couple of hours. Can you make it?"

"Uh…yeah, I've just got some things I need to do. If I'm more than fifteen minutes late, go without me, I'll find my own way."

"We'll see you then."

"Sure, Dad."

Hunter closed the phone but kept it in his hand. Grandda was dead. It was impossible. The man always looked like he was going to live forever. He could still hunt and field dress a deer without help, something most of his staunchly Democratic friends didn't know. He had always loved hunting in his woods.

Just minutes ago, Zoe had told him about a vision, about talking to Grandda. Now he was gone? When did he die and how the hell had he talked to Zoe? The connection between the two events chilled Hunter. He understood it was all true—both Zoe's conversation and Grandda's death.

And nothing was ever going to be the same.

Hunter stood. "First, I've got to find somebody to take care of Zoe, and then I've got to make that helicopter."

He looked out the window and saw the lights still on at the house next door. Thank God Zoe's closest neighbor was a well-known night owl. He scrolled through his cell phone until he found the number and called.

"Bernie! Hey, it's Hunter. I'm at Zoe's, and I need a big favor."

Chapter 8

I jerked awake from a nightmare filled with blood. Pain in my head and neck stilled me, and my brain automatically went back to Kinley's broken body.

I knew she was in trouble, but I got there too late.

My mother had also been in my dream. She'd been beside Kinley with a bullet hole in her chest. It wasn't surprising that I dreamed of my mother's murder tonight. In the dream, she was still and soulless, just as she had been when my dad came home and found her.

I stacked my pillows so I could sit up, glad Hunter had left the light on. I didn't want darkness.

My arms and chest were sore from falling face forward. I had a tender chin and my neck felt like it had been twisted.

I closed my eyes again and thought of my mother. I was fourteen when she died. The housekeeper and I had been in the house, but Mom was killed in the master bedroom suite. We hadn't heard anything.

As an adult, I'd seen the crime scene photos and knew the hole in my mother's chest was small. The scene wasn't bloody except for the pool that had spread under her back.

Pain shot through my head with the memories. I was beginning to feel the full effect of the attack now. Tomorrow was not going to be a fun day. I squinted at the clock beside my bed. Just after eight a.m.

Correction—today wasn't going to be fun.

"Zoe?" a female voice said from the hallway.

"Who is it?" I opened the nightstand, frightened when my gun wasn't there. It took me a moment to remember the police had taken it. I'd have to get my spare out of my gun safe tomorrow.

"It's Bernie, Zoe, you need anything?"

"Bernie?" I started to sit up more, and then immediately regretted that decision. "Where's Hunter?"

"He had to leave." Bernie came into my bedroom. "Let me check on you since you're awake."

Bernie was Bernadette Murphy Feldman, my dear friend and neighbor, who had been a nurse since World War II. She retired from her husband Ira's medical practice when he'd died twenty years ago. I suspected she'd said goodbye to eighty several years ago, as well.

As usual, she was dressed in a cotton house dress she called a "duster," with the snaps down the front, which made it easy to get on and off. Her misshapen hands were the result of rheumatoid arthritis, and some mornings I knew she struggled getting dressed because it was difficult to get her fingers to move.

Her snow-white hair was short and parted on the left. She kept it clean and combed and didn't worry too much about style. She and her husband had built the house next door where she had lived there for the past forty years.

An old-school neighbor, she often brought over leftovers.

As Bernie held my wrist and checked my pulse, I said, "What are you doing here? I thought Hunter was staying with me."

Bernie sat down on the side of the bed and held my

hand in her left hand. She reached up with her right hand and felt my forehead. "Your pulse is good and there's no fever." She patted my hand and looked at me closely. "Do you remember Hunter waking you up and talking to you?"

"No, I was so tired."

"He had to leave," she said.

I sat up, uneasy. After last night, maybe I didn't want to know what had happened now.

Dizziness came in a wave and passed. "Help me up."

Bernie helped me get to the bathroom, but allowed me to go in by myself. After using the toilet and washing my face, I put on a robe. I was suddenly cold to my core.

Glancing out the window, I saw it was snowing. How appropriate. The world was cold and white too.

And dead.

Bernie was waiting for me.

"Tell me about Hunter."

"His grandfather is dead."

"Shit." I wavered, and Bernie caught my arm.

"I have to talk to Hunter." I slipped free of her grasp and headed downstairs.

Bernie followed, fussing the whole time.

In the kitchen, she steered me toward a chair. With the efficient movements of a long-time nurse, she took my face in her hands and studied me. Her fingers were gentle despite the ravages of her arthritis. She lifted my eyelids, and then put her fingers to the pulse in my wrist.

"I was worried after Hunter told me what happened. What a terrible thing. I'm so sorry about your friend." She lifted the bandage on my head and peeked under it. "A little butterfly bandage but no stitches. That's good."

"Hunter's friend Taylor Bradford fixed me up."

"Oh, James Bradford's grandson. James was a surgeon Ira and I used to work with him at Wayne Memorial." Bernie sniffed in distaste. "He's in Palm Beach now with a wife who's forty years younger. But his grandson is handsome and single."

"Bernie," I said, recognizing the matchmaking gleam in her eye. "What happened to Mr. MacRae?"

"You need something to eat and drink." She turned back to the refrigerator. "Maybe some ginger ale and a few crackers. I've already got a nice chicken soup planned for lunch."

Bernie likes to talk, which she did at a fast clip as she filled a glass with ice and opened a sleeve of saltine crackers.

I cut through her chatter, taking the glass of ginger ale. "Tell me what happened."

"I don't really know," Bernie said. "Hunter was in an awful hurry."

I took another drink and stared numbly into space. Knowing Mr. MacRae was dead added an air of other worldliness to our conversation. Had he come to me before or after he died? I had no problem believing in ghosts; I just had no personal experience with one.

Bernie laid vegetables on the table. "I told Hunter he should call a cab, but he said he packed the clothes he had here and went to meet his family at the helicopter pad in Manhattan. Can you imagine flying in a helicopter any time you want to?"

"The MacRaes have an executive helicopter that

has room for several passengers and probably someone who keeps Hunter's mother in drinks. I've traveled in it several times with Hunter's family to his grandparents' home."

Bernie folded her shopping bag and put it on the counter. "Want me to fix you some breakfast? I'll be happy to fix whatever you want."

"No, I don't think so." I sipped my ginger ale again.

"You should be hungry. You haven't eaten in hours, and you need to regain your strength."

She opened the refrigerator. "I can fix some dry toast and soft-scrambled eggs."

The thought of the eggs made my stomach turn. "Let's see if I can keep these crackers down and then we'll talk about more food later." I reached for the plastic sleeve she'd laid on the table and took out some saltines. "Did Hunter say he would call?"

"He said he'd be in touch as soon as he had details." Bernie began washing carrots and celery in the sink.

I drank more ginger ale, sat at the table, and listened to Bernie prattle while she chopped celery and carrots and put a hen on to boil. It was kind of nice to have someone preparing something special for me.

"Did you go to the grocery store this morning?" I asked when she took a breath from chatting about her Mah Jong group.

Bernie sliced into an onion. "I had a hen in the freezer, and I always keep vegetables around."

The thought of her delicious homemade soup made me feel better. I smiled. "You're the best neighbor a person could have. Thank you."

"Any good mother could do it for you. I just happen to be the one living next door," she said with a laugh.

Bernie's nonchalant reference to a "good mother" didn't apply to mine. She'd never been a Betty Crocker or a June Cleaver, or for that matter, not even much of a mother.

She did try to find good nannies and always liked to shop with me. I didn't realize how much I enjoyed those times until she was dead.

The phone interrupted us and Bernie handed it to me. I was relieved to hear Hunter's voice on the other end. I carried it into the living room and stretched out on the couch.

"I feel like the world is falling apart. I'm so sorry about your grandfather."

He sighed. "I know. It doesn't seem real. How about you? How's the head this morning? Is Bernie taking good care of you?"

"Of course. She's making me chicken soup. What happened your grandfather? Is that why he came to me?"

"I'm not sure." He sounded hesitant.

"Hunter?" Fear made my stomach churn again as he remained silent. "What's wrong?"

"He was attacked by some kind of animal. His body was a mess. I went with my dad to identify the body. It was bad, Zoe, really bad." His voice broke.

"Where did it happen?"

"He'd been at the cabin for a couple of days. Shamus went to take him supplies and found him in the woods. It must have happened shortly before Shamus got there. Grandda was still alive. For some reason he told Shamus to take care of me, and now that old coot thinks he's moving back with me. Can you imagine Shamus living in Jersey City?"

"Your grandfather told me you were in danger. To tell me and Shamus to watch out for you, he must have thought—"

"He was an old man and he was dying. Remember, you'd been hit on the head hard enough to be unconscious. You probably hallucinated."

Hunter's voice was laced with frustration; still, I could sense the fear under his words, the tension that made him snap at me.

"But, I—"

"Let it go, please."

I was hurt, but I knew he would hang up on me if I pressed him further. In this area he was like his father; his temper had a hair trigger at times, especially when it came to family.

I decided to try another avenue. "Do you know any details?"

"The county let us pay for a private autopsy. Fortunately, it's such a small town that the local GP is the sometimes ME. He was glad to let somebody else handle it, and we hired a friend who knows about Grandda's strange DNA do the autopsy. We should know something by tomorrow."

"Can you imagine what the tabloids would report if it leaked?"

"Money may not buy happiness, but at least it will keep our secret for a while longer."

"How's your grandmother?"

"Nana's strong, but she's grieving. She asked me to stay with her a few days."

"Are you going to?"

"I don't think she needs to be alone. I've called Brad to take my open cases."

Brad Evans was another divorce layer in Wayne. He and Hunter backed each other up for vacations and time off.

"I need to come up there for the service. When is it?"

"No details yet. I'll let you know."

There was a voice in the background. Hunter said, "Gotta run. I'll call you tonight."

I pushed the end button on the phone and laid it on the table, feeling rejected. Hunter and I were seldom this far apart and I missed him, especially in light of what had happened to Kinley...and me.

It had been years since Hunter and I were separated when one of us had a problem. We were always there to provide support. It didn't seem right that I was down here sitting on my butt doing nothing when he was in need.

Even though it was unreasonable, I was also hurt at Hunter's attitude. I was sure when he called me this morning that he'd insist I come to join him immediately.

Instead, he was distracted. Maybe it was his family. His parents weren't nice to each other at the best of times. The tension had to be multiplied with an unexpected death like this. Nothing stirs a dysfunctional family more than a death, especially when it's the family patriarch. A man who was also a shapeshifter.

I headed back to the kitchen.

"How's Hunter?" Bernie asked.

"Not good," I poured more ginger ale. I wondered

if I'd ever feel normal again. I watched big, fluffy flakes falling outside the kitchen window wishing I knew a way to make myself get better faster.

"What did he say?"

"Very little," I sipped my drink. "He and his dad had to identify his grandfather." I didn't tell her about the wild animal or the attack. She might unknowingly say more to someone than the MacRae family wanted out in the public.

Bernie patted me on the shoulder, but I felt so alone. I was sorry I hadn't been more compassionate with Hunter. All I could think about was how it affected me. No doubt Hunter would call back later today and give me details on the funeral. I knew he would want me there for the service.

I stood, determined to get myself out of this stupor. "I'm going to get a shower. Just answer the phone if it rings and come and get me if it's important."

"Leave the door open so you can yell if you get dizzy or need me."

After showering and drying my hair, I heard voices in the living room. I donned blue jeans and a Rutgers sweatshirt before I headed downstairs.

"Oh, my late husband knew lots of the cops around here," Bernie was saying. "Did you know a Vince Scala?"

"Yes, ma'am, he's my great uncle. He was a cop and my grandfather was a fireman," a deep voice said. "My brother and I are both cops, and my sister is married to a cop."

"Well, your mother must worry all the time."

I walked into the doorway and Mike Scala rose to his feet. No surprise to see him here, of course. He had a murder to solve.

"There you are," Bernie said. "You've got a visitor, honey, a nice policeman."

"Thanks." I took a seat beside her on the couch.

He sat in the chair closest to mine.

Bernie popped up. "I'm going to check on my chicken soup and make coffee."

I gave Mike a rueful smile. "I guess we'll have coffee."

Mike pulled out his notebook and a pen. "I'd like to go over what happened last night, if you're up to it. How's your head?"

"Better." Mike was reading through his notes, so I asked, "Have you talked to Eric?"

"Yeah, early this morning."

"What do you think?"

"He was at his mother's house with his two daughters and everyone was asleep when we arrived. His mother said he'd been with her and the girls all evening, playing games and reading to them. They had homemade soup and sandwiches for dinner and went to bed early. Nothing we saw indicated anyone left the house during the night."

I pushed down my anger. Mike could only go by what he had to work with, but I was sure Eric Russo murdered his wife.

"If it's any consolation, we don't believe him either," Mike said. "We've just got to do some good detective work and find the clues that lead us back to him. This was a brutal murder. It had all the earmarks of a crime of passion. Whoever did that to Kinley Russo hated her, and from what I've learned from family and friends already, that's a short list."

"You're right, of course. I stayed at her house Friday night after she'd had a scene with Eric. I should have continued to stay with her."

"How did you end up at her house last night?"

Oh, boy, this was going to be fun. How could I explain to a police officer who dealt in facts and absolutes that I had a vision that Kinley was in trouble and went running to the rescue a little too late? Apparently I was taking too long to answer him.

Not taking his gaze from mine, he said, "Why don't we start with Friday night. Why were you there?"

I told him everything, including the new locks that were installed on Saturday.

"Did she call you again last night?"

"No, I…uh…" I made it up as I went along. "I became concerned about her and decided I'd go over and check. I felt something was wrong."

"You thought he might try to hurt her again?"

"Eric's predictable. I knew he'd be frustrated when his set of keys no longer worked. I decided to just pop in and see if I could surprise him."

"You surprised somebody," Mike said. "Tell me again what happened."

Closing my eyes, I thought back to when I got out of my car last night. Slowly, with as little emotion as possible, I recalled for Mike how I found Kinley's body.

"Then I felt a horrible pain in my head and everything went black."

"That's all you remember?" He didn't sound as if he believed me.

I thought about my conversation with Hunter's grandfather, but kept it to myself. "I remember you woke me up." He frowned again. Before he could probe any more, I asked, "Who called the police?"

"The next door neighbor saw you sneaking around and called 911. I was headed home and was only a couple of blocks away when patrol asked for an ambulance. Of course I didn't know it was you until I got there. "

"Yeah, me again," I said weakly, keeping my hands on my knees in a relaxed pose.

"You and your partner."

Mike studied me for a moment. "Four nights, two dead bodies and the two of you."

And now Hunter's grandfather.

That fact clicked into my head with such force I was afraid Mike could hear it. I said quickly, "Kinley has nothing to do with the man found in the woods. We don't even know who he is."

"His name was Jess Dugard. His family identified his body this afternoon."

"I don't know that name."

"He's from North Carolina. We put a photo out on him Saturday, and the North Carolina state troopers identified him Sunday. In fact, one of his cousins is a trooper who brought the mother in. The Dugards come from some tiny place up in the mountains in the eastern part of the state. They're making arrangements to take the body home with them for burial."

"What was he doing here?"

"Family says he liked to travel."

"To New Jersey in the dead of winter?"

"Yeah, it didn't add up to me, either. But the guy has no record. His mother was all broken up, but she said she didn't have any idea why he was here or why he would have been murdered."

I eyed him for a moment. "You don't believe her."

Mike closed his notebook with a snap. "I do believe he has nothing to do with Kinley Russo's murder."

"Kinley's husband killed her," I said again.

"And maybe, just maybe, you and MacRae happened to be in two very bad places where there were two very dead but completely unrelated bodies."

"Believe me, I wish I hadn't been at either place."

"I believe you about Dugard." Mike's voice lowered and he leaned forward. "I think you wish you'd been five minutes earlier at the Russo's house."

I looked away.

"I think you wish you had shot Eric Russo dead."

I pursed my lips. It was no good, however. I just couldn't lie. So I looked him straight in the eyes. "You're right."

He didn't flinch. Instead, with something like admiration in his eyes, he reached out and took my hand in his. "I don't blame you for feeling that way. We don't have proof yet that he did it. We're going to pursue any avenue that opens up. But if he did it, he'll give himself away. Then he'll pay. "

"I want to help." I didn't resist when he kept holding my hand.

"I'll keep you in the loop." He was placating me, of course. This was "police business" and he wasn't telling me anything I couldn't read in the newspaper.

But I smiled and let him hold my hand until Bernie appeared with coffee. Mike Scala's big, masculine hand felt damned good. Of course, I was also calculating what he might say when he discovered there was another death in Hunter's life. Even I knew the bodies were piling up pretty fast for a hotshot divorce attorney and a mild-mannered PI.

What in the hell was going on?

Chapter 9

Hunter's family was gathered in the massive drawing room at the family estate. The room was silent save for the crackling of the wood fire. It was evening, barely twenty-four hours since his grandfather's death. They had received neighbors from the nearby town and the estate's employees and their families tonight.

There would be a memorial service in Manhattan at a later date for the firm's business associates. Tonight had been for those who knew and loved the real Fraser MacRae—husband, father, grandfather, friend, shifter, and leader of his clan. Tradition dictated that his body be cremated and his ashes spread within two days of his death. So tonight, they said goodbye.

Hunter missed Zoe and wished she could be here, as well. But she needed to get over her concussion, and she'd be there for him later. Just like always.

For the most part, Hunter had spent this evening listening to stories about Fraser. Now he struggled to accept the finality of it all.

Grandda was dead.

Anger surged through him, and he wondered at the silence of his family.

Seated on a sofa facing the huge fireplace, his grandmother, Isobel, was regal in a dark gray dress with pearls at her throat, her hair a shining white crown of braids. His father was at her side. As usual, Stirling was solicitous, broad of shoulder and square of jaw, the faultless son. Hunter's mother, Margaret, was in a chair to the side, sipping yet another fortifying glass of wine. His sister, Meagan, was curled into a chair upholstered in deep red. Her face was pale against the rich color.

A color like blood. Like the streaks of blood he had seen on his grandfather's flesh.

"How can we just sit here?" Hunter snarled.

Stirling's gaze was steady on Hunter's. "Have some respect, son."

"Respect?" Hunter retorted.

"Mind your manners," his mother slurred, sounding more than a little drunk.

Hunter whirled to face her. "How can we worry about manners when Grandda is dead, murdered by God knows what kind of monster?"

Meagan gasped and dropped her head into her hands.

Stirling stood. "You're upsetting everyone."

"So we do nothing?" Hunter demanded. "I know we're supposedly waiting on autopsy results, but we both saw the body. We know Grandda was ripped to shreds, but we're just supposed to sit here?"

Before Stirling could protest again, Isobel took her son's arm. "Be still." She looked hard at Hunter. "Both of you be still."

In the sudden silence, the scream of an animal could be heard from outside.

Hunter leapt toward the bank of French doors to his right. Over his sister's sobs and his father's protests, he wrenched them open. Cold air spilled inside. Hunter smelled something alien. Another scream cut through the night, cruel and triumphant.

His skin tingled as he strode to the edge of the icy, brick patio. Summoning the second nature inside of him, he roared, his instinct to challenge whatever was prowling the mountains beyond the estate.

"Hunter, no," Isobel demanded from behind him. "Now is not the time."

Following her command as he would have his grandfather's, Hunter clenched his fists. His body strained against his clothes, anxious for a change, yearning to stalk the beast that had killed his blood kin.

His grandmother touched his shoulder. Her voice gentled and settled him. "Think of your sister and your mother. They don't understand this part of our world."

"Listen to her," his father said, stepping to his side. "You can't do anything about this tonight. Your grandfather's men are mourning him. They deserve that. They shouldn't have to worry about you, too."

"I don't understand," Hunter protested.

"I know you don't," Isobel said, regret lacing her tone. "I'm sorry you're not better prepared. Your grandfather thought he had more time. He thought you deserved to be carefree before you knew the truth."

"What truth?"

"You know we have enemies," Stirling said. "I know he told you that much."'

Chymera. The creature his grandfather had told him about. The mutant Fraser had warned Zoe about in her vision. No doubt Chymera had his own clan.

Hunter remembered the legends, the stories of how his family had become shifters, of the enemy who had sworn a blood oath against them. But had he truly believed those stories before now, before Grandda's savage death?

"I need to know," Hunter said, turning toward his grandmother.

"And you will." She turned back toward the door. "Come back inside where it's warm." She sounded strong and sure of herself, but in the lighted doorway, she swayed a bit and reached for Hunter's hand.

"Nana?" he said, suddenly alarmed as she faltered another step.

Swearing, Stirling stepped forward to take his mother's arm. He guided her to the sofa.

Meagan went quickly to Isobel's side, glaring at Hunter. "What's wrong with you?"

Isobel patted her granddaughter's hand. "I need to talk to Hunter."

He closed the doors behind him. "And I need to hear the truth."

"No," Meagan said, a note of firmness in her voice that Hunter wasn't used to hearing.

She glared at him again. "Nana's exhausted. Tomorrow, she's spreading Grandda's ashes at the cabin. Whatever she needs to say to you can wait until after that."

"I need to know now," Hunter protested.

"And of course the mighty Hunter should get what he wants," Meagan retorted. "Just like always."

Hunter fell back a step, surprised by Meagan's bitterness.

"That's enough." Stirling helped Isobel to her feet. She protested, but it was clear that she was in no shape to continue this conversation.

"Tomorrow," she whispered to Hunter. "I promise tomorrow we will talk. You take care tonight."

With a last grumble from Stirling and a disgusted

glance from Meagan, Isobel was helped from the room. Hunter stood in front of the fire, staring after them.

From the chair where she had remained seated, his mother chuckled. He stared at her. She raised her glass to him and then drained it dry. "The fun's just beginning, my dear boy. You may be sorry when you know all the secrets."

Hunter swore, and she laughed again. "I know. I know I disgust you. But if you ever marry, we'll see how well your wife copes with the MacRea heritage."

Turning on his heel, Hunter went to the foyer and through the heavy front doors into the cold, winter night. He couldn't breathe in this house. Despite his grandmother's admonition to take care, he needed to change.

He raised his face to the sky and began to run, shedding his clothes as he changed into a sleek black panther. Lifting his head again, he let out a loud roar, fully realized, fully feline. Panthers can roar as many other cats do not. Cats like bobcats, cougars, and even housecats can purr, but they cannot roar. Hunter roared again, eager to silence the other creature who had dared cry out on his family's land.

Behind him, he heard voices. He recognized Shamus, calling his name. But Hunter took off, racing through the gardens, scaling a tree and breaching the walls of the estate. No one could catch him when he took this form. Black panthers were called ghosts in the forests because they were difficult to see among the trees and undergrowth.

As he ran, the anger inside him subsided. He remembered running in this same forest with his grandfather. He could feel Fraser's presence. On a hill overlooking the house, he stopped and roared again, imprinting his grief on everything around him. He waited for an answer, but he heard nothing. He felt dominant and in control as he tore his way up and down trees.

Gradually, he calmed. He went back toward the estate wall. Then he smelled the enemy.

The evil was close. He looked around, sniffed the air, and moved to hide in nearby weeds.

He waited, but the enemy stayed hidden. Chymera didn't attack. And Hunter was canny enough to realize this was part of the battle. His grandmother had been right. Tonight was not the time. But the time would come. Hunter knew that as well as he knew this land.

He climbed a tree and went back over the wall. Just beyond the broad, front porch, he shifted again and found his clothing had been placed on an iron bench among the porch's furniture.

Shamus stepped out of the shadows. A rifle gleamed in his hands. "You can't tear off like that again, Master MacRae."

Master MacRae? The address surprised Hunter into silence. This was what Shamus had called his grandfather. He ignored the man and pulled on his clothes.

"There's a demon afoot," Shamus said. "Your grandmother cannot take another loss. Aye, none of us can take it."

Remembering the strength he had felt on the hill overlooking the house, Hunter forced out a laugh. "I'm not afraid."

"You should be."

Before Hunter could reply, his cell phone rang. He

pulled it from his pants pocket and saw that it was Zoe.

"Are you all right?" she asked breathlessly when he answered.

He turned away from Shamus and went inside, firmly closing the front door on the scowling bodyguard.

"I'm fine." Hunter crossed the foyer to his grandfather's study.

"What do you think it was?" Zoe asked.

"What was?"

"What you heard in the woods. You felt something, smelled it. I saw you."

"You're talking crazy. Do I need to call Bernie and get her to take you back to the hospital?"

"You were in the woods, as a panther."

Hunter frowned. "How did you know that?"

"I saw you, Hunter, I saw you running through the woods. I was just sitting here, thinking about you and your grandfather, and then I could see you. You were so sad and so grief stricken it broke my heart. You ran wild through the woods like a black streak."

How could Zoe know what he had just done?

"Your grandmother told you not to go, but you went anyway."

This was downright creepy. He and Zoe had always been in tune, but she was peeking into his brain. "So you saw the scene with my family, too?"

Zoe sighed. "I can't explain how I see these things, but I do. I know you were warned not to go into the woods and went anyway."

"How much of my life can you see?"

"Oh, my god, Hunter, only stuff involving your second nature," I said with impatience. "Anything else and I'd poke my eyes out. Now what was going on tonight?"

There was another long silence before Hunter sighed. "I felt like I was going to explode if I didn't run, and there's this thing out there, howling in the night..." Hunter steadied his voice and told Zoe about his grandmother's talk of his family's enemies. He described the primal scream that had spilled over the mountains and valleys.

Zoe barely stifled a gasp. "So you ran off to issue your own challenge? And you're already thinking about going back. Aren't you?"

He was silent.

She groaned in frustration. "Oh my God, I can see you searching through those woods again. This is what your grandfather meant in my vision. He said we had a special connection, that I could see you. I have just enough precognition to know what's about to happen, but I can't do a damn thing about it. Just like with Kinley."

"Zoe," Hunter murmured. "There's nothing you could have done about Kinley."

"I can't lose you."

"You're not going to."

"Your grandfather told me to protect you."

"Shit." Hunter dropped into the chair behind his grandfather's broad desk.

"There's so much I don't understand. Like Grandda's body. He didn't change. He took all that punishment as a human. That just doesn't make sense. He could change in half the time it takes me. What would cause him to remain human when he was being attacked?"

"You need to listen to your grandmother," Zoe said. "I know she can explain this to you."

"Tomorrow I'm taking her to the cabin to spread Grandda's ashes. She promised we would talk."

"Is it safe to go there?"

"Grandda's men are armed to the teeth. They'll be standing guard."

"They couldn't contain you tonight."

"I didn't give them a choice," Hunter admitted.

"Don't take chances," Zoe warned. "Please, promise you won't. I feel as if something bad is about to happen."

"Worse than what's already happened?"

She had no reply to that. Hunter sat back in his grandfather's chair. "Don't worry. I'll be back at work in a few days. We'll be back to normal."

"Normal?" Zoe's laugh was low and without mirth. "I don't know, Hunter. I think ever since you found that body in the woods behind our office, nothing has been normal."

Hunter clicked off the phone and listened to the sounds of the house settling around him. He had always felt safe here. Now he wondered if he would ever feel safe again.

The following afternoon, Hunter pulled an ATV up to the porch of his grandfather's cabin. The rustic hideaway still looked much as it had when he'd come here as a teenager. The snow that had fallen yesterday had largely melted. Sunlight filtered in streaks through the bare limbs of the giant trees that surrounded the haven of Fraser MacRae.

This would be his final resting place.

Beside Hunter, his grandmother sighed. "Fraser

was always so happy here. He loved the woods and spent a good part of his life wishing he could spend more time here."

Hunter got out of the vehicle and extended her a hand. She stepped out, one arm cradling the urn with Fraser's ashes. Nana had regained her strength today. Her eyes were clear and bright. Acceptance had settled over her features.

Hunter had been surprised that it was just the two of them who would spread the ashes. But Nana said that's what Fraser had wanted. How did being excluded make his father feel? And what did Stirling think of how Shamus and the other employees kept deferring to Hunter?

His parents and sister had been very quiet this morning, as if last night's family fracas had never happened. Margaret and Meagan departed for the city after a somber family brunch. Stirling was back at the house, going over financial records and meeting with attorneys, already moving forward to settle Fraser's estate.

His grandmother's soft sigh brought Hunter back to the business at hand. He turned to her. "Are you ready to do this?"

"Almost," she murmured, looking again at the sun-dappled forest. "Fraser brought me here when we conceived your father. Those four days were among the happiest of our married life."

"Nana, please," Hunter said, pretending to shudder.

She chuckled. "Your grandfather was a lusty, loving man. Our life together was a wonderful romantic adventure. It should make you proud to know that."

"It does, but can we talk about something else

now?"

Isobel passed the urn containing her husband's ashes to Hunter. He took it calmly, although he couldn't control a grimace.

"Don't be so squeamish. You're just holding a part of your grandfather. He will be so happy when he's resting peacefully in his beloved woods."

Looking down at the urn, tears stung his eyes.

"I know, *ogha*. Life will never be the same for either of us. He was a vigorous, happy man, more so with me than anyone else." She glanced around, her expression soft with memories. "When we moved here, there was almost nothing here. He built our house and set about bringing people here to build the town and create a place where he had everything he needed. With easy access to New York City, we were set."

"Were you happy living way up here most of the year?" Hunter set the urn on the steps of the cabin.

Isobel laughed. "Not at first. I left the small town where I lived in Scotland and looked forward to living in America and experiencing new things. I wanted to live in the city. Fraser was astonished at my reaction. He said, 'I thought you'd love it, Izzie, it's a great deal like your home in Giffnock.' I said, 'That's why I wanted something different, you big ass.' We had a hell of an argument."

Now Hunter laughed, remembering his grandfather's famous temper. "How long were you two mad at each other?"

"Until your grandfather grabbed me and kissed me and said, 'Ah, lass, you're gorgeous when you're spittin' fire. Give us a kiss, and I'll take you anywhere you want to go.' And he did. Did you know we've visited every one of the continents? I've had a good life, a very good life." Tears gathered in her eyes.

"It's not over, Nana, you can still travel and enjoy yourself."

"Maybe after a while. I'm thinking about going back to Scotland. Your great aunt Agnes lives in Giffnock. I'm going to stay with her for a while. She's in our family's big old home, so there's plenty of room. It'll be nice to be with family and visit old friends."

She wiped the tears off her face with her hands.

Hunter's chest tightened. It would be like losing both grandparents with his grandmother living so far away. "Are you sure you want to leave the house where you lived with Grandda?"

"It holds nothing but loneliness for me now." Her words were whispered. "The staff will stay on at the house and maintain it. It'll be here whenever you're ready for it. Your grandfather made arrangements to provide everything for them, and for you. He wanted you to have this estate. It's never been important to your father."

"Why is that? Why do you think Father is so different from me and Grandda? It's not just the shifting. Father and I are nothing alike."

She put her hand on his cheeks. "He's very much like my own father, reserved and ambitious. When he visited my parents in Scotland, your father would go to town and sit for hours in my father's office at the bank. He was obviously a very observant child. He has used all he learned at my father's knee. They don't think like we do. For them it is all about what you possess, how you appear to the world."

"He does know how to make money," Hunter said

without affection.

"As did your Grandda," Isobel said, her voice stern. "And it's not a bad thing. You resent it because it's not as important to you, but so many people envy what you've always had. Appreciate it and use it wisely. Emulate your grandfather, Hunter. Use what you've been given to help others and make Fraser proud."

She stepped back and nodded at the urn resting on the porch step. "It's time."

Hunter was afraid he would give into tears if he tried to talk now. He picked up the urn containing his beloved grandfather's earthly remains and followed his grandmother to a spot just south of the cabin. The winter sun was beginning to dip in the sky, but it was still strong enough to warm the shadows here.

Isobel took the urn from Hunter, lifted the lid and turned in a slow circle. Fraser's ashes poured out in a silvery stream. After several moments, his grandmother stopped, bowed her head, and her lips moved soundlessly. She looked up, smiled, peaceful as she handed the urn to Hunter.

He took it, not knowing what he should do or say. But once the container was in his hands, he felt his grandfather. He could feel Fraser's essence merging with the land he had loved so much.

As the last of the ashes scattered, the emotions Hunter had been holding at bay took over. He dropped the urn to the ground and sobbed.

Isobel enveloped him in a rose-scented hug and let him weep on her shoulder. "It takes a strong man to cry, my grandson. It is good that you loved your grandfather so much."

Hunter eventually backed away, pulling a white linen handkerchief out of his pocket. His initials were embroidered in the corner. Having a clean handkerchief was something his grandfather had taught him. The older man told Hunter that girls liked it, especially if they cried during a movie and needed it.

When he had composed himself, Isobel put her arm through his, and leaned her head against his shoulder. "We always knew this day would come, Hunter. We Scots are nothing if not practical."

Her voice became almost businesslike. "Your grandfather's attorneys know what to do. The estate is set up to provide for you and me and to give Stirling his share, which I'm sure he will continue to invest wisely and increase accordingly. I believe Meagan shares his talent for financial wizardry."

She pulled back to study him. "You're the one I'm worried about. You've inherited your grandfather's mantle, his blessing and his curse."

"The shifting. And the family enemy." Hunter returned her steady gaze. "You promised you would tell me what I need to know."

She nodded and stepped away. "I know you don't realize this, but you're the only thing Fraser and I truly disagreed about."

"About me? Why?"

"He wanted you to be carefree as long as you could. He wasn't able to do that, you see. He had to take up the reins of the family honor." She looked hard at Hunter. "He had to fight."

Hunter frowned, not quite following her. "As in physically fight?"

"Sometimes. Leading the MacRaes is a big job.

You're the one who has to continue the line."

"You're talking about reproducing, having children—"

"I mean protecting this family. I was furious with Fraser that he hadn't prepared you for your role as protector. Your father and I argued with him about it many times, but it was no use. He had his own timetable set in his head. He wouldn't have it any other way."

"Grandda called me this weekend. He said we needed to talk. I should have come straight here. If I had, he wouldn't have been alone."

Isobel shook her head. "He was stubborn and foolhardy at times. You need to learn a lesson from what happened to him. You have to respect Chymera's daring and strength."

"Respect that thing we heard screaming last night? Never."

"You must respect your worst enemy," his grandmother insisted. "Think about when your grandfather taught you to shift and showed you how to prowl this forest like a king. What did he tell you?"

Hunter closed his eyes, thinking back to those long months here at the cabin, when his first change had come upon him. He remembered the nights he and Fraser had roamed for miles, crossing the territories of other predators. His grandfather taught him to be confident, but to know that a false step, an unguarded moment, could give other creatures the opening they needed.

When he looked back at Isobel, she was smiling. "He taught you well, didn't he?"

He nodded.

She gestured for him to follow her as she crossed the clearing and back to the cabin's porch. "It's time for you to know everything, Hunter. But first, I have a little surprise for you."

She pulled off her coat and laid it over the wooden banister of the steps. Stretching her arms up, she closed her eyes and the air around her crackled with energy and change. Hunter stood with his mouth gaping as his grandmother became a beautiful snow leopard. Before he could say anything, the air was alive with electricity as she changed back. Seeing Hunter's face, she burst out laughing and squeezed his arm.

"You look so amazed," she said, her bright laughter ringing throughout the woods. "It was your grandfather's idea to keep our secret. Fraser, and now you are the only ones I've ever revealed myself to. I do understand how you were trained. He trained me, as well."

Hunter legs went weak. He rubbed his face with his hands, still not certain of what he'd just seen. "I'm...I'm astonished. How...what?" He stopped and took a deep breath. "Have you always been like this?"

"Your grandfather changed me," she explained.

Hunter was dumbfounded.

Isobel smiled as she explained, "I became pregnant about three months after your grandfather and I married. We were so happy, so excited, and a little afraid because of his family's genetic problem. But others in the family had gotten through it—"

"Others?" Hunter sputtered.

"There are many shifters in the MacRae family. Surely you didn't think you were the only one."

"But Grandda never told me. He never said—"

"The family is spread throughout the U.S. and Europe. As you know, we have enemies."

"So we hide?"

"Of course not!" Isobel protested. "How can you say that when your grandfather became such a successful, prominent man here in the U.S?"

"But if there's a family, isn't there strength in numbers?"

"Our numbers are dwindling."

"If Grandda could change you, then why not others?"

She sighed. "It's not that simple, Hunter. What happened with Fraser and me has rarely been replicated. It happened soon after your father was born."

She took a seat on the porch steps and gestured for him to sit beside her as she explained, "I had a wonderful pregnancy. Fraser made sure I had whatever I craved. He even sent Shamus' father Henry into New York one night to get me a piece of the chocolate cake from Sardi's."

"I can't imagine him being so indulgent," Hunter said.

"He was a marshmallow with me, I admit it, and I shamelessly took advantage of it. When I went into labor, Dr. Connor came out to the house, of course, with his nurse, and Henry's wife was a midwife, so I had plenty of help. My labor was long and hard, though, and when Stirling was finally born, I was torn badly, and my uterus collapsed. There was a lot of blood. I don't remember most of it because I passed out, but I do remember the fear in the nurse's face.

"When I woke, Fraser was connected to me, giving

me a transfusion. He literally saved my life. In the next two weeks, I had to have two more transfusions and eventually a hysterectomy. It broke my heart because Fraser and I wanted lots of children. Still, I was glad to be alive."

"I guess it helped that Dr. Connor knew our family secrets," Hunter commented.

"Fraser brought him here because of that. And his son who is taking over the practice already knows the truth, as well."

"Did you feel differently after the transfusions?"

"I felt stronger and much closer to Fraser, but I thought that was because we'd just had a baby and a big scare, and we were both so happy. As the months went along, however, I noticed other things. When he went out to run at night, I wanted to go with him for the first time. He laughed at me and said I was just feeling hormonal."

"What happened?"

She laughed. "You probably aren't going to like this, but one night a couple of months later, we were making love. It was always wonderful with your grandfather, but this night was very intense."

Hunter gritted his teeth. "Do I have to hear this part?"

She patted his arm. "Don't worry, I'll spare you the details. This time I felt...I don't know, electric. I was terrified at first because my body felt on fire. I thought I was dying. Instead, I became a snow leopard. Your grandfather was so frightened that he changed without even realizing it. We stared at each other for a few moments, and then he changed back. He walked me through the process. Then we made love and went for a run together. It was beautiful."

Her voice softened. "For the first time, I was a part of Fraser's whole life. We were truly one, and you're lucky enough to share that trait with us."

"Oh, yeah," Hunter said. "I'm the lucky one."

"Can you imagine your life without the splendor and excitement of becoming a cat?"

Hunter paused, then admitted the truth. "No, no, I can't." He stood and leaned in to his grandmother. "You've got to tell me one thing."

"Anything."

"How do you shift without taking off your clothes?"

Smiling, Isobel put both on her hands on his face. "It's just mind over matter, *ogha*." She used the Gaelic word for grandchild. "And it's magic, just plain magic."

"Where does the magic come from?"

"I like to think it came from my Celtic ancestors. My great-great-great-grandmother was a white witch. Did you know that?"

"No, I didn't," Hunter admitted. "It seems there's a lot about my family and my gift that I didn't know."

"There's more," Isobel said. "We have much to teach you."

"Does that mean I'm going to meet the whole family?"

"In time." She got to her feet. "You'll start by listening to me and to Shamus. You're already the MacRae clan head by birthright. Shamus will be filling in some of the gaps in your education that Fraser neglected." She lifted a hand, and as if by magic, his grandfather's devoted servant appeared at the edge of the woods, his rifle at the ready.

As Hunter watched, other men and women melted out of the forest. He recognized the faces. These were the people who worked on the estate and lived in the town nearby. They were old, young, and middle-aged. He had known them all of his life. Taken them for granted, really, as just part of his grandparents' home in the mountains.

"We're here to protect you now." Shamus stepped forward.

Hunter looked helplessly at his grandmother and then back at the two dozen or so men and women who stood in a semi-circle. All of them were armed. Many were looking over their shoulders, obviously on alert. Surely this was a joke.

He was about to wisecrack about having his own private Secret Service. But one of the younger men caught his eye. Evan Egan was his name. He was around Hunter's age. Hunter also recognized Evan's older brother, Craig, who was Shamus's second-in-command. Hunter remembered Craig and Evan from summers he had spent here when he was a child. Now, something in Evan's gaze made Hunter bite back the witticism on his lips.

"It's late," Shamus said. "We need to get back to the main house."

Hunter's feline senses prickled to life. While he and his grandmother had talked, the afternoon's shadows had lengthened. It wasn't safe out here. No matter that Nana could change into a leopard capable of tearing out a man's throat—

A cat's scream broke into Hunter's thoughts. It was the same horrible sound that had intruded on his family last night. He was reminded that this was no man. This was monster.

He gestured toward Evan. "Take my grandmother home. Quickly."

But it was Craig who came forward to escort Isobel to the ATV. She murmured a word of caution to Hunter, but followed Craig without hesitation. The ATV headed off with about half of the guards as well. In moments, the engines of other vehicles came to life in the forest.

Hunter scowled at Evan. "Why didn't you take my grandmother?"

"Evan stays by your side," Shamus said. "As do I. You are the MacRae, and we are sworn to serve you."

"She is part of me."

"Part of all of us. Craig would lay down his life for her, as would the others. But for now, you want to hunt Chymera. And we're here to help you."

Hunter realized that the lessons his grandmother had mentioned were about to begin. He was about to take his grandfather's place. Anticipation quickened inside him. "Let's find the bastard. I'll lead."

Like lightning, the change took him. In panther form again, he led them into the forest.

Chapter 10

I'm a lapsed Catholic. I stopped regularly attending mass when my devout nanny departed my father's employ the day after my eighteenth birthday. But just about the time I figured Hunter and his grandmother had finished spreading Fraser MacRae's ashes, I felt a strong need for the ritual and peace I had often known in church.

I had a sense of foreboding about Hunter. I couldn't summon what connected me to him last night. We had talked earlier today, before brunch with his family, and he hadn't sounded good. Worse, I was sure he was keeping things from me. My visions were freaking him out. But hell, they were freaking me out, as well. Especially since I couldn't call up a vision at will. What good was this kind of gift if I couldn't use when I wanted to?

I tried praying, meditating, and listening to classic tunes by Jersey's own god, Springsteen. Nothing helped.

"So I might as well go to church," I said to my reflection in my dresser mirror. I headed downstairs, hoping to sneak past Bernie.

Unfortunately, I had to stop in the hallway to get my coat and purse. From her perch in front of the television, Bernie looked up from a Maury Povich interview with mothers whose daughters had chosen prostitution over college. She got to her feet, arms crossing in determination. "You're not going anywhere, Zoe."

"I'm not driving." I pulled my good wool coat over my clothes. "I'm walking to the church just down the street. I won't be long."

"I'll go with you."

"No, Bernie, really—" I stopped and bit my lip.

She looked at me. "So you've had enough mothering, have you?"

Bernie had insisted I didn't need to return to work until Thursday and she should stick close by. The result had been non-stop conversation unless I was napping in my room. I knew she loved me, and I didn't want to hurt her. But Bernie had to go home.

Now I went to her and kissed her soft, wrinkled cheek. "Thanks for everything."

She took the hint. "I'll take myself home while you're gone. Supper's already waiting for you in the kitchen."

I gave her a last hug and left.

The temperature was in the high thirties, and much of yesterday's snow was dirty, gray sludge at the edge of the street. My steps quickened as I caught sight of the church's slim steeple.

It wasn't a large building, but the red brick exterior had mellowed with age. Inside the chapel, beautiful stained glass windows told the story of the Good Samaritan from the book of Luke.

The late afternoon sun illuminated those windows. I gazed at the colorful pictures of the familiar parable and thought of how I had failed Kinley. Where was her Samaritan when needed? I felt my heart breaking.

Those little girls had lost their mother in a most horrible way. If I had been a few minutes earlier, I might have stopped it all. Regret consumed me.

I stopped about a third of the way to the altar. The old, wooden pew creaked as I made the sign of the cross and sat. Dry, furnace-forced air blew the scent of candle wax my way. A few others sat with bowed heads. An older couple lit a candle at the front.

I bowed my head to pray for Kinley and her little girls. Then I prayed for Hunter and his family. I felt such a responsibility to keep him safe. But how was I going to do it when he was so far away?

This new psychic awareness I had, as foggy as it was, seemed a heavy burden, and I wasn't ready for what it required of me.

I have always believed in God and have studied the bible a great deal. I enjoy debates where beliefs are presented with religious experts discussing their tenets and perspectives. I understood so much more about what others believed now and wondered if it was difficult for God to be so many different things to so many people.

I closed my eyes, giving myself over to the pain of Kinley and Fraser's deaths and Hunter's absence. A long-forgotten bible verse ran through my head, "Peace I leave with you, my peace I give unto you: not as the world giveth, give I unto you. Let not your heart be troubled, neither let it be afraid."

It's amazing what the child learns that the adult recalls. I knew it was from the book of John. That I could remember it was comforting.

Maybe the peace of the church was what did it. Because that's when I tapped into Hunter.

I felt him moving through the forest. I saw him, his body sleek and black, golden-green eyes glowing. He wasn't running as he had last night, but prowling through the undergrowth, twining around trees, huddling at the base of rocks. Often, he stopped to sniff the air. A low growl rumbled in his throat. The forest was deeply shadowed and growing darker by the moment.

Was this happening now or was it a future event? I had no idea. My mind was spinning, hundreds of miles from the quiet church. But my spirit was with Hunter, and he was stalking something.

Chymera.

I concentrated on the scene in my head. I heard voices in the distance. I saw Shamus. Fraser's loyal bodyguard with other men, close on Hunter's trail. I saw the high-powered rifles they carried. At least Hunter wasn't alone and unprotected. But what was he thinking? He was an alley cat who used his shifting abilities for fun. Did he really think he could battle the monster that killed Fraser?

At the same time, I realized it had been too much to think he would hold off going after his grandfather's murderer as soon as possible.

It gave me a jolt to realize Hunter was going to kill someone. But maybe Chymera was just some thing, and maybe it didn't matter.

I wasn't sure I liked thinking that way about a life, any life.

But Hunter's life mattered at this moment. My heart pounded as he picked up speed. The men were shouting at him. As if I were inside him, I felt his anger, his animal instinct to hunt, to pounce, to kill.

While I couldn't see exactly what Hunter was trailing, I felt the same dark presence that had been in the forest last night. There were shouts from the men. An inhuman howl tore through my brain, quickly answered by Hunter's roar and an explosion.

"Oh God, no." I covered my ears and rocked forward. I knew what I heard was a gunshot. I felt Hunter's fear.

"Are you all right?" A concerned voice cut through my connection to Hunter, snapping it off as quickly as it had begun.

With a sharply indrawn breath, I looked up to find a priest standing beside me.

"Are you ill?" he asked.

"I'm fine." The ingrained instincts of a Catholic schoolgirl die hard. I didn't want to make a fool of myself in front of a man of the cloth.

"You called out. Several times."

"I was thinking about a friend," I replied, fumbling for an explanation. If I told the priest I was having a vision, he might call for help, maybe recommend an exorcism—or a straitjacket.

He frowned. "A friend? Is the friend in trouble? You've been here a long time." He assumed I was talking about myself.

"What?" I got to my feet, noting that sunlight no longer came through the windows. How long had I watched Hunter in the woods?

"You were sitting here when I came in about forty-five minutes ago."

"Oh my God, I mean oh my...goodness."

"Do you need to talk?" he asked, his expression kind.

"No." I grabbed my purse. "I have to go."

"Please."

But I hurried down the aisle, not looking back. I dug through my purse for my cell. Hunter didn't answer. I left him a frantic message as I rushed down the front steps into the early winter evening.

Frantic, I scrolled through my contacts until I found the phone number for the MacRae estate. The phone rang several times before a deep, cultured voice answered. It was Hunter's father.

"Mr. MacRae." I felt awkward and inadequate when I spoke with him. I smoothed my hair, as if he could see me. "It's me. Zoe."

"Yes?" He sounded irritated.

"I'm trying to reach Hunter." My voice shook. "Is he there?"

The man drew in a deep breath, and my heart fluttered.

"Is Hunter okay?"

"He's not here," Stirling replied, speaking as he might have to a child. "He hasn't returned from the cabin."

"Is he all right?"

Stirling cleared his throat. "I certainly hope so. He had someone escort his grandmother back to the estate. He's apparently on some sort of expedition."

"So it's true," I murmured. "He's out in the woods. That idiot."

"My feelings exactly," Hunter's father retorted. "Is there a message, Zoe?"

"Tell him…" I paused. What could I do? Tell Stirling MacRae about my vision? I couldn't imagine it. "Just tell him I called."

"Of course."

I stood on the sidewalk, shivering. It wasn't that cold. But I was chilled to my core. Was Hunter dead? Was that why my link to him had shattered so completely?

I rushed home, my plan to book a flight and a rental car as soon as possible and go to Hunter. But what good would that do? It would take hours to get to the estate. What if I was on a plane when Hunter needed me? With my cell phone at my side, I willed Hunter to call.

Somehow, some way, I needed to link with him again. I went to my laptop to look up precognition on the Internet. I immersed myself in trying to learn more about this strange ability.

There's a lot of weird stuff out there when you start looking for things of a psychic nature. I concentrated mostly on information from universities and studies.

I was astonished to learn scientific study of precognition began in 1927. A British Premonitions Bureau was established in the 60s to attempt to use precognitive data to avert disasters.

That was my mission now, should I choose to accept it. Did I have a choice?

Fraser had been adamant that I was the first line of defense for protecting Hunter. I'd have to be with him all the time. Was that even possible? With his late-night antics?

My head was aching when I gave up a bit after nine. Since my bump on the head, that had been happening often.

I made myself warm some of the beef and cabbage casserole Bernie made earlier in the day. I was putting the leftovers away when my cell phone rang. It was Hunter.

"Thank God you called," I said by way of greeting. "What's happened?"

"Shamus is dead."

I dropped into a kitchen chair, stunned. "What? How?"

"The same creature that took Grandda." Hunter's voice broke. "It was horrible."

"You were in the woods, and Shamus had a rifle. There was a shot."

"And it was too late. Shamus moved away from the group, trying to keep up with me. Chymera doubled back and took him. By the time we got to him Shamus was dead." Hunter drew another shaky breath. "His throat was ripped out."

I didn't know what to say. Sorry was inadequate. "When did this happen?"

He explained how Chymera had surprised them at the cabin. "It was about six-thirty when he was attacked."

I was in the church, watching it all unfold just before Shamus was shot. Maybe if I'd shared my vision with Stirling, I could have prevented the tragedy. I wasn't sure I could tell Hunter that, however, over the phone. I settled on, "I'm coming up there."

"No, you're not! Right now, I'm working on getting Nana out of here and in to the city. It isn't safe."

"Not for you, either," I protested. "He's killed two people now."

"He won't kill another."

"Hunter, please get out of there."

"Grandda didn't raise me to walk away from a

fight."

"But you need to think, to plan."

"Oh, I am," Hunter said. "I'm planning how he will die."

He was dead serious. But death was what I feared most for him.

There were voices in the background. "The men are here with a report. I have to go."

"But what—"

The phone clicked off. I started to call Isobel. She must believe he was being foolish too.

Or maybe she had lived long enough with Fraser MacRae to know what Hunter had to do. I sat holding the phone against my chest as if that would keep the connection alive between us.

I was still sitting there when it rang again. Sure it was Hunter calling back to beg me to come rescue him, I grabbed it but was surprised to hear another male voice on the line. "Hi, Zoe, it's Mike Scala. How are you?"

"Fine, Detective. Is something wrong?" I was wary. Did he have more information about the man found dead behind the office? The news of Fraser's death had hit the media, although a hunting accident had been listed as the official cause. Were the police wondering, like I was, why everyone was dying around me and Hunter? Or worse, had they discovered our lie?

"Are Kinley's girls all right?" I asked.

"As fine as they can be, considering what has happened. Although the oldest one hasn't said a word since they told her Kinley was dead." His voice was laced with genuine concern.

"That's terrible. Kelly's such a little sweetheart.

Maybe I should go see them."

"That might be a good idea."

What a nice guy. I could use a man like that in my life. But was this the time to be dating a cop, just when my partner and best friend was planning to kill someone? I needed to end this. "Is there something I can help you with?"

"Uh, yeah, actually." Mike cleared his throat. "I was wondering if you might want to grab a bite to eat tomorrow evening."

I started to say no, but I couldn't get the word out. I mean, here I sat alone. My best friend needed me, sure, but he was pushing me away. And did I really blame him?

Hell, I didn't know anything about hunting half-man, half-beast creatures, and my psychic hotline to Hunter wasn't ringing in time for me to protect him. For about the hundredth time, I wished for an instruction manual on how to be a shifter's first line of defense.

But on the other hand, what did any of that have to do with my romantic life? A hot man was on the phone asking me for a date. That was as rare as a good hair day.

"Zoe?" Mike prompted in the silence, sounding nervous. "You still there?"

If nothing else, getting to know Mike would keep me in touch with Kinley's murder investigation. And be a contact for future cases. "Dinner sounds nice." We made plans for him to pick me up at seven.

"Unless I catch a case, of course," Mike said. "That's the difficult part of homicide. People don't die from nine to five."

I said goodbye, praying I wouldn't also be involved with more dead people tomorrow. It would be a pity to have to tell Mike I was breaking our date to drive to New York and post bail for Hunter.

Chapter 11

Hunter didn't call back. I wanted to reach out to him again, but I knew he needed some space. Wondering about what was happening at the MacRae estate would drive me insane if I let it. What I needed was work. I didn't usually sit around doing nothing. So what if I had been home on doctor's orders. I still felt like a lazy slob.

The mild weather continued on Thursday, and the snow was almost gone. At the office I found our small parking area blocked by a stretch limo. Darla's car was on the street, but I wasn't about to do the same. Leaving my car running, I walked over to the driver's window and rapped it with my knuckles.

The electric window slid down and the driver gave me a bored look.

"You're in my space," I said.

"Mr. Howerton told me wait here," he said.

Howerton, as in Lizzie Howerton? Maybe her father? How interesting.

I pulled my cell phone out and glared at the driver. "If you don't move this barge in fifteen seconds, I'll have the police tow it."

"But Mr. Howerton—"

"Doesn't own this property. I do." I pointed to the street. "Move it. If Mr. Howerton can't walk the additional twenty feet, we've got a wheelchair inside."

I went back to my car and waited while the limo glided down the street. I parked in my usual space and stomped inside. That kind of thing just took the sparkle out of my morning.

Darla met me at the doorway, her entire body tense. "There are two men waiting for you in the conference room," she whispered. "I offered them coffee but they refused because we didn't have coffee from Hawaii. They've been here about ten minutes and seem pretty angry."

She handed me Douglas Howerton's embossed business card. I am psychic—it was Lizzie's father. I stuffed the card in my pocket and headed for my desk. "Don't worry about it. I'll take care of everything."

Enjoying myself as I imagined the men stewing in the conference room, I didn't rush as I took my things out of my briefcase and checked my schedule on my phone.

"Miss!" a voice boomed from the conference room. "Has Zoe Buchanan arrived?"

I leaned around my cubicle wall and signaled for Darla to say nothing, and then I headed for the back. As I passed the conference room, I stuck my head in. An older man sat beside a bored-looking younger one. They both looked up as I said, "You sure you guys don't want some coffee? It's awfully early to discuss things without benefit of caffeine."

"No, thank you," the older man said, his voice dripping disdain. "We simply want to get this done."

"Perhaps you should have shown the courtesy of making an appointment," I said with a smile. "I'm always here when clients phone ahead of time."

Douglas Howerton's mouth gaped. The younger

man squirmed in his seat and I wondered if everything he had was puckered as tightly as his lips.

Lizzie's father was in his late fifties. His gray hair was thin and patchy. He was overweight, though his Italian suit fit him beautifully. Amazing what good tailors can do.

"I'm Zoe Buchanan, by the way," Instead of rising to greet me, he nodded and didn't even bother introducing the young man with him. "And you'd be Lizzie's father. I'll be right back."

The elder Howerton grumbled as I went to the break room and fixed my coffee. I also picked up couple of donut holes from the box left on the counter.

In the conference room, Howerton sat at the head of the table with the mousy assistant on his right. I deliberately sat at the other end of the long table.

"What can I do for you gentlemen?" I broke one of the little pastries in half and popped it in my mouth.

"I am here to insist that you stop taking advantage of my daughter," Howerton said. "She is a young, vulnerable woman, and you should be ashamed of yourself for taking her money on false pretenses."

I ate the other half of my donut hole.

"Well," he bellowed. "Do you have anything to say for yourself?"

I washed the pastry down with coffee and kept my tone mild. "Lizzie hired me to find her sister, the sister you insist she doesn't have, but one she distinctly remembers having until her third birthday. And since she hired me, she is the only who can break the contract."

Howerton held out his hand. "Winston."

The younger man opened a briefcase. He reached

inside for a paper he gave the older man.

"This is a check for one hundred thousand dollars," Howerton said. "That's what I'm willing to pay you to tell my daughter the truth—that she has no sister."

"If it's the truth, why do you need to pay me to tell her? Wouldn't I eventually discover it on my own?"

Slapping his hand on the table, Howerton shot to his feet. "Young woman, I demand you stop scamming my daughter!"

I also stood, deliberately brushing my jacket back so my gun was visible. "Mr. Howerton, I suggest you sit down and speak quietly if you wish to continue this conversation."

Though he scowled ferociously, the older man sat. Young Winston went even paler than before. Sometimes, especially with self-important types like this, I loved making like David Caruso from "CSI: Miami." I only wished I had some aviator sunglasses.

"Now, listen closely," I said after we sat back down. "I made my agreement with Lizzie, and she's the only one who can break it. I don't want your money, and I won't heed your threats. I fully intend to give Lizzie an answer when I get the right information."

I looked from one to the other. A muscle twitched under Howerton's left eye. Faded, squinty brown eyes, I noted. Nothing like Lizzie's beautiful blue eyes. Young Winston couldn't even look at me.

"Now, is there anything else?" I picked up my second donut hole and broke it in half.

Howerton's face was almost burgundy with fury. I'd hate to think what his blood pressure was. "This is the best offer you're going to get."

"I didn't ask for an offer. I want the truth for

Lizzie. What I'm wondering is why it's worth so much to you to keep me from finding it."

"Good God," Howerton muttered as he shoved himself to his feet. "Lizzie's got you believing these delusions of hers."

"Anything worth a hundred grand from you must be a secret worth finding." Dramatic pause. "Considering your current financial situation."

He looked like he wanted to rip into me with his bare fists. Winston was actually trembling. But instead of taking a swing at me, Howerton snatched up his overcoat and strode out of the room. His minion scampered behind, struggling with the check, his briefcase, and coat.

I leaned back in my chair and called, "You might want to give your driver a call. I had him move the car out of my way, so he's probably been circling the block." My only answer was the slam of the front door.

As I headed for my office, Darla and I shared a satisfied glance and a chuckle.

"What an unpleasant man." She handed me a couple of file folders.

"Hopefully he won't be back."

Darla dismissed the pair, more concerned about Hunter, when he would be returning to the office, and how he was coping with his grandfather's death. She adored her boss and wanted to do something special for him when he returned. It wasn't easy to be honest with Darla. I mean, how was I supposed to explain that Hunter wouldn't be back for a while because he was plotting how to get rid of a half-human cretin? Darla was pretty sophisticated, but I didn't know if she was ready to learn about one of her employer's supernatural abilities.

Instead I switched the subject to Hunter's current cases and asked how Brad was doing. She said he was in court and would be all day, but he and Hunter had discussed everything active.

"I'm caught up on all my work," Darla added. "Is there anything I can do to help you?"

I thought for a minute and hit on a great idea. I wanted to work all day, but I also needed to go to Manhattan. I planned to visit Kinley's little girls this afternoon at Lydia's. I'd missed the funeral so I wanted to take the girls something special.

I asked Darla if she'd mind making a shopping trip for me.

"Are you kidding?" she said with a laugh. "Shopping in New York on somebody else's dime? I'm there. What do you need?"

"I want a couple of those beautiful stuffed animals from FAO Schwartz. I'll give you my credit card so it shouldn't be a problem." I reached for my purse. "I want a cat and a dog, two really pretty ones, not too big, but not too small either. Can you take care of that?"

"Sure." Darla grabbed my card.

She left and I dug out Lizzie's file. As I was reading my notes, my thoughts wandered to Hunter too often to concentrate. Unable to resist the urge, I called him. When he didn't answer, I called the estate again.

The person who answered identified himself as Evan. I didn't recognize his voice and didn't appreciate his tone as he informed me that Hunter was in a meeting and couldn't be disturbed.

"This is his partner, Zoe Buchanan."

"He cannot be disturbed," he repeated.

I frowned. "I'm sure he would speak with me."

"His father gave me my instructions."

Stirling left instructions. That explained why I was being cut off. I sighed. But, starved for information, I said, "When is Shamus's funeral?"

If anything, Evan's tone became even more guarded. "I'm sure Mr. MacRae will give you the details soon. I'll tell him you called."

Just like that, I was left holding the phone. "And thank you very much," I said.

I had to put this mess out of my mind. I took a call from Brad about a divorce case Hunter and I had worked last month, and then I turned my attention back to Lizzie Howerton. This job felt more urgent after my two visitors this morning.

Today I focused my Internet search on Charles and Elaine Hayden, the doctor and nurse who owned the Hayden Clinic where Lizzie was born. I followed up on every lead I discovered. Charles died in 1993, but Elaine was still alive and living in their New York apartment in The San Remo, a historic building that overlooked Central Park. The Haydens moved there when they'd retired.

I checked The San Remo out on the Internet and recognized it immediately. Its famous twin towers loom above Central Park. The Haydens shared space with famous neighbors like Tiger Woods, Bono, and Glen Close. The lovely Rita Hayworth spent her last years there.

The Hayden Clinic had been a favorite among the elite women in the New York area. The elegant birthing hospital just outside Manhattan in Secaucus was a state-of-the-art obstetrical center in its heyday. The doctors, among the best in the country, were pioneers of many of the fertility options used today.

I knew the first American test-tube baby was born in 1981 and the fertility industry—a profit-motivated enterprise—had been growing steadily ever since. There were many people who opposed the practice of creating humans in labs instead of sperm meets egg during sexual intercourse. Of course there was always the fear that kind of influence would create a kind of mad scientist with a god complex.

In a way, I guess, that was a valid fear. Dr. Hayden was remembered by many parents as a saint who gave them the children of their dreams. But could he have been involved in something sinister? I definitely needed to explore that option.

According to an announcement in the New York Times, Elaine had remarried. A few clicks of the mouse gave me a phone number in her new husband's name. I called and got a maid who said Mr. and Mrs. Richards were unavailable. I left a polite message for her to call and referenced Lizzie Howerton's birth at the Hayden Clinic. Hanging up, however, I was none too sure the maid even understood, and I was frustrated.

"Dammit," I said to the silent office. I needed a genuine lead, any kind of lead. Whatever Douglas Howerton was willing to pay to hide could be found.

I began another Internet search, trying to find out if Elaine Hayden Richards owned any other properties. Hours sped by as I searched for clues, learning more about the Haydens, test-tube babies, and the Howertons than I would probably ever use. But nothing pointed to a hidden second daughter.

Could Douglas be right? Was Lizzie just a

vulnerable woman grieving her mother's death? Maybe she just yearned for family other than an uptight father.

I was surprised to see it was almost three o'clock when Darla came back to the office toting an array of shopping bags. I hoped most of those purchases were on her credit card, not mine.

"Looks like you bought out FAO Schwartz."

Darla gave a short laugh and reached for two bags in the back. "These are yours. The rest are mine. I couldn't resist the sales."

I pulled out two plush furry animals. I rubbed the adorable chocolate Labrador puppy and the gray striped tabby kitten. "These are so cute. Thanks so much. I can take them by this afternoon."

Darla handed me another small bag. "This is from me to Kelly and Claire. I went to the funeral, but they were so upset, I didn't try to speak to them. Tell them I'm thinking about them both."

"That was so sweet of you."

I looked at my watch. If I left now, I'd have time to see the girls and get home to freshen up before Mike came by at seven. Darla said she'd lock up and I was sure it would be within the next thirty minutes, but I found I didn't care.

As I drove down the tree-lined streets, I remembered the determination and fierce love in Kinley's face as she had talked about her girls and their future. Now it was up to Hunter and me to see her wishes were honored. Eric's abusive past and his being a person of interest in Kinley's murder should ensure Kelly and Claire stayed with their aunt and uncle.

There was a hearing next week about temporary custody. I hoped Hunter would be here to handle it.

Brad was an excellent attorney, but this was personal.

I was getting the shopping bags when the front door opened and a bundle of energy bounded down the steps.

"Zoe!" Claire wrapped her arms around my legs.

Kinley's youngest daughter was five years old with an insatiable love of life.

"I'm so happy you came to see us. What did you bring?" she asked, taking my hand as we walked up the sidewalk to the steps.

"Claire, be nice," Kinley's sister Lydia stood in the doorway.

"I am nice. Miss Johnson says I'm one of the nicest peoples in my class."

"I'm sure she's right." I squeezed her hand. "I've got some surprises in my bag. Let's go inside so I can talk to Kelly too."

"Kel-leeee," Claire yelled. "We got company."

As we reached the porch, Kelly came down the stairs to the living room while Claire chattered. Claire scooted up beside me on the sofa, grinning and enthusiastic. Kelly sat at a child-sized table and chairs, where she began doodling on a piece of paper with a crayon.

"Here you go," I handed her the smaller bag. "This is from Miss Darla at our office. Remember how you and Kelly used to sit with her while your mother talked to me and Hunter? She thought you and Kelly would like these."

Claire opened the bag and went still. "Wow," she said, her voice filled with awe. "Barbie dolls! My favorites." She laughed in delight. "Barbie kind of looks like Miss Darla."

147

Darned if she wasn't right, I thought, smiling.

Claire ran to Kelly. "Look, it's Barbie in a bikini. They're just alike. One for you and one for me!" She handed the second doll to Kelly and whirled back to her aunt. "Aunt Lydia, I can't get it open."

"I'll get the scissors." Lydia went to the kitchen. "Zoe, do you want a Diet Coke?"

"No, I'm fine."

Kelly studied the doll through the plastic container but didn't try to open it. After a moment she returned to her coloring.

Lydia came back, working on opening Claire's Barbie. I took the shopping bag and joined Kelly. The little wooden chairs looked sturdy so I sat across from her.

I studied the picture she was coloring. "That looks great." It was a creative drawing for a seven-year-old. A little girl lay in a bed looking across the page at someone standing a distance from her, a figure dressed in red, which Kelly continued to color until the red crayon broke. She picked up a broken half and began coloring again.

I reached in the bag for one of the stuffed animals. When I brought the gray-striped kitten out, Kelly put her crayon down and reached for it.

"Oh, I'm so glad you like her," I said and patted her lightly on the arm. "I love kittens too. They're soft and cuddly."

Claire raced over. "What about me?"

She pulled the stuffed puppy out with a little shout of happiness. "I'm going to call him Brownie 'cause he's so soft and looks like Aunt Lydia's brownies." She hugged the puppy to her and then squealed again as her aunt freed Barbie from her plastic prison.

"What do you say, girls?" Lydia asked.

Claire hugged me as much as she could with her arms filled with the toys. "Thank you, Zoe. Thank you so much. Tell Miss Darla I love my Barbie, too. I'm going to my room to show Brownie and Barbie where they will be sleeping." Like a miniature tornado, she raced up the stairs.

"Kelly," Lydia said. "Don't you want to thank Zoe for the gifts?"

Kelly's sad eyes met mine. My heart broke at the grief in her pale face. I could share that I knew what it was to be a little girl whose mother died. But I sensed Kelly needed patience and simple kindness, not a lot of words.

"I'm glad you like the kitten," I said, unable to resist giving her a little hug. "And the Barbies that look like Miss Darla." I looked back at the picture on top of the little wooden table. "Maybe you can make me a picture of your kitty. I can hang it in my office."

Once again, she nodded but said nothing.

"Do you want me to open your Barbie?" Lydia asked.

Kelly shook her head and took her toys upstairs without saying a word. Lydia was wiping tears when I turned back. "I'm sorry," she said.

"I understand. Detective Scala said she hadn't been talking. Have you found a counselor for her?"

"There's one at their school. I like her very much. She was with us on Tuesday and yesterday, and came by this morning, as well. Kelly won't speak to her either, but we're going to use her because she's someone Kelly knows. The kid was already pretty torn up by Eric and Kinley's troubles, but this..." Her voice trailed off.

Lydia cleared the top of the little table, putting crayons back in the box and stacking the papers.

"That's the third red crayon she's broken. She really loves red." She took Kelly's latest artistic work. "I'm going to put this up on the refrigerator."

I followed her into the kitchen. "Hunter's going to be out of town for a few more days, but I'd be happy to help you in any way I can. Did Brad get you a copy of Kinley's will?"

"My husband and I are thrilled that Kinley was specific about what she wanted," she said. "Eric hasn't said anything about contesting the will, but that doesn't mean he won't. His silence has been frightening, especially with what his mother has been saying. She thinks the girls should live with her."

Eric was behaving uncharacteristically well, letting Lydia keep the kids without a fuss. There had to be a reason for that. Maybe he was lying low to avoid more suspicion about Kinley's death. Or simply planning to take the girls.

"Bill's getting us a new alarm system," Lydia continued, "and the detective said he'd have a patrol car driving by periodically. I just hope Eric doesn't try to kidnap them or something worse."

Her voice broke on a sob, and her shoulders shook as she cried. I helped her sit and reached for a glass. Using the controls on the front of her refrigerator, I fixed her some ice water and sat down beside her at the kitchen table. After a few moments she regained control and took a drink.

"Thank you. Every time I feel like I'm all cried

out, I break down again." She took another sip. "The police say Eric has an alibi. But who else would do this to Kinley?"

"I can't think of anyone."

"Claire says she, Kelly, Eric, and his mother all had hot chocolate and went to bed early," Lydia said rubbing at the tension in her neck. "That puts Eric at home all night."

"The mother backs that up?"

"Of course." Lydia rolled her eyes. "That woman would say her son was Superman if he wanted. She dotes on him. That was half the problem with him being a husband and father. He didn't know how to put anyone's needs before his own. I just worry what we'll do if he wants the girls. I mean, Kinley spelled out her wishes. She wanted me and Bill to raise them. We can't have children of our own, and she knew…" Her voice broke again. "Kinley knew we'd be good to them."

Zoe patted her hand. "She wanted you to give them a safe and happy life."

"Aunt Lydia," Claire called from the top of the stairs. "Barbie wants a granola bar and some milk. Can I have some too?"

Lydia wiped her eyes and rose to get the snacks. "Sure, come on down. Ask Kelly if she wants something."

We heard Claire run back down the hallway, and then she was coming down the steps. "Kelly said no."

Lydia poured Claire a half a glass of milk and opened the granola bar. Back in the living room at the child-sized table, she moved Kelly's art supplies and put Claire's snack down.

"I need to go," I said, walking over to get my

purse. "Are you sure there's nothing I can do?"

Lydia hesitated, and I realized she wanted something.

"Please," I assured her. "I'd love to help in any way I can."

"Would you mind going over to Kinley's and getting some more of the girls' stuff? Bill and I got what we could, but we don't want to go back right now."

Which was understandable. "Just tell me what you need and I'll get it."

Lydia scribbled a list and pulled a set of keys out of a desk drawer. "These are Kinley's. Detective Scala gave them to me. He said to call if I needed to get into the house."

I took the keys, popping open the small leather case attached to them. It contained adorable photos of Claire and Kelly. I stuck them and Lydia's list in my purse as I said goodbye to Claire and headed for the door.

"There is something else," Lydia said as we stepped out on the porch. She leaned her head back inside. "Claire, I'll be right out here if you need me." She closed the door and spoke softly, "Kinley has a quilt on her bed that she and the girls made with pieces of their baby clothes. I thought it might help Kelly to have it on her bed."

"That's a wonderful idea. I'll be sure to get it," I hesitated, wondering if I should stay longer. "Are you going to be all right?"

Lydia straightened her shoulders. She reminded me of Kinley—fragile on the outside but strong where it mattered. "Thanks, but Mother and Dad are bringing dinner over tonight, so I don't have anything to do but enjoy the girls. I'll be fine."

We said goodbye again, and I got into my car. I didn't look forward to going back to Kinley's house, but it was better for me to do it than Lydia.

Chapter 12

Hunter sat at the desk in his grandfather's study, a room that now belonged to him, as did the rest of the house and its acreage. Despite the tragedy of Shamus's death last night, Stirling had insisted that Hunter go over the will today. It was evening now, and his father had just dismissed the quartet of lawyers.

The estate was his with a contingency that his grandmother could live here until she died. Hunter knew it was a challenge, taking over for his grandfather, but he was proud of the older man's faith in him.

The house had more than ten thousand square feet of living space, with an indoor pool, a bowling lane, and a small skating rink. It boasted a wrap-around porch lined with comfortable wooden rocking chairs, Adirondack chairs, and gliders for relaxing and enjoying the quiet setting along the Hudson River. The outside was rustic but beautiful, the inside elegant but comfortable.

The house's accessories made it easier to convince the grandchildren to visit when they were younger. Meagan and Hunter were curious and adventurous as Fraser and Isobel taught them the unique history of the beautiful woods that had been saved from ruin by the industrialists who'd built their retreats among the lush trees in the mountains.

As they grew older, they brought friends along but eventually spent more time at their parents' home in the Hamptons because most of their friends summered there.

Then, of course, there had been Hunter's sixteenth summer, when his whole world had changed.

Now it was changing again.

Hunter studied shelves filled with an array of first editions his grandfather had collected over a lifetime. The books had been just one of Fraser's many passions. He also loved art and owned several paintings by Gordon White, the Scottish artist known for his renderings of Scotland's famous golf courses. There were also Wyeths, an O'Keefe, and even a Warhol that Stirling had given his father, which said a lot about how little Stirling knew the older man.

Now it belonged to Hunter. Megan had inherited the rent-controlled apartment in New York City.

Stirling got the family home in the Highlands of Scotland, a home that could never be sold or inhabited by anyone outside the MacRae family.

Hunter sighed, a sound of quiet resignation. It was too soon. His grandfather should have lived many more years, like most of the MacRae clan.

Chymera had done that, the damned mutant.

Hunter now knew everything about his family's enemy. Last night, after he and Craig had brought Shamus's body home, Isobel and Stirling had told him what they knew about Chymera.

In the human world, he was called Michael Killin, a financial genius dubbed the Lion of Wall Street by the media. He was older than Stirling, though he looked absurdly young. Like most shifters, he didn't age like a normal human. Rumor had it that Killin was the inspiration for Gordon Gekko, the ruthless hustler of the 1980's movie, "Wall Street."

Fraser always spoke of Killin with contempt but had neglected to tell Hunter who Killin really was, what he really was, a monster leading a family at war with Hunter's own.

Each Killin leader took the name Chymera when they changed.

Hunter was angry that he didn't know this before now. His grandfather had not prepared him for the battle ahead. It was small comfort to know that Isobel and Stirling agreed with Hunter, but they allowed his grandfather make the decisions. Now Fraser was dead.

Despite the loyal men and women who were his protection detail, he felt very alone. He missed Zoe, but he didn't want her here now. Besides his concern for her safety, he was wary of her new ability. His grandmother said that over the centuries the MacRaes had worked with other humans who had special psychic abilities, which made Hunter wonder why they'd both been left in the dark. Their meeting as young teens now seemed fated. Which just raised more questions.

His grandmother left this morning with a full complement of guards. She would be in New York until the Manhattan memorial service, and then she was headed for her sister's home in Scotland. Other guards had been placed with Meagan and Margaret. Though the imminent threat from Chymera seemed to be at the estate, the creature straddled the human and supernatural worlds. He could strike at any time.

According to Isobel and Stirling, the MacRaes had relatives who might help, cousins in North Carolina,

Wyoming, and Canada, as well as in Scotland and, of all places, Russia. Isobel was certain Fraser had been in touch with them before his death. Hunter needed to meet the extended family soon.

But these kindred's numbers had dwindled over the last century. Many families were like Hunter's, where the shifter gene had skipped a generation. A few had been changed the way Isobel had, with a blood transfusion, but that procedure had failed at five times its rate of success. Worse, several MacRaes had fallen to the Killins in the early part of the twentieth century. That was one reason they had spread out, to break up the target area.

On the other hand, Isobel and Stirling said the Killin clan was growing. Killin was rumored to have children with several women, and there were whispers of rapes. His own protection detail included a couple of brothers who were devoted to him. Lions traveled in prides. They didn't enjoy a solitary life, and that meant Chymera had his own army with him all the time, whether he was human or cat.

Hunter was up against some fierce odds. He was especially saddened—and disheartened—by the death of Shamus. Tomorrow they would bury Grandda's main man in the estate cemetery. Shamus trained Craig, but the older man knew more about these pursuers than anyone beside Fraser. Perhaps that was why Shamus had to die, to render Hunter more vulnerable.

Hunter braced his elbows on the desk. Was it only days ago that his main worry had been how to score with a hot redhead at a doughnut shop? Or how to avoid Mandy's husband? Now he was burying another of his clan and plotting how to kill his enemies.

He sighed. Did that make him a good guy or a bad guy?

He wasn't a pillar of any community. He was impatient with talk of duty. Certainly, he had no interest in the firm Fraser founded and Stirling had turned into an empire.

Hell, the most he'd ever done that came close to being charitable was buy two hundred boxes of Girl Scout cookies every year. And that was because he loved Do-Si-Dos and Tagalongs. Zoe picked out their pro bono cases. He didn't look for those who needed his help. Now lots of people depended on him. Not just his family, but Craig, Evan, and other men and women and their families. He was now the MacRae, they had told him. The MacRae.

Hunter rubbed his eyes. He needed rest and exercise to build his strength. But most of all, he needed to get his life in order to understand how he was supposed to go on living despite Michael Killin's death wish for him and his people.

That started now, Hunter decided as he stood and walked to the bookshelf that housed the entire Sherlock Holmes collection. He pulled out *The Valley of Fear*, and the shelf opened without a sound, revealing a room filled with everything needed for guerilla warfare. Craig had revealed this room last night.

Hunter scanned the array of weapons. Now that the lawyers were out of the way, he would join the security detail patrolling the estate. They searched for signs of Chymera all day, but found nothing. Hunter would meet them after dinner. He wanted to begin as human, to see if and how Chymera reacted. The guards had AR-15 rifles with night scopes. Did the monster prowl only at night?

What if he appeared as Killin, as the human? Hunter studied the secret room full of guns. He hadn't thought how to react if he faced a human. Would the men shoot to kill?

It was something to discuss with Craig. Hunter put on a side holster and shoved his favorite nine-millimeter Beretta into it.

He laughed softly. No wonder Zoe liked wearing her gun. He felt powerful and invincible. Zoe could outshoot him though. She was at the gun range at least once a month doing target practice. If the bad guys got in her sights, they'd go down with one shot.

He walked back into the study and pushed the bookshelf back in place. He needed food to get through the night, so he headed to the kitchen. In the foyer, however, his father called out to him. He found Stirling alone, watching the Bloomberg channel on an eighty-inch television in the den.

That's entertainment.

"Where are you going?" Stirling asked, sipping a tall gin and tonic. Hunter raised an eyebrow at that. Stirling didn't drink often.

"Out to do a security check."

"Why the hell are you doing that?" his father asked and stood. "Those people know what they're doing. That's why they're here. You're the head of the estate now. Do you think your grandfather went out patrolling with his hired help?"

Hunter rested his hands on his hips. "Yes. I can't see him waiting quietly with a threat like we have now."

Stirling's face went red, and he snarled a curse.

"Oh, right, because he was the great shapeshifter, sworn to protect the family's secret. And now it's your job." Spitting out another curse, he threw his crystal glass to shatter in the fireplace.

The move stunned Hunter. His father never lost that steely control. Was he angry that Hunter about the will? In silence, Hunter watched Stirling stalk to the bar and pour himself another drink.

"You know what happened to Grandda and Shamus," Hunter said quietly. "We have to take control of this situation."

"If Father had let me deal with Michael Killin, perhaps I could have bested him in the boardroom. If he weren't so successful in both worlds, would he pose such a threat?"

Hunter paused, surprised by the bitter tone in his father's voice.

"We're in trouble now because your grandfather was too stupid to kill Michael Angus Killen, Chymera's grandfather, when he had the chance," Stirling said. "When your grandfather and Angus fought, they were true gentlemen. Each allowed the other to walk away. Now the Killins have multiplied like animals, their leader is ruthless, and our backs are against the wall."

Stirling surprised Hunter again as he set down his drink and reached for one of the Bradmore swords on the wall. He took a fighting stance, waving the sword through the air with a skill that Hunter had never seen.

"I was a fencing champion at Harvard," Stirling said.

"You never told me that."

"I do most of my thrusting and lunging with words and money now, but at one time, I was the national champion." He moved out of his stance and studied the sword.

Hunter saw such sadness in his father's eyes that he felt heaviness in his own chest. His father was grieving just as much as he was, only he couldn't let loose of his control in order to show it.

When Stirling looked back at Hunter, he picked up his drink again. "Go play soldier with your little friends." He toasted Hunter with his glass and returned to his seat in front of the big television.

Hunter wondered if he should suggest his father come with them. He couldn't imagine such a thing, however, so he left, calling Craig as he walked toward the kitchen at the rear of the house.

****

Hunter could smell Chymera, but tonight there were no cries rending the air. He didn't feel the dark presence of evil as he had before. But still, there was…something out here in the night.

His security force was dressed in black. Many had blackened their faces in order to blend with the night. They looked menacing. Hunter felt confident. Evan carried a formidable looking crossbow.

Hunter now knew the Egans had worked for the MacRaes for centuries. Their roots went back to the same little village in the Highlands, though they were not shapeshifters.

The Egans and their descendants lived according to the Marcian Statutes, handed down from the goddess and warrior, Marcia Proba. She believed in equality and knew that women were truly as strong as men. A Celtic warrior queen who lived around the third century, BCE, her Statutes were purported to be the guide for the

161

Magna Carta, though the latter document refused to recognize women as equals to men.

The two families joined forces when the big cats of the MacRae family saved the Egans' homeland from being seized. In return, the Egans promised to be warriors and protectors of the MacRae secrets. There were three husband-and-wife teams in the security force.

Hunter had complete faith in Craig Egan, knowing Craig and his wife Bree knew the estate well and supervised the guards with a ruthless discipline. Craig handed out assignments for the two-person teams as they began their search.

Partnered with Craig, Hunter stayed close. The night was cold and cloudless, the moon rising in the sky. They walked cautiously through the dense greenery, making as little noise as possible. Night vision goggles made it easy to see. Occasionally Hunter heard whispered reports in his earpiece, but he didn't use the mic on his jacket lapel.

Hours passed. At the west side of the estate, Hunter stilled when he heard movement in the nearby bushes. He was alone. Craig had moved to the left. He raised his rifle, focusing on the spot in the thick shrubbery. The bushes moved again, and Hunter watched in horror as an angry beast rose up on two legs. With its teeth bared and its claws released, it reminded him of nothing less than a demon.

Though it had stocky human legs, the upper body was covered with a shaggy mane and the blonde fur of a full-grown lion. There was a rumble deep in the animal's chest as he gazed at Hunter hungrily, licking his lips with anticipation.

There was no roar as the animal advanced on him. Hunter froze. Hearing stories of this beast had in no way prepared him for seeing it live in front of him.

A tiny movement to the left put Craig in Hunter's peripheral vision and he stole a quick glance at the other man. Though Craig showed no shock at what he was seeing, Hunter's stomach clenched again.

They were facing his grandfather's murderer.

Chapter 13

I was having a good time. I was in a restaurant with a very good-looking man who wasn't my best friend.

I admit it. I was pretty turned on.

It had been a long, dry spell. I mean, the last time I felt this way was when I was watching a Ben Affleck movie. You can guess how that ended. But as I sat beside Mike Scala, enjoying food and some sexy repartee, I sensed my luck was about to change.

The evening had started well. I had time after leaving Lydia and the girls to go home, shower, and do my make-up and hair. This was a definite improvement over my previous meetings with Mike. I dressed in my best and tightest jeans and the red cashmere sweater Margaret gave me for Christmas. I knew her personal shopper had probably picked up one in every color for the unimportant people on her list, but this color looked good against my fair skin and dark hair.

Maybe it was the clothes, maybe it was the mascara and red lipstick, but Mike seemed to be enjoying the view. I beamed in return, because he looked nothing short of delicious in black jeans, a cable knit sweater, and a bomber jacket. He was sexy, confident and tough. I liked that combination, especially in a real man instead of an image on the screen.

He was sitting close, helping me finish off my

Pollo Parmigiana. We were at an intimate restaurant called Gabriel's instead of the casual place he mentioned last night. It was a more romantic setting. Gradually, while we drank wine and made our way through bread and salad and entrees, his chair had moved closer to mine, until the side of his leg was pressing against my thigh. I normally don't share food with strangers, but the butterflies in my stomach were fluttering so hard, my appetite was off.

"You look nice." Mike leaned in closer. "And you smell wonderful." He had been saying things like that since he picked me up.

"I think that's the garlic," I joked in return. "And you're not so bad yourself."

"So, not sorry you came out with me?"

"I love Gabriel's. Thanks."

He slanted a sideways look at me. "I was wondering if you liked the company."

I'm really not the best at romantic chitchat, which might explain my dry spell. Instead of cooing something back Mike's way, I said, "I thought we'd talk about Kinley's case."

Mike burst out laughing as I blushed almost as scarlet as my sweater.

He made me feel better, however, by teasing, "So you're just going to use me for information?"

"Of course not," I said, still flustered. Where were the witty remarks when I needed them?

"That's good" He leaned back in his chair to study me. "You know I can't comment on an ongoing investigation."

"I know Eric killed her. I'd like to help prove it."

"Leave the investigation up to us. We're doing

everything we can."

"I'm sure you are," I replied, already regretting losing the flirtatious mood. "But I feel responsible."

His gaze sharpened. "Why?"

"Hunter and I promised to keep her safe."

"We're pursuing any and all leads, including Eric."

"Other leads?" My interest quickened. "You can tell me about them. It's not like I'm just a civilian. I'm a licensed investigator."

"In my eyes, you're a civilian. I'm not discussing the case with you."

"I had a professional relationship with Kinley."

Mike leaned forward and took away the knife I was waving around. "I asked you out because I felt a special connection with you. I thought you were interested, too. Did I read you wrong? Are you and Mr. MacRae more than just business partners?"

It was a minute before I realized he was asking about my relationship with Hunter. I wasn't used to anyone calling him Mr. MacRae. Now I laughed. "Oh, we're much more than business partners."

The detective frowned, not reassured.

"Hunter's my best friend," I explained. "We've been a dynamic duo since middle school. A nerd and nerdette who became business partners."

"I can't imagine you as a nerd," Mike replied.

"Oh, I had the braces, the wild hair, and the thick glasses." I bit my lip, willing myself to shut up. Why in the world would I paint myself as a dork to this man?

"Your partner definitely grew out of his nerdiness. Word around town is that he's quite a ladies' man. Rich, too."

I took a sip of wine. Just as I feared, Mike had

investigated Hunter thoroughly.

"Yes, Hunter's family is very rich."

"And he practices family law just for fun, right?"

"Hunter enjoys his work." And meeting attractive women.

"But he doesn't have to work."

"No."

"Must be nice."

"He works hard."

"He left town and hasn't returned."

"His grandfather passed away unexpectedly."

I felt my confessing compulsion come to life. If I didn't shut up I'd be telling him everything about a shifter and a seer. Shit, what was I doing here with a cop?

"Naturally, I ran background checks after Friday night," Mike continued. "I knew about his grandfather's death."

I shot him a look.

He had the grace to squirm under my stare. "That sounded like I'm a stalker. And I'm not. I just..." He paused and grinned at me. "You found a body. I had to check you out."

I nodded. I knew about the details of an investigation. "Anything more happen with that poor guy we found? You said his name was Dugard."

"His family arrived yesterday and made arrangements to take him home."

I frowned. "That's kind of quick to release a murder victim's body, isn't it?"

"I told you he had connections to law enforcement." Mike frowned. "Orders to release the body came straight from the top. The autopsy was complete, so we let it go. Cause of death was evident."

I shivered at the memory, but before I could reply, Mike leaned in close again. "You know, this is my first night off in eight days, and I wanted to spend it with a gorgeous woman. Not talking about murder."

"A gorgeous woman, you say?" I glanced over my shoulder. "When's she going to join us?"

He kissed me, leaning over to cup my face, draw me close, and fasten his sexy mouth on mine.

God, I wanted him.

We gazed at each other. Then Mike moved back and raised his hand for our waiter. I thought he was going to ask for the check and we would do the horizontal bop in the backseat of his SUV. Instead, he said, "Coffee, please. Black. How about you, Zoe?"

I ordered a cappuccino and sat back, thinking, oh, but this man is really smooth, playing patient and controlled. I liked him and his style.

We sat close together, talking easily—movies, pop culture and books. I was excited to learn Mike was addicted to the cable series "Justified," was a rabid Robert B. Parker fan, and loved Stephen King as well.

"My last Stephen King was *Cujo*," I said with a laugh. "I saw the movie, but it scared me to death. I slept with the lights on for three nights and swore I'd never have a dog."

Mike laughed, and I enjoyed the way his face changed completely. "I guess I'd better keep Barney in the garage if you ever come to my place."

"Barney would be your dog, right?" I said, disappointed. I was, for obvious reasons, a cat person.

"Don't worry. They don't come any friendlier or dumber than Barney. I've seen him lie still for thirty shoulder.

I leaned back and looked up at him. "I really wanted dessert at the restaurant. Didn't you?"

His answer was a long, deep kiss that curled my toes and started a heat in my belly that spread throughout my body, making it sensitive to the brush of my clothes in strategic places.

He stepped back, dropping his arms and reaching for my hand. "Lead the way."

Fumbling with my keys only slightly, I opened the door and pulled him inside. We shed coats and shoes along the way to the bedroom. Just inside my room, I dumped my purse, cell phone, and gun. Mike unhooked his shoulder holster and dropped it on my dresser as he reached for me again. My bed was rumpled and unmade, but that was actually kind of convenient as we fell onto the cool Matouk sheets I had splurged on as a Christmas gift to myself.

By the time we hit the bed he was pulling my sweater off and pushing my bra aside.

"I want to see you." He turned to click on the bedside lamp.

Then he was beside me again, kissing my breasts, lifting them, and running his thumb across my nipples. Desire went through me like a warm wave.

It had definitely been a long time since I had shared this bed. I got his shirt off as quickly as I could and pressed my breasts into the mass of soft, dark hair on his chest. He hugged me tighter against him and bit my earlobe. I went to work on getting his jeans off and out of the way.

We both struggled with snaps and zippers and finally stood to remove the rest of our clothes. I took a foil package out of the nightstand drawer and dropped it on the bed. "We might need to check the expiration date on this," I said, talking too much, as usual.

"Like any good cop, I have back-up," Mike retorted.

We were laughing by the time we were naked, but stopped to study each other in the lamplight.

His muscles were tight and well defined. His body, to my mind, was perfect—from his chin with the sexy dimple to his penis, that saluted me with a little twitch when I reached for him.

I wrapped my fingers around him. I felt his knees give, but he quickly caught himself and held on as I caressed him, feeling him grow harder and longer at my touch.

"Slow down," he whispered.

"Not a chance."

We hit the bed once again, and he was immediately touching me everywhere. I was wet and waiting when he slid two fingers inside me. With his thumb rubbing my clitoris, my orgasm built.

I came really fast. It was like light exploded throughout my body. While I was trying to catch my breath, he put the condom on and moved over me. He slid slowly inside me and I clenched my muscles, making him groan and stop for a moment while he regained control. Then he was kissing me and moving inside me with quick, deep strokes. I responded eagerly, opening up to him.

When my orgasm grew again, I couldn't stop my cries of encouragement. I came with a scream, digging my fingernails into his arms as my body arched against him. He drove into me one last time with a triumphant minutes while my eighteen-month-old nephew hit him with a stuffed hammer. I think Barney would rather be hurt himself than do anything to anybody else."

Mike told me about his family. There were three sisters between him and his older brother. "Lots of estrogen in the house," he said. His brother, Dominick, had been a member of the New Jersey Army National Guard. Dom, as he called him, had died in Afghanistan protecting a wounded buddy during a firefight.

The open admiration and pure love in Mike's voice touched me. He said he spent many of his days off at Dom's house doing odd jobs for his sister-in-law and two nephews.

"I feel like I need to be their male role model," he explained. "They're great kids. Anthony's fifteen and Michael's twelve. They both play basketball and hockey and love the Yankees. We try to get to at least two or three games every year."

"Kids definitely get under your skin," I agreed. I told him about my visit that afternoon with Kinley's daughters.

"I want to try to help Kelly."

"So she's still not talking."

"All she did while I was there was draw pictures. She used a lot of red, pressing down on the crayon like she'd never get enough color on it."

"Expressing her anger, maybe?"

I shrugged. "I promised Lydia I would go over to Kinley's and pick up a few things."

Mike glanced at his watch. "It's not quite ten. How about we go by tonight? I can help you."

I hesitated. This was not the sexy end to the evening I had in mind. On the other hand, his company would be nice on this difficult task.

****

Kinley's little house looked lonely in the moonlight as we pulled into the driveway. I closed my eyes. Unfortunately, all that did was make me think of the vision from Fraser. I hadn't thought about Hunter in the last two hours. But now, very clearly, I could hear Fraser telling me to protect him.

"You okay?" Mike asked as he unbuckled his seatbelt.

"Sorry, I didn't think it would bother me so much to be here," I lied.

"If you need to wait out here, I'll get the stuff Lydia wants."

He put his hand on my shoulder, and I immediately felt better. There is great value in human touch. I handed him the house keys while we walked up the steps. I waited while Mike cut the crime seal and unlocked the front door.

I felt Kinley's presence everywhere, and I was filled with a suffocating sadness. Mike put his hand in the small of my back, and we stood, absorbing the grief that surrounded us.

Mike flipped on the lights as we went upstairs. I read off items on Lydia's list and he gathered. He was surprisingly knowledgeable about kids' toys and clothes. He told me he had six nieces as well as the three nephews he had already mentioned. Together, we packed a couple of suitcases we found in the hall closet. He helped me fold the quilt from Kinley's bed, and we carried the bags downstairs.

Mike did a quick walk-through of the house. As we passed the kitchen, I glanced inside and noticed the refrigerator was covered with childish artwork.

"Hang on a second." I stepped into the room to study the pictures.

Most of the drawings were done by Kelly. They were actually a story of her family. There were pictures of a house with the mom, dad, and two little girls standing in grass with flowers at their feet. At the top was what I assumed was a newer picture of a mother and two girls standing by the same small house, with the flowers and grass in place.

These pictures were a stark contrast to the ones Kelly was drawing now.

"Something wrong?" Mike asked from behind me.

I turned and headed for the living room. "I'm sorry. This is such a sad place now. Kinley wanted it to be a happy home."

As I walked down the sidewalk to the car, I looked back and shivered. Mike locked the front door and put the police seal back in place. I hoped I never returned here.

We put the bags in the backseat of Mike's car. "Why don't I take these over to Lydia's in the morning?" he suggested. "I need to talk to her anyway."

I agreed. Out of the corner of my eye, I thought I saw something. A man?

I whipped around and saw Hunter's grandfather standing just at the rear corner of the garage. Gasping, I ran forward.

"Zoe?" By the time I reached the spot where Fraser stood, Mike was at my side with his gun drawn.

And there was nothing and no one there.

"What is it?" Mike asked.

"I just thought—"

A bolt of silver shot past us, and we jumped. Then a cat's plaintive meow sounded from the darkness.

"Hunter?" I murmured, stepping forward again.

"What?" Mike touched my arm. "What about Hunter?"

What was I supposed to say, something like, "Hunter becomes a cat all the time. I thought he might be checking up on our date." Instead, I just shook my head.

Mike walked around the garage but found nothing, of course. He paused and looked at me but said nothing as he holstered his gun. He took my arm. "Let's get you out of here," Mike said. "This place is nothing but bad memories."

Maybe that's all it was, I thought on the drive to my house. Perhaps being back at the scene of Kinley's murder made me jumpy. Just to be sure, I pulled out my cell phone and checked. Nothing from Hunter. No phantom texts from Fraser telling me what to do next.

"Expecting to hear from someone?" Mike asked.

I put the phone away. "Just a client."

I don't think he believed me. He was quiet when we got to my place.

But as we stood in the circle of light from the lamp beside the door, his expression softened. He put his arms around me and pressed a kiss along my jaw line. His voice was a deep caress against my skin. "I'm really glad I met you," he whispered.

Boldly, I slid my arms around his waist and pulled his body against mine. He didn't resist. The chill began to leave my body as he hugged me tight against his heat. In his arms, I didn't feel so lost, alone, and worried. His mouth made a trail of soft kisses to my shoulder.

I leaned back and looked up at him. "I really wanted dessert at the restaurant. Didn't you?"

His answer was a long, deep kiss that curled my toes and started a heat in my belly that spread throughout my body, making it sensitive to the brush of my clothes in strategic places.

He stepped back, dropping his arms and reaching for my hand. "Lead the way."

Fumbling with my keys only slightly, I opened the door and pulled him inside. We shed coats and shoes along the way to the bedroom. Just inside my room, I dumped my purse, cell phone, and gun. Mike unhooked his shoulder holster and dropped it on my dresser as he reached for me again. My bed was rumpled and unmade, but that was actually kind of convenient as we fell onto the cool Matouk sheets I had splurged on as a Christmas gift to myself.

By the time we hit the bed he was pulling my sweater off and pushing my bra aside.

"I want to see you." He turned to click on the bedside lamp.

Then he was beside me again, kissing my breasts, lifting them, and running his thumb across my nipples. Desire went through me like a warm wave.

It had definitely been a long time since I had shared this bed. I got his shirt off as quickly as I could and pressed my breasts into the mass of soft, dark hair on his chest. He hugged me tighter against him and bit my earlobe. I went to work on getting his jeans off and out of the way.

We both struggled with snaps and zippers and finally stood to remove the rest of our clothes. I took a foil package out of the nightstand drawer and dropped it on the bed. "We might need to check the expiration date on this," I said, talking too much, as usual.

"Like any good cop, I have back-up," Mike retorted.

We were laughing by the time we were naked, but stopped to study each other in the lamplight.

His muscles were tight and well defined. His body, to my mind, was perfect—from his chin with the sexy dimple to his penis, that saluted me with a little twitch when I reached for him.

I wrapped my fingers around him. I felt his knees give, but he quickly caught himself and held on as I caressed him, feeling him grow harder and longer at my touch.

"Slow down," he whispered.

"Not a chance."

We hit the bed once again, and he was immediately touching me everywhere. I was wet and waiting when he slid two fingers inside me. With his thumb rubbing my clitoris, my orgasm built.

I came really fast. It was like light exploded throughout my body. While I was trying to catch my breath, he put the condom on and moved over me. He slid slowly inside me and I clenched my muscles, making him groan and stop for a moment while he regained control. Then he was kissing me and moving inside me with quick, deep strokes. I responded eagerly, opening up to him.

When my orgasm grew again, I couldn't stop my cries of encouragement. I came with a scream, digging my fingernails into his arms as my body arched against him. He drove into me one last time with a triumphant

Chapter 14

Hunter tried to move but he couldn't. He heard his men yelling and running but he could do nothing. His face was wet with what he thought was his own blood. His lungs were screaming for oxygen.

"Come on," Craig yelled. "Help me get this bastard off him."

They struggled. It took Craig, Evan, and two others to lift the heavy body off Hunter, and when he was free, he could do nothing but drag in air. He felt like a turtle, on his back unable to turn over. Finally, he controlled his breathing and rolled to his side. When he did, he came face to face with a huge, shaggy lion's head.

For hours they had tracked the beast through woods around the estate. Hunter began to think the creature was playing a game with them, but when the attack came it was sudden, violent, and aimed straight at him. Thankfully, Evan had a clean shot.

The beast's mouth was open, and Hunter shuddered at the size of the large feline teeth. They were almost four inches long and would have killed him with one bite. Evan saved Hunter's life with a well-placed arrow that went straight through the chimera's heart while the animal was in mid-air above Hunter. One of the massive claws had scraped Hunter's head as it fell, bringing the blood that was chilling on his cold face.

Craig and Evan each offered Hunter an arm and helped him stand. When they let go, he staggered but straightened at last. Still drawing deep, ragged breaths, Hunter looked down at the animal, half lion and half man.

"It's Patrick Killin." Craig crouched beside the big body. "Michael's younger brother." He looked up at Hunter. "There's only one person Michael Killin loves more than himself and that's his mother. She adored Patrick. He was her youngest, and she will push Michael relentlessly to kill you in the most painful manner possible."

Hunter wiped his hand across his mouth. He was trembling. He was sure it was shock. He felt cold, clammy sweat all over his body, and his heart was still banging in his chest.

"How do you know it's Patrick?" he asked when he could.

"I recognize his mane." Craig touched the tawny, black-tipped fan of hair around the beast's face.

"How?"

"We've been studying these predators for years." Craig got to his feet. "A lion's mane is like a fingerprint. We managed to get pictures so we could identify all of them. They're out to destroy the MacRaes, so your grandfather made it his business to know who he was dealing with."

One of the others pressed a handkerchief into Hunter's hand. He held it against his forehead.

"Why didn't Chymera come after me himself?"

Craig shrugged, reaching for Hunter's arm. "Let's get you back to the house and see how badly you're hurt, and then we'll talk. Evan, radio ahead so the doctor will meet us."

Hunter stared down at the huge beast again. The regal lion's head was enormous, and the shaggy mane was waist-length. Sharpened claws were still visible in the huge paws at the base of the lion's forelegs. He shuddered again thinking what would have happened if Evan weren't an expert archer.

"Thank you, Evan," he said.

"He left himself wide open," Evan replied. "Makes me think he didn't expect so many of us to be out here. Come now, let's get you inside."

Hunter was fascinated by the beauty of the feline portion of the creature. It could well have been the mystery man in the story of "Beauty and the Beast."

"What will we do with him?" Hunter walked away between Craig and Evan.

"We'll drag him further into the woods, and Killin's men will find him," Craig said.

Hunter looked at the man's stoic face; there was no hint of concern or fear. "Wouldn't it be easier if we just buried him?"

"It's not our way, Hunter," Craig said earnestly. "Even in a war, a man has a right to have his body returned to his family."

"I see," Hunter said, though he really didn't. He felt like he was in a time warp, and he knew without a doubt he needed to get back to the city. His life might never be normal again, but more familiar surroundings might help him get his bearings.

ATVs appeared to take them back to the house. It was late, after midnight, and from the bite of the wind, there would be a frost tonight. Hunter shivered as clouds covered the moon.

When they entered the house, Dr. Connor, his grandfather's physician, was waiting. Stirling scowled at his side. Hunter's father appeared to have sobered up while they'd been working.

Dr. Connor directed them to the kitchen "I've got everything ready."

Hunter sat heavily on a chair in the kitchen where his Nana used to bake cookies. He winced when the doctor pulled away the big, rough handkerchief Craig had tied around his wound.

"Doesn't look too bad," Dr. Connor said. "Shouldn't take more than a few stitches to fix it right up. Craig told me the big cat was already dead, but he managed to wound you anyway."

"Those claws are long and razor sharp," Craig said. "Thank God the bastard was on the small side."

Hunter yelped as the needle pricked his forehead. "He felt mighty damn big to me."

Craig laughed. "His brother is older and bigger and a lot meaner. You'd be wise to get into better shape for the time you'll meet him."

It took ten stitches to close the cut at the edge of his scalp. This was clearly more than "a few" in his opinion, but he kept that to himself. When he complained about how long the process was taking, the doctor reminded him this was a spot that would be seen and, therefore, needed a little extra care to keep him from having a bad scar.

Finally, Dr. Connor was satisfied. Hunter went upstairs to shower and change out of his bloody clothes. After getting dressed in comfortable jeans and a sweatshirt, he grabbed the cell phone that had been ringing almost constantly since they'd returned.

He punched speed dial for Zoe and she picked up before he even heard a ring.

She answered, "Oh, my God, are you all right? I've been scared to death. I had a vision and I kept calling and you didn't—"

"I couldn't get to the phone. I'm sorry. I'm fine, Zoe. Everything's fine," Hunter said as he gingerly touched the bandage on his head. He knew Zoe would have a fit when she saw it.

"What happened? I saw a monster jumping for you. Was it Chymera?"

"His brother."

"He has a brother?"

Hunter sighed. He really didn't want to explain all of this to her just now. "I had to have a few stitches, and the monster is dead. One of the monsters, anyway."

Zoe's tone turned to anger. "You've got to come home. Surely animals like that won't come to the city. You'll be safe down here."

Hunter thought briefly about the "Lion of Wall Street," but decided it was best not to tell her about Michael Killin over the phone.

"I'll be home tomorrow, I promise."

"That makes me feel better," Zoe said, although she didn't really sound calmer. "I need to see you, Hunter. I need to see for myself how badly you're hurt. And how can I help you if I'm not with you?"

Hunter ended the call and returned to the den. The doctor had departed, but Craig, Evan, and Stirling were waiting for him.

"Tell me what happened out there," Stirling said from the deep, leather chair he occupied.

Craig recounted the stalking and killing of Patrick

Killin while Hunter took the chair across from his father. Evan poured him scotch in a heavy crystal glass. It wasn't his drink of choice but tasted good tonight.

"So you killed one of them." Stirling sighed.

"We saw only one," Hunter replied, feeling defensive.

"But there were more," Evan said. "Many more."

Craig agreed as he turned back to Hunter. "Our ancestor's village was wiped out in a fierce attack one night. Dozens of these savages came through and killed everyone they found. The only ones who survived were a group of hunters who were away hunting to stock the town's larders for winter."

"The murderers were the Killins," Stirling said.

"Why can't they change completely?" Hunter asked.

"Our scientists say it's due to aplastic anemia," Stirling answered. "That's the only constant they could find in their research. They believe the mutation was caused by the reduction in red blood cells."

"I'm no scientist," Evan added, "but I know a human chimera can occur when one fraternal twin dies in the womb. When that happens the other twin absorbs the genetic material and can have two different DNAs."

Hunter waved his glass in impatience. "No matter what causes their problems, these creatures are our enemies."

"They've been waiting," Stirling said. "Michael Killin waited until Father was growing old. Killin's been watching us closely. He knew Hunter wasn't ready to take the reins, and Fraser was vulnerable." He looked hard at Hunter over his glass of scotch. "Killin put that body in the woods behind your office as a test.

And you failed it."

Hunter stared at his father in surprise. "How did you know about that body?"

"Jess Dugard was one of us," Evan answered in the sudden silence. "Part of the MacRae clan."

"Someone who lived here?" Hunter demanded.

Craig shook his head. "Dugard was a North Carolina MacRae. He worked under cover. He had infiltrated Killin's group."

Hunter looked puzzled. "How is that possible? Wouldn't the Killins know he belonged to us? Smell us on him."

"Like you smelled Chymera near Dugard's body?" Stirling challenged.

"I did sense…something." Hunter remembered his unease that night, the smell that he couldn't place, the danger he had sensed. If he had known what it was, that is was Chymera, would Grandda be alive?

"But you didn't know what it was," his father said, clearly reading his thoughts. "Thanks to your grandfather."

"Dugard was a protector like Evan and me. Members of our family are with all the MacRaes," Craig said.

"Did Grandda know Dugard was with the Killins?" Hunter asked.

"Someone among us is always trying to get close to the chimera." Craig's face was dark and sober.

"We realized Dugard was missing on Sunday," Evan said. "He missed a check in, which was unlike him."

"Your grandfather made some calls," Stirling said. "He found out about the body left behind your office.

We have contacts in the police department. People with special...abilities. They confirmed that it was Dugard. Calls were made to his family. They've already taken his body home to rest in their mountains. Just as we'll bury Shamus tomorrow."

Hunter couldn't help but wonder what kind of creatures were standing shoulder-to-shoulder with humans in the thin blue line. His grandfather had kept too much from him. .

"Then Chymera came after your grandfather," Craig said.

"And he killed him." Hunter downed the last of his scotch, wishing the burn could consume the grief inside him. "How can we be sure it was Michael Killin and not his little brother, Patrick, who did the killing?"

"Shamus was sure," Stirling said. "I didn't need any other proof."

The room was silent save for the wind that pushed against the windows.

"What's our next move?" Hunter asked.

"It's kind of like chess," Craig said. "We made a move tonight. We'll see what they do."

"But if this is a game, they're ahead," Hunter insisted. "They killed this Dugard man, then Grandda and Shamus. Should that go unanswered?"

"I'm not waiting here," Stirling said. "I'm heading back to the city tomorrow. As long as Father was alive he wouldn't allow me to challenge Killin openly in the business world."

"But now you will?" Hunter asked.

Stirling stood. "Killin's quite proud of his financial prowess. He enjoys destroying others literally and figuratively. We can hurt him in many ways. Not just by chasing him in the woods."

The controlled fury in his father's voice surprised Hunter. "You hate him, don't you?"

"More than I can say," Stirling replied. "I suspect he is already far from these woods, on his way back to civilization. That's my playing field."

Though Hunter saw the wisdom in Stirling's words, he wished his grandfather could advise them. How could the clan survive with The MacRae so unprepared?

Craig agreed that it was doubtful the chimera would attack them here again. "Evan will be going with you," he told Hunter. "Shamus was to go back with you originally, but since he's gone, it'll be Evan."

Though Hunter owed Evan his life, he didn't like the idea of bodyguard. He had respected Shamus, but he had never understood why his grandfather had required a twenty-four/seven shadow. Even now that he understood the threat that Fraser had lived with, he felt he could defend himself.

He got to his feet, protesting, "I don't need a babysitter. I've always been able to take care of myself."

"Your grandfather thought that too," Stirling said sternly. "You'll take Evan with you. There'll be others you won't see watching us all. Craig needs to stay here, but Evan is well-trained. He's ready to protect you."

"In addition to what he learned from Shamus and me throughout his life, Evan was with the Rangers in Iraq until a year ago," Craig added, "Like all of us, he knows how to do this job. Hell, it's in our blood."

"But in the city it's different," Hunter said. "It's more difficult to hide there if you're part animal and

185

part human."

"The chimera go everywhere and anywhere," Evan's tone was even, as if he were describing the habits of a housecat. "Your grandfather preferred living here because it reminded him of his home in the Highlands, but we've had members of our clan killed in St. Louis, Atlanta, and even Los Angeles."

Stirling said, "Michael Killin lives in a penthouse near Central Park. He owns the building. The rest of the residents are on his staff in some capacity."

Hunter continued to shake his head. Craig got up and grasped his shoulder. "Patrick's death means Michael will be hunting in a rage. He'll want to spill your blood with his own hands. You need Evan. You've got to change your life. You'll have to be vigilant every minute, or you'll die. It's that simple."

They looked up as one of the guards came through the doorway, his rifle at his side. "The Killins have already taken the body. Maeve and I were doing the late patrol, and discovered it was gone."

"Michael Killin knows for sure his brother is gone," Stirling murmured.

A look passed from him to Craig and Evan. The somberness in their faces carried an edge of fear. Hunter felt a chill down his spine.

"And so it begins," Evan said.

To Hunter's ears, Evan's voice carried a note of bloodthirsty anticipation. He wondered if that was what he wanted in a bodyguard.

What would Zoe think?

Chapter 15

The helicopter was like dozens of others that dotted the sky over Manhattan, but I didn't take my eyes off the gold and black striped craft while it hovered and then set down. I was waiting atop The Stirling Building on Fifth Avenue just off 51st. Fraser MacRae had built it in 1950 and named it in honor of his son born the same year. Though other buildings towered over it, this one was still impressive with its classic granite exterior.

The helicopter's engine roared and wind whipped my hair about my face, but I didn't even notice. Though I've been up here many times with Hunter, I never feel comfortable being so close to helicopter blades. The tightness in my chest eased, however, as the blades slowed and Hunter's familiar, dark head popped out of a door.

"Hold on," said the woman beside me. Stirling's faithful and efficient administrative assistant, Marie Nelson, held me back when I would have run straight to Hunter.

He stepped out and I couldn't wait any longer. I had to be sure he was truly here, safe, and whole. He dropped his duffel bag on the concrete and pulled me close, swinging me around as he hugged me tight enough to cut off my breathing.

"Oh, my God," I gasped. "I'm so glad to see you."

Hunter set me back on my feet. "I thought you

could see me anytime."

I stepped back. "Eyes on you, buddy, all the time. You'd better believe it." I pushed his hair up to look at the neat row of sutures that lined his scalp. I frowned. "You're almost healed."

"The claw just scraped me." Hunter stooped to pick up his duffel bag. He slung an arm around my shoulders as we walked toward the doorway where the patient Marie hovered.

The older woman greeted Hunter with a hug. In quiet tones, she told him how sorry she was about his grandfather. I knew Hunter was appreciative.

Dear Marie. For as long as Hunter and I have been friends, she had been as involved in Hunter's life as his parents. Maybe even more so. She arranged for permission for school trips and scheduled doctor's appointments, and made sure he was outfitted with the right sports equipment and clothes. Marie was more like a doting aunt than an employee.

Long ago, Hunter thought his father and Marie were romantically involved. I wasn't sure. But I wouldn't blame anyone who preferred Marie's warmth and kindness to Margaret MacRae's brittleness.

We followed Marie down a short corridor just inside the building. The family firm occupied the top five floors and seemed to grow bigger every year. Marie led us straight to the familiar oak-lined lounge where corporate guests who arrived on the helipad were usually greeted with refreshments and smiling, fresh-faced assistants. Today, the room was empty, although sandwiches, ice, water, and a pitcher of orange juice had been set up on the dark granite bar. Marie never missed a thing.

Pausing to hold the door after Hunter walked through, Marie gave Stirling a soft smile. "Welcome home, Mr. MacRae."

I blinked in surprise. I hadn't even noticed Stirling getting off the helicopter. As usual, his brow was furrowed and his eyes were glued to his phone. The man was always attending to business. He didn't even acknowledge Marie's greeting.

I was about to say something to him when I noticed another man walking behind him. He was young, with tawny, close-cropped hair. His bearing military-straight. His features were strong rather than handsome, and his shoulders were about as broad as the doorway. He had on worn jeans and a black leather coat, the collar turned up against the cold. He hefted three bags with ease as he followed Stirling into the room.

Holy crap, he was gorgeous.

His brown-eyed gaze swept the room and I realized he would know the second anything changed. He was on guard.

"You must be Zoe," he said.

I put out my hand. "And you would be—"

"My babysitter," Hunter sneered.

"Bodyguard." Evan set the bags down and took my hand in his large, warm one. "I'm Evan Egan."

I studied him. So this was the "rube" Hunter had fumed about when we talked this morning. He had been raving about a group of warriors assigned to be his protectors, with one in particular designated as his official guard. The whole situation infuriated Hunter.

Evan wasn't what I expected. I'd met Shamus and assumed Hunter's man would be like him—old and grizzled. The two of us had made plans to ditch the bodyguard as soon as we made our getaway from the Stirling Building to hit New York's nightlife. After all, we knew our way around this city. Evan didn't. Marie had a limo downstairs waiting for us.

I was looking at a man who wouldn't be easy to evade. No wonder Hunter was pissed. So was I. Fraser told me I was Hunter's first line of defense. Why did he need this oversized ape man if he was with me? Why did Hunter need Evan?

As if reading my mind, Evan directed his gaze like a laser at me. "I'll be with Hunter," he said. "All the time."

"That sounds great, doesn't it?" Hunter said with false enthusiasm. He turned to Marie. "Is the limo ready? I want to go out for dinner here in the city and not have to worry about how to get back to Jersey later." His voice dipped into sarcasm as he looked at Evan. "Are dinner and drinks permissible?"

Not rising to the bait, Evan gave a nod of approval. He turned and politely introduced himself to Marie, who displayed no surprise about Hunter's new bodyguard. She knew everything about this family. I looked from Marie to Stirling, but there was no indication of them being more than colleagues.

Stirling finally looked up from his phone, his frown deepening to a glower. "Hunter, please don't make things difficult. You know Evan will be going wherever you go."

Hunter ignored him and said to Marie. "You did order the limo, didn't you?"

"The service is bringing a car to the executive entrance right now," Marie answered. If she had any reaction to the unpleasant undercurrents swirling in this room, she gave no hint of it.

"I'll send someone for your bags," Marie said to her boss. "Is there anything else you need right now?"

"No, but thank you. I'll be down in the office directly." Stirling gave her the kindest look he had spared for anyone since getting off the helicopter. "We'll go over the final details for the memorial service when I get there."

"Yes, sir." Marie nodded to Zoe, Evan, and Hunter and left the room.

"We need to talk," Stirling said to his son.

"We've talked for days," Hunter replied, sounding weary. "Can't it wait?"

"Why don't we all go have a drink at the club?"

I stiffened, anticipating Hunter's response. The Metropolitan was an exclusive club for affluent men started in 1891 by J.P. Morgan. Stirling met there often with associates and friends as diverse as Donald Trump and Bill Clinton. But I knew Hunter thought that place was pretentious and overbearing.

"We should present a united front to the public." Stirling's turn toward me was unexpected. "I'm sure you know all about the situation that we're in. Don't you think we would look stronger if we appeared together in public? Killin has spies everywhere. He'll know when we go in the club we're not hiding."

"I'm not afraid," Hunter retorted before I could answer, "and I don't have to prove that to anyone. I'm just going to live my life my way."

His father sighed and shook his head. "Everything has changed. You have a responsibility now."

"I know that," Hunter snapped.

"You have to take your place with the family,"

Stirling continued. "How long do you think it will take you to shut your firm down? You can take your grandfather's office."

I looked at Hunter with wide eyes. Shut down the firm? What the hell was this?

Hunter's face was grim. "Why would I want Grandda's office?"

"Because you're needed here." A muscle twitched below his father's eye, betraying his emotions. He glanced uncomfortably from me to Evan. As usual, he didn't want to make a scene when anyone was watching. To Hunter, he said, "I didn't even think this would be an issue."

"We've been over this before." Hunter had no qualms about displaying temper. "I don't practice corporate law."

"Things are different now. Your grandfather is gone, and this is a family law firm. You need to take your rightful place here," Stirling said as if that settled everything.

"Meagan is already part of the firm—"

"Your sister isn't cut out to lead," Stirling said dismissively.

"That isn't true. Meagan is a born leader. She's everything you've only wished I would be."

"But you're my son," Stirling replied without the least apology for his misogynist sentiments. "You are the MacRae."

I was shocked. The MacRae? Okay, I was cool with the shifting. I understood Hunter was now in the crosshairs of an ancient family enemy. Looking at Evan, I realized I could even accept the warrior-servants who would die themselves to protect Hunter.

But the tone in Stirling's voice sounded like Hunter should be taking a throne, not accepting a position in a multinational law firm.

Apparently Hunter had some doubts about it, too. "I'm not coming to work with you."

I'd never seen Hunter so firm with his father. The new title also brought out his Alpha tendencies.

Stirling said nothing, but his blue eyes darkened and the tic under his left eye worsened. "Hunter, I thought you understood. It's time for you to step up and be the man you're supposed to be."

"Maybe that would be easier if someone had explained all this a long time ago," Hunter said. "You begged me to join the family firm, but never gave me concrete reasons why. If I had understood, maybe I would have…" His voice broke. "Maybe I…"

The muscles in Hunter's throat worked, and I realized he thought he could have saved his grandfather if he'd had this knowledge sooner.

That was it. I wasn't going to stand here while his father exploited Hunter's guilt. I slipped my arm through Hunter's and gave Stirling a challenging glare. "I think Hunter's had a lot to absorb this week. Do you really need to discuss his future right now?"

Stirling's gaze was calculating, as if he wanted to dismiss me like an underling. I lifted my chin and was surprised when a small smile crossed his lips and he nodded.

Hunter wasn't ready to let it go. "I would never have wanted to be part of this firm. I understand my place in the family. But it's not here. Be smart and give Meagan a chance to step up," Hunter continued. "She's got a great head for business, much better than mine.

You paid for her MBA from Harvard. Marie says she's well-respected here. There's one other thing that will make her more successful than I could ever be—she adores you and would do anything for your love and approval. Give her a chance."

"You've made yourself clear," Stirling was angry and wasn't going to say anything more in front of Evan and me. "We'll talk about the firm at another time."

"Let's go," I said before Hunter could protest again. "You need to clear your head."

"An excellent idea," Stirling agreed.

Knowing Stirling agreed with me made me want to argue, but I knew that wouldn't help Hunter.

With a nod of goodbye, I picked up Hunter's duffel bag and led him and Evan out of the room. Evan took the bag from me, and the three of us were silent in the whisper-quiet elevator that whisked us to the executive garage level where the limo was waiting.

Once inside, Hunter told the driver to head to Times Square. He made a quick call for reservations for dinner at Marea and then popped the cork on the champagne sitting on ice in front of him.

"Sweet, wonderful Marie," he said as he handed me a flute. "Count on her to know what I needed."

I chuckled, then said primly, "She won't approve if you overindulge."

"Then we'll keep that between you and me," Hunter handed a drink to Evan and poured his own. "God, it's good to be here. Ever been to New York City, Evan?"

"A few times," Evan said. "I'm not really a city person."

"I'm going to show you another side of it." Hunter raised his glass for a toast. "Here's to the night life!"

Evan only sipped his drink while Hunter had two glasses of champagne and I finished one.

We began with some of the places Hunter liked to party: China Club, Sound Factory, and the infamous Studio 54. The women hung off him, many of them calling him by name, acting like I wasn't even there.

Evan didn't escape their notice, however. With his looks he could have had any woman he wanted. He turned down overt invitations from several.

It was just the three of us as we sat down to dinner at Marea.

"Enjoying yourself?" Hunter asked Evan.

"I have to admit, the nightlife is much better here than in Glasgow, which is where I go when I'm in Scotland," Evan said with a laugh. "The women were certainly forward."

"Most men find aggressive women a turn on." I sipped a club soda and lime.

"I'm not most men." His unwavering gaze made me want to fidget in my seat.

"I'm not most men, either," Hunter said with a slight slur. "I'm a deadly cat."

"Shut up, Hunter." I peered around to see if anyone was paying attention.

Evan put a hand on Hunter's shoulder. "Calm down. We're going to have a nice, quiet dinner, and then we'll go home."

Hunter nodded. "We're going to have a nice, quiet dinner, and then we'll go home."

Hunter surprised me by remaining subdued during our meal. He fell asleep in the limo before we were out of Manhattan.

"What did you do back there?" I asked Evan.

"I enjoyed a great meal."

"You know what I mean. Hunter can get mouthy when he's drunk. That's why he doesn't let it happen often. But something you did stopped him cold."

"I just told him to calm down."

"It was more than that. I know it was more than that." I lifted one of Hunter's eyelids.

"What are you doing?" Evan asked.

"I'm trying to see if he's been drugged."

"You know what to look for in the pupils?"

"No, it just seemed like the right thing to do."

Evan laughed. "Don't worry. Hunter's fine. He just had too much to drink."

I smoothed Hunter's hair and took his hand, watching him sleep. His breathing was steady and looked comfortable.

"So Hunter is 'The MacRae.' The Killins want to kill him first, right? To make a statement?"

I took a deep breath, digesting that simple, bald truth. The limo slowed in the traffic inside the Lincoln Tunnel, and Evan was quiet. My anxiety about Hunter's situation increased as the tiled walls seemed to go on forever.

When the limo reached my house, Evan stepped out to help me. I looked back at Hunter again, still concerned about his odd behavior.

"Why don't you guys stay here tonight? I have a guest room. He stays here a lot."

Evan scanned my house and made a quick decision. "All right."

Evan and the driver walked Hunter inside and up to

my guest bedroom. Evan let the driver out and brought the duffel bags upstairs. I eased off Hunter's shoes, but left him dressed and pulled covers up around him. He'd come around soon and make himself comfortable.

"Would you like some tea?" I asked Evan. "Or you can go to bed. The sofa in the living room pulls out. There are sheets, blankets, and a pillow in the hall closet."

"Tea sounds good," he replied, and we went downstairs.

I left him in the living room with Craig Ferguson on TV while I fixed tea.

"It's been a long day." I handed him a steaming mug. I hadn't relaxed since I'd had the vision about the attack on Hunter last night. I thought of Mike. Would he ever forgive me? Should I approach him or just leave it alone?

Evan looked as fresh as he had at the beginning of the evening. The military could have injected him with something to give him super powers? Or maybe he wasn't real. Like a cyborg. If there were shifters in the world and if I could be connected psychically to Hunter, couldn't there also be other half humans out there?

I sent Evan wary glances. What would I do if he went all Terminator on me?

His ability to sense my thoughts was eerie. "Nothing I do will come between you and Hunter. He'll explain everything to you."

Now I felt like an idiot. I focused on the television and worked to get my head back in balance.

"There's a quote I like that I think works here," Evan said in the awkward silence. "It says 'cats are intended to teach us that not everything in nature has a function.' No one knows who said that, but I think it's very wise and applies to this situation."

Okay, maybe he was a cyborg/psychic/philosopher. How weird was this?

I jumped when he reached over and hit the remote to turn up Craig Ferguson talking with his guest.

I'd had enough of Evan Egan for tonight. I stood. "This couch is comfortable and I'm sure we won't be getting up too early. If you need anything, please tell me."

"I'm comfortable wherever I am."

"I'm sure you are." I backed away, keeping my gaze on him.

He appeared ready to stay up all night on guard duty. Did I need someone else not human in my life?

Trying not to picture him morphing into an armored monster, I headed upstairs and wished I had a shot of brandy for my mug of cooling tea.

Chapter 16

I woke with a head full of cotton and a mouth full of sand. I felt like I'd spent the night wrestling with a hot man, but I was as alone in my king-size bed as I had been since my "unfortunate incident" with Mike Scala. My only wrestling had been with my pillow.

The sunlight trickling into the room told me it was late. The bedside clock said it was almost nine. I could smell coffee, and for a moment, I thought Bernie was still in my house. Then I remembered I had two male houseguests. Someone was already up. I threw back the covers and hustled into the bathroom to take a quick shower. Rather than my usual Saturday morning attire of ratty robe and faded sleep shirt, I made myself decent in jeans and an off-white sweater.

While I touched some blush to my cheeks and a little mascara on my lashes, I told myself I was stupid for thinking about the good-looking hunk who had spent the night on my sleeper sofa. Hell, what was wrong with me? Did I wish I was wrestling with Mike or the warrior-prince downstairs?

The smell of bacon and eggs greeted me at the top of the stairs. My stomach growled in appreciation. In the kitchen I found Evan at the stove flipping eggs, and the table was set for three.

"Good morning," he said as I crossed the doorway. He looked at home.

I poured coffee. "That smells wonderful. Do you always cook a big breakfast?"

"At least once a week, especially after I've had a good run."

I speculated on why a cyborg would need to run as I sipped my coffee. "So you left Hunter alone in the house in order to run?"

"I figured you had it covered," Evan said, his brown eyes glinting.

Touché, I thought, but didn't reply.

"I went six miles today. This is a great neighborhood. The small hills make it challenging." Evan slid his eggs from the skillet onto a plate. "How do you want your eggs?"

"Just one, over medium. Thanks."

I sat, feeling useless in my own kitchen but pleased to have a handsome man preparing a meal for me. Maybe the fact that he ate real food meant he was human, after all.

After fixing my egg, Evan turned everything off and grabbed the toast that popped up, a masculine move. He buttered both slices and put one on each of our plates. He sat down across from me and smiled, "I'm sorry I didn't have any potatoes and haggis to add to the breakfast."

I shuddered. "I had haggis in Scotland, and that's something I will never do again. I don't buy potatoes because I tend to forget about them until I have a funny smell in the pantry. Same goes with onions and stuff."

"I try to keep staples on hand because I never know when I'll get the urge to cook something." His smile was disarming. "My mother always said the only person who could let you go without was yourself, so she made sure my brothers and I knew what we needed to get around a kitchen."

I laughed, thinking of my parents. "It's safe to say my mother never cooked in her life. I'm not sure my dad could get coffee if he couldn't find a Starbucks."

"But I hear he can shred a witness in a courtroom."

I wondered how he knew my father was an attorney. Maybe Hunter had said something?

"Dig in," he said. "What are you doing today?"

"Going in to work." I hesitated. "Is there something else I need to do? For Hunter?"

Evan shrugged. "Not that I know of. I'm not sure of his plans."

"Well, I'd like to work," I said, irritated to feel that I needed to explain myself to Evan. "I've got a case I'm working to find a lost sibling."

"How does one lose a sibling?" Evan asked, adding milk and sugar to his coffee.

"She didn't actually lose her, she just remembers having a sister when she was very young but that sister disappeared."

"That must make it a real challenge, like trying to find a needle in a needle factory."

I opened my mouth to say something, and then closed it. He'd thrown me off guard when he hadn't finished with the familiar cliché. He seemed adept at that. He was becoming more of a mystery and that wasn't good because I enjoyed solving mysteries.

As we finished breakfast, he asked more about the case and I found as I talked that I was sorting out points that had been confusing me. Hunter and I usually did this, but he was out of commission and might be that way for a while.

Evan stood and took both our plates to the sink and ran water over them, just like he knew the egg yolk would stick without a soak.

"I could get used to this." I smiled up at him. "Leave the dishes. It's only fair that I clean up since you did all the cooking."

We both turned as a moan came from the stairs. Evan grinned and said, "Well, at least it's alive."

We waited, hearing Hunter groan every time his foot hit the floor. When he came to the kitchen doorway, Evan handed him a mug of coffee and Hunter sat across from me. He was wearing boxers and a Cold Play T-shirt and all the evidence of his drinking last night was on his face.

"God, who's idea was it to go clubbing last night?" he asked in a whisper.

"Yours," I said cheerfully. "I had a great time. I slept well, and I'm ready to get to work."

My little headache was gone after my good breakfast. "Are you coming in today?" I asked Hunter.

"Isn't it Saturday?" he grumbled.

"Since when does that matter?"

He moaned again. "I'm not even sure I'm entirely human this morning."

I gave him a long look up and down and said, "I don't see any signs of fur."

He raised his finger in a universal obscene gesture and I laughed, making him grimace.

Before I could get in another dig, the doorbell rang. Evan was heating the skillet to fix Hunter some eggs as I headed for the front door. When I looked through the peephole and saw the top of Mike's head, I was the one who moaned. I had a feeling that my "unfortunate incident" was about to have a second act.

I opened the door, and he gave me a tentative smile. "I hope it's okay that I'm just dropping by. You said you get up early, even on the weekends."

I darted a look over my shoulder. "Sure."

He paused. "Can I come in?"

Knowing the inevitable was about to happen, I moved back. Mike stepped around me.

I turned just as he saw Evan and Hunter in the doorway to the kitchen.

Mike darted me a dark look. "I see you haven't spent your time moping about me."

"Did you think I would?" I let anger overrule my discomfort. Hunter made a sound that was close to a growl. I spared him a warning glance. I could handle this.

"Is there someplace we can talk alone?" Mike's chin jutted out in challenge. "I don't like the idea of talking in front of lover boy there."

His tone was infuriating. We had been out one time and slept together. What rights did that give him? "These two men are my friends, and you'd do well to watch what you say. They anger easily. Let's go to my office."

Hunter watched us through narrowed eyes. Evan never took his gaze off Mike. We headed down the hallway to the small den I used as my office.

I shut the door and took a seat behind my desk, feeling like I needed a position of power in this conversation. Mike continued to stand, his entire body emanating anger.

So I took the lead. "I'm sorry about what happened the other night, but I can assure you that Hunter is just a friend. We've been best friends for many years, and we have a...a real connection." I stumbled to find the right words. "We're very close, and I sometimes know when he's in trouble—"

"Oh, come on, Zoe, you can do better than that," Mike said through gritted teeth. "Just tell me the truth. You were enjoying the sex. You just weren't enjoying it with me."

"That is absolutely not true!"

He gave me an unyielding glare. "I know when people are lying."

"I'm trying to tell you the truth. Hunter was...hunting and was in an accident. I had a vision—"

Predictably, that made him sputter. "A vision? For God's sake, just tell me the goddamn truth. Are you trying to make him jealous with me? Or are the two of you just into kinky stuff with other people."

Footsteps clomped in the hall. Evan's voice came through the door. "Everything all right, Zoe?"

"Everything's fine, thank you." I hated that Evan and Hunter might be hearing this exchange. I turned back to Mike. "Look, it's obvious we're not going to agree on this. All I can do is ask you to believe me. Hunter and I are not lovers. I'm sorry for what happened. I certainly didn't intend to hurt or embarrass you. I'm not using anyone."

"That's what you say," he said, his expression sad and distant. "But I'm a cop. I deal in facts, and the facts tell me a different story."

"Sometimes you just have to accept things on faith."

I watched him process my words, his expression growing even darker. "I'm a homicide detective. Faith hasn't been part of my life for a long time." He opened the door and stepped into the hallway. "I'm sorry I came here this morning. I thought maybe we could figure this out."

"I could never be with a person who doesn't trust me."

"Maybe trust has to be earned."

"We obviously don't look at life in the same way at all."

He glared at me in silence.

"Bye, Mike," I said without breaking my gaze.

He turned his back, walked down the foyer and out the front door. I resisted the urge to watch him walk to his car. As I closed the door, Hunter's arms came around me from behind and pulled me against his broad chest. "What was that all about?"

I turned and wrapped my arms around his waist. "I was just enjoying some male company and things didn't go exactly as planned."

"Did he break your heart?"

"The heart hadn't become involved yet."

"Want me to send Evan to beat him up at the playground after school?"

I laughed. "Could you turn into a tiger and scare the shit out of him?"

"You bet," Hunter said in all seriousness.

He would do it for me. And I knew for someone as pragmatic as Mike that would be a mind-blowing trip. It was tempting, but I shook my head. "I'm kidding, Hunter. Leave the cop alone. I'll be fine."

Evan called out that Hunter's breakfast was ready. We walked into the kitchen, and Evan told me, "Don't worry, Zoe. It will get better."

His confidence was disconcerting. I avoided his gaze and loaded the dishwasher while Hunter ate breakfast and took over the conversation. I only half listened, still mulling over Evan's strange comment. Like Hunter, he sounded sincere. I couldn't help wondering what he might know about my future. Was he a seer? Did he have visions, too? Maybe he could help me with mine?

I gave myself a mental shake as I turned on the dishwasher. I honestly didn't know what to make of the whole lot of us, and I felt like I needed to put Hunter, Evan, and Mike out of my mind.

Thankfully, there were practical matters to consider. Hunter had driven his car to the city the night his grandfather died, but the always efficient Marie had made sure it had been returned to his apartment in Jersey City. So I took them home, then backtracked to the office.

I went straight to work on Lizzie's file. I needed to organize my thoughts, so I pulled out a new legal pad to write down what I already knew.

Lizzie had been born in Secaucus, New Jersey, at The Hayden Clinic, but had grown up in London. The Hayden Clinic was closed now; Mrs. Hayden was still alive though remarried. Lizzie had an image of herself and her sister standing at the bottom of the stairs in matching Easter dresses for a photo. There was no evidence of this picture or any other sign that Douglas and Camilla had more than one child together.

And one last fact: Camilla left everything to Lizzie, and had taken Douglas out of her will. Was that because of his financial indiscretions or because he had messed up her family?

That was the definitive question. Was Camilla trying to tell Lizzie something by hitting Douglas in the place she knew would hurt him the worst—his wallet? Like many wealthy families, these people were completely dysfunctional and their one connection was their money. That motivated most disagreements.

Geez, I wondered how families like that were described before dysfunctional entered our vocabulary.

One thing I knew for certain—I needed proof, proof there had been more than one biological child in the Wilkinson/Baines family tree.

I tried again to reach Elaine Hayden. This time, not even a maid answered, so I left a voice mail with my name and phone number and told them again that I was calling about Lizzie's birth at the Hayden Clinic. I hoped the woman would be interested enough to call me or contact Lizzie.

Until then, there had to be something I could do. That's when inspiration struck. Bernie and her husband had been an active part of the New Jersey medical community for many years. Maybe she knew something about the Hayden Clinic and specifically about Charles and Elaine Hayden.

Rather than call, I headed for my neighborhood. Bernie answered her doorbell immediately.

As always, Bernie was delighted to see me. "Come on back to the den," she said. "I was just about to get comfortable and watch some stuff I had taped. My grandson taught me to record any program I want to see. I don't have to wade through all of that trash to find something entertaining."

I followed her to the small den that adjoined the kitchen at the back of the house. The house was very warm and had the lingering aroma of food.

"Do you want some coffee or a glass of juice?" she asked, ignoring my answer and pouring us both some cranberry juice and filling a plate with homemade cookies.

I smiled as I took a seat on the oversized leather sofa. "I'm working on a case that involves a doctor and his wife, and I wondered if you knew them."

Bernie set my juice and the plate of cookies on the table beside me and took a seat in a recliner nearby. Her eyes were bright with interest. "Who are you investigating? What did they do?"

I explained that I needed information about Charles and Elaine Hayden and the Hayden Clinic.

"Ira and I were friends with the Haydens. In fact, we were in the same bridge club and played together every week for at least fifteen years. Professionally Ira and Charles were very different, but as bridge partners they were unbeatable," she said with a laugh. "The four of us won most of the local tournaments."

"How were Ira and Charles different?"

"Oh, Ira was always a very involved doctor. He believed he needed to get to know the patient to understand what made them sick. Charles was always a bottom-line kind of guy. He kept up with the latest developments in obstetrics and when he opened his own clinic, I guess you would have called it 'state of the art.' He always had a staff of young doctors and medical students to order around," she said with a wave of her hand. "He liked being in charge and certainly had a strong sense of self-importance."

"Anything else?"

Her eyes shifted and she put her hands on her

knees. It was obvious she wanted to tell me something but wasn't sure about it.

"Nobody will know where this came from," I said. "I'm doing research for myself here."

"Well, this sounds silly now, but Ira always had suspicions about Charles and his 'fertility' work." She used air quotes.

"Why? What about it bothered him?"

"It seemed that everybody who came to the clinic had a baby, and, well, I think we all know you can't be successful all the time with women and fertility. Ira wondered how Charles managed success so often. Women came from everywhere to see him."

She stopped and shook her head for a moment and then shrugged. "Then again, maybe he was just a good doctor."

"What about Mrs. Hayden?"

"Elaine was, and is, all about status. She couldn't wait until they were making enough money to live in Manhattan. She was born in Newark, but she'd never tell anybody that. When they asked, she'd always say she grew up in the New York area."

"When Charles was passed over for chief of obstetrics and gynecology at Wayne Memorial, she was the one who pushed him to get his own clinic. She was also the one who got the investors and brought in the money to get it opened. Ira always said she had the balls in the family."

We talked some more about the Haydens as I munched cookies. I wasn't sure if what Bernie told me was anything more than speculation, but at least it lent a framework to start my investigation of the Hayden clinic.

Thanking Bernie for her help, I stood.

"I have some leftover lamb chops if you'd like them for dinner," the older woman said.

Knowing nothing made her happier than feeding someone, I agreed and walked next door with the wrapped chops. As usual, there was enough for several people. Maybe Evan and Hunter would like to share.

I had just put the chops in my refrigerator and got out of my coat when my cell rang. It was Kinley's sister Lydia.

"Hey," I said, glad to hear from her. "How are you and the girls doing?"

"I have such good news that I wanted to share it with you," she said in a rush.

"Is there a break in the case?"

"Not that good, but last night Kelly started talking to the stuffed cat you gave her. She's just whispering, but we all feel like it's the beginning of bringing her back." Lydia's laugh was joyful. "When we first heard her on the baby monitor, I thought I was hearing a ghost."

"That is good news. Is she saying anything in particular?"

"Just about going back to school, saying she misses her mother, things like that. I haven't said anything to her about it because the therapist said it might be better to leave her alone and just observe for a few days. But it's hard not to push her."

Kelly was such a bright, sweet little girl. It was good to know she was finding her way out of the darkness.

I thought of the pictures the little girl had been drawing last time I'd seen her. They were so different from what I'd seen on the refrigerator at her home. Dark, almost violent. I couldn't help feeling those pictures were key to getting inside her mind. How did we unlock it?

"Zoe?" Lydia prompted. "You still there?"

"Sorry, I was just thinking about what more I could do to help Kelly."

"You've been so kind, and the cat is very special to her." She sighed. "The girls have their first visit with Eric tomorrow."

I shuddered, uneasy about the man having access to his daughters. Friday, Brad had tried to block Eric seeing them. But with the police unable to prove he was involved in Kinley's death, the courts had no reason to stop him.

"His mother wants them to come and spend the night," Lydia said, her voice now laced with anxiety. "Thankfully, Eric agreed that they need to stay here. He's just going to come over and visit for a while."

That surprised me. "Being cooperative is not Eric's style."

"He has checked on the girls every day. I can barely stand to talk to him, but my husband thinks it's important to be cordial until after the custody hearing. So I let him talk to Eric most of the time, and he says the guy is very shaken by Kinley's death."

"More likely shaken by the thought that he's guilty," I muttered, then sighed. "Hopefully this will end soon. Somewhere there's proof of what Eric did. I want the girls to get on with their lives."

I said goodbye to Lydia with a promise to check in again soon.

I moved through my house, putting my coat in the

closet and heading for the stairs as I thought about Kelly whispering to the stuffed cat I had given her. Another thought struck me. If Kelly would whisper to a stuffed kitten, could we possibly get her to talk to a real cat?

I just happened to know a cat that would fit the bill.

Chapter 17

Hunter's phone beeped. It was Zoe, but he was reluctant to answer. He knew she wanted to talk about the chimera, about Evan, and what had gone down with his father yesterday afternoon. She had let him off the hook last night and this morning, but he knew her too well to think that would continue. He didn't want to face any of it. Even with Zoe.

Standing at his condo's bedroom window, he watched evening shadows drag their way across the urban landscape of Jersey City. He was so on edge, his skin prickled and itched. For the first since discovering his feline nature, Hunter understood the trauma of being a caged animal. He never thought he'd feel so trapped in his own place.

He didn't blame Evan. He also understood he needed Evan's special brand of protection. He just wanted Evan to do the protecting from a distance. This had been a long afternoon.

After Zoe dropped them off this morning, Hunter gave Evan his pick of the two guest bedrooms in the condo. Of course, the guard had chosen the one closest to Hunter's. Evan unpacked, and then went over every foot of every room in Hunter's home—living and dining rooms, kitchen, three bedrooms, and three baths and Hunter's pride and joy, his small home gym.

After being sure the windows and doors were

secured according to his standards, Evan questioned Hunter about neighbors.

"Hell, I don't know," Hunter answered in irritation. God, he just wanted the man to shut up. "I don't know them. Chymera could have his lieutenants in every condo in the place and I wouldn't know."

Smiling in an indulgent way that made Hunter want to bare his teeth, Evan replied, "Your grandfather had grown older and a bit lax, but he would never have allowed you to be living among chimera. I'm sure he checked out everyone moving in and out of this building." He dug out his cell phone. "I'm going to call Craig and get him to send me the files on the tenants."

"How does one spot a chimera?" Hunter muttered. "Or one of the chimera's faithful servants?"

"Always lead with your nose," Evan said matter-of-factly. "That scent you caught the night Dugard died? The smell you chased in the forest? That's the stink of chimera. And even when they change fully into humans, it's always there, especially when you know to check for it. It's similar to the smell of a true shifter, only there's something faintly rotten about a chimera."

"So I smell, too?" Hunter lifted his arm to sniff himself.

"Yes, but it's pleasantly musky, like a well-groomed cat," Evan said.

Hunter was about to protest that commenting on his scent in such a way was a little too cozy for his taste. But Evan was on his phone. After talking to Craig, the guard retreated into his bedroom with his laptop. Relieved, Hunter paid bills online and returned some of the most pressing personal and professional emails and voicemails that had come in during his absence.

What pressed him most of all was the fact that he was horny. Mandy had called several times, cooing sympathy and promising a hot romp. Hunter closed the door to his bedroom as he dialed her number.

"Hey, there," she answered on the first ring.

"I'm sorry I've been out of touch," Hunter replied.

"I heard about your grandfather. My condolences."

"I got your messages, but I've been busy."

"Of course." Mandy's husky whisper dipped even lower. "I've missed you."

Damn the woman could make him hard with just her voice. "How about later?"

She sighed. "We're throwing a dinner party tonight." A bell chimed faintly in the distance. "In fact, the first guests are already arriving. Charlie and the other guys will be smoking and drinking until all hours while I entertain a bunch of stupid, trophy wives."

"Couldn't you sneak away?"

"Not tonight, baby. Maybe tomorrow? Charlie will be taking a nap tomorrow afternoon after this party. I can tell him I'm going shopping."

Tomorrow was Grandda's memorial service. He wanted to see her, but he didn't think he should take a chance on getting hung up with Mandy and being late for the reception. Plus, how was he going to ditch his new jailer/roommate?

Reluctantly, he told Mandy he would call next week.

So, feeling trapped, he stood at his bedroom window, hands clenched on the glass as if he were a tomcat ready to climb a window screen and claw his way to freedom.

Almost as much as he needed a woman, he needed to get out of here.

He looked down at the waterfront walkway along the Hudson River. His mind was made up in a flash. He changed out of his jeans and T-shirt and into cold weather gear and running shoes.

The living room was empty. A low voice came from beyond the half-open door to Evan's room. No doubt, the gallant servant was on the phone with other warriors, strategizing their next move. Hunter cared about that. God, he really cared about his own life and his family's safety. But he was going nuts. And he had been protecting himself for a long, long time. So he was busting out.

He moved silently through the condo, into the kitchen and out through the utility door to the back hallway. In moments he was down the stairs, pushing through the service entrance into the chill February dusk.

His building was three miles from Liberty State Park, with its dazzling view of the Statue of Liberty's backside and New York's financial district. It was all connected by the Hudson River Waterfront Walkway that started just above the old Central Railroad of New Jersey and would eventually cover the eighteen miles from the Bayonne Bridge to the George Washington Bridge. It was the perfect place to run, walk, or ride a bicycle.

Hunter jerked his black hoodie over his head and glanced up at the darkening sky. He started to run, veering right toward Liberty Park. This was exactly what he needed. The cold breeze from the water felt good on his skin. Out here alone, away from the bodyguard he never wanted, and didn't want to need, he could think and relax.

His father's words from yesterday had hit harder than he wanted. Did he have an obligation to join the family firm? Already, his life had changed in a million ways. But did he have to give up his practice, too?

Thoughts churned as he picked up speed. He knew he'd had every advantage in the world handed to him before he ever opened the practice with Zoe. They were able to afford to buy a building and live on family largesse for the first year. But for two years now, their practice had done very well. They had built something together. Together, he and Zoe helped people navigate turning points in their lives.

Hunter ran harder as family duty warred in his brain with his natural inclination to do what he wanted, when he wanted.

Dimly, he was aware of the others scattered throughout the area where he ran. Singles, as well as couples strolling hand in hand, made the walkway a busy place this evening. There weren't as many as there might be on a warm summer night, but the dedicated runners and walkers were out in droves, passing each other along the trail. He sped past them without looking and found he was almost alone as he neared the park.

Maybe, just maybe, he would be able to ditch his clothes somewhere and shift. God, that would feel good.

He was considering the options when someone called his name. Damn. Although he had told Evan he didn't know his neighbors, he was casually friendly with a number of people who lived in this area. He darted a look over his shoulder.

Unexpectedly, there was Cyn.

He came to a halt as the sexy redhead ran toward him. A long, flame-colored ponytail was threaded through her dark ball cap and glinted as she sprinted under the streetlights. Slender and tall in black leggings and an oversized black zip-up sweatshirt, she was the last person he expected to see.

"What are you doing here?"

She bent over, one hand at her waist as she caught her breath. "Trying to keep up with you."

"Me?"

She darted a look around. "What are you doing out here?"

"Didn't I just ask you the same question?"

Again, she scanned the area around them, clearly anxious.

"You seem nervous," Hunter said. "What's up?"

"I wanted to talk to you..." She faltered, then continued. "About your grandfather. I'm sorry."

"I guess you saw it in the news."

Once more her gaze skittered away from his. "Yeah, well, I'm kind of well-connected to the news."

"Because you write for *Out There*?"

"That too," she replied, confusing Hunter. What was she saying?

"I saw you running," she said.

"You must live close by."

"No."

He frowned, realization dawning. He grinned. "You came looking for me."

Cyn laughed, regaining some of the cockiness he liked. "Don't flatter yourself, okay? It's a nice place to run. I simply saw you take off and came after you."

Hunter wasn't sure, but he felt she wasn't telling him the truth. Before he could say anything, however, his head jerked around, drawn by a sound, a movement, a familiar scent. Yes, he could smell chimera. Just like Evan had said.

The walkway was deserted for the moment. On one side was the swirling Hudson River and on the other side grassy areas off limits to the public. Through the water and high weeds, Hunter thought he saw movement. Two bright eyes glowed in the gathering darkness. A stray dog? Or something more?

He stepped in front of Cyn. She protested, and he snapped, "Be quiet. There's something here."

She went still. She was close enough that Hunter could feel her heart beating. Heat came off her body in waves, and her deep, primal fear touched something in his second nature. He had to fight to keep from growling. Peering into the darkness beyond the lighted path, Hunter searched for the eyes again. They were gone. Now he could smell only water, earth, and sky. He stood alert for a moment, then slowly relaxed.

He turned to Cyn. "I guess it was nothing."

Her gaze was steady on his. "I felt it, too."

Hunter frowned. What was she saying? What did Cyn know about what he felt?

They stared at each other for a second. Then pounding footsteps came from the direction they had come. Hunter stepped protectively in front of Cyn once again until he saw it was Evan racing down the path.

"What the hell are you doing?" Evan challenged.

Annoyance surged back through Hunter. "I needed to run."

"You're supposed to take me everywhere you go."

Evan grasped his shoulder. "You're not to go out alone."

Jerking away from Evan's steel grip, Hunter said, "I've never had to live by that rule and I'm guessing that this is going to be problem if you don't give me some space."

Ignoring him, Evan turned his laser-focus on Cyn. "Who are you?"

She stood her ground and returned his glare, but said nothing.

Slowly, as he studied her, Evan's expression changed, calmed. He put himself in between Hunter and Cyn, and asked in a much more deliberate tone, "Who are you?"

"This is Cyn, a friend of mine," Hunter retorted. "Why are you acting so weird?"

Evan kept his attention locked on Cyn. "Are you really a friend?"

"Definitely. But not everyone is." She looked toward the tall weeds.

Evan stared toward the weeds and took a deep breath, "He's been here. Close by."

Hunter glanced around, relieved to have had his instincts confirmed. "I kept thinking I was seeing something in the shadows. I smelled it too."

Evan took a deep breath. "Like meat gone a day too long in the fridge."

"Exactly," Cyn whispered, stepping closer.

Both men looked at her in surprise. .

"I should go," she said to Hunter and nodded at Evan. "Nice to meet you."

"But wait—" Hunter protested.

She took off like a shot back toward the more

populated areas of the walkway. Hunter started after her, but Evan caught his arm again.

"Cut that crap out," Hunter said, shaking himself free.

"Let her go," Evan ordered.

"But if there's something out here and she knows what it is, then she could be in danger."

"She'll be fine."

Hunter glared at Evan. "What do you know about her?"

"That she knows what she's doing. She was smart enough to catch up to you, keep you from going any further along this path." Hunter stepped away from Evan. "Shouldn't we look for our stalker?"

"Not tonight," Evan muttered. "We don't go looking for trouble. Come on. Let's get home."

Reluctantly, Hunter started in the direction Cyn had disappeared. It went against his grain not to challenge the chimera.

Evan picked up his pace. Hunter fell in step beside him, and they were quickly back with the crowd. Cyn was nowhere in sight.

Beside him, Evan barely panted in exertion. "At least you smelled him. You're using all of your senses. That will help you survive."

"I'm not going to walk around sniffing these animals."

Evan punched Hunter's shoulder hard enough for Hunter to grab it in pain and come to a halt. "You've got to start using your brain," the guard said fiercely. "This bastard is out to get you. He's a cool killing machine, and he wants you dead. How long before that sinks in, man? It won't be an easy death. Did you see all those slashes on your grandfather's body? They were made one at a time while someone held Mr. MacRae down. Do you know what that means?"

Hunter looked away from Evan unable to think about what his grandfather must have endured. "Why are you doing this?" he asked angrily.

"Because you can't go off alone like this again." Evan got in Hunter's face, practically bumping chests with him. "You know what kind of danger you're in. You know how a cat plays with a mouse before killing it? That's what the chimera wants to do with you."

"You honestly believe he would try to take me here?" Hunter said in disbelief.

"Not here." Evan gestured to the people around them. "But back there..." He pointed toward the path to the park. "If he had surprised you, he could have dragged you in the weeds before anyone noticed."

"Then why didn't he take me and Cyn?"

Evan rubbed at his chin. "Now that I don't know. I'm not sure what she is."

"What she is?" Hunter repeated. "You mean she's not just a hot, sexy redhead who was looking to scratch my itch tonight?"

"Surely the gifts you inherited from your grandfather told you the minute you met her that she was much more than just a hot redhead."

Hunter sighed, though he stubbornly refused to answer. What he really didn't like about Evan is that the guy was always right.

Evan put his head down for a moment and when he looked back at Hunter, his eyes were dark and angry. "I'm not sure who or what she is, but you have to take care. You can't be taking up with new people and going off on your own like a stray cat. You're not doing that on my watch."

The raw emotion in Evan's tone startled Hunter.

"Your grandfather died on Shamus's watch," the guard continued. "But there were many, many times when he saved the MacRae. That's my plan, saving you."

"I'd like to save myself," Hunter retorted.

"Since the end result is one and the same, I don't understand your resistance."

Hunter stood with his arms helplessly at his sides, feeling like his chest would explode. What he began to realize several days ago was coming into focus. The freedom he had relished for so long was gone.

He looked across the water. Lady Liberty stood with her back to Jersey City. New York spread like a wonderland of lights in front of her. Hunter felt as frozen as she looked. He began walking, forcing himself to cool down. He sensed rather than saw Evan moving behind him, shadowing his every move.

The silence continued on the elevator and up to Hunter's floor. At the door to his place, however, Hunter stood back, knowing Evan needed to go in first, in case there were any surprises. He might not like this bodyguard business, but he knew when to back down and accept the inevitable.

There was a surprise inside. Zoe was waiting for them. "You bastard," she yelled at Hunter as she leapt off the couch. "You damned idiot. If I'm going to be saddled with knowing every time you're in danger, then why can't you answer your damn phone when I call?"

Hunter was afraid she would punch him. Instead, she threw herself into his arms and burst into tears.

Chapter 18

I didn't cry. Not ever.

I prided myself on the fact that I kept a tight rein on my emotions. But what had I just done? Had a frigging crying meltdown in front of Evan the Warrior Prince.

I stared at myself in horror in the mirror in Hunter's bathroom. He knew how much I hated this kind of blubbering, weak female crap. That's why he had hustled me away from Evan and into the master bedroom suite. He had left me alone in here for twenty minutes or more, no doubt while he tried to convince Evan that I wasn't a lunatic who should be banished from the kingdom of MacRae.

But was that true? Maybe I wasn't well. Maybe these visions I was having, these spells, were the result of being knocked in the head the night Kinley was murdered. I certainly couldn't control them. Even when I could see Hunter being stalked, as I had at my house not an hour ago, I couldn't do anything about it. Maybe I should exit stage left and leave the protecting of Hunter up to those whose forbearers had been doing it for centuries.

I was beginning to hate Evan Egan.

A knock sounded at the door. "Zoe, you okay?" Hunter said.

I opened the door. "I'm fine. Is Evan still here?"

Hunter sighed. "He's never not going to be here."

"Shit."

"Yeah. Shit."

I sank down on the edge of Hunter's bed. "What are we going to do?"

"I have no idea." Hunter put his hands in the air in surrender.

"I didn't think they'd come after you here."

"According to Evan, there's nowhere I can hide. Michael Killin is a clever enemy. He is surrounded by a huge clan that is fierce in its loyalty and its desire to do whatever he wants."

"And you've just got me," I said sadly.

"Along with Evan and others who are prepared to die for me." Hunter looked as if the weight of that responsibility was shackling him to the ground as he sat down beside me.

"What's going on? You don't sound like yourself."

"Let's just say I'm having trouble adjusting to my new life." He filled me in on his attempt to escape from his watchful guard.

"I saw you running," I said. I had been at home when I had the vision that had sent me in a frantic rush to his condo. "Something was watching you."

"A woman?"

I frowned and shook my head, trying to see it as it had played out in my mind. "I assumed it was Chymera."

He told her about Cyn and how the reporter said she had sensed the monster's presence as well. "Evan hinted that she…may not be quite human."

"Oh that's just great. All I need is for you to get mixed up with some alley cat that will secretly sell you out to the enemy. Did she lure you down that path tonight?"

"She's not like that." Hunter looked thoughtful. "I think she kept Chymera away."

"Then let's get some of her mojo."

"Let's go talk to Evan about it some more," Hunter said as he stood.

I groaned and scrubbed hands through my short, tangled hair. "I wish I didn't have to see him."

"He's not judging you."

"Really? Because I am judging myself. I suck at this psychic guide stuff."

Hunter put out a hand and hauled me to my feet. "Neither of us knows what we're doing. Evidently, Evan's been training for his role since he was a baby. Let's go pick his brain."

We went into the living room. Evan was calm, almost Zen-like, waiting in one of the deep chairs Hunter's decorator had arranged in front of the gas fireplace. The fire was on, warming the room. Evan pointed to a wine bottle and some glasses on the coffee table. "I thought you might want some wine," he said to me.

Yes, I definitely hated this man, I thought as I picked up a goblet of red wine and took a grateful sip. I reflected on my hatred and Evan's incredibly sculpted features as I curled on the corner of the sofa closest to the fire. I chugged down some more wine.

"I ordered pizza," Evan said. "One of our men will pick it up and bring it here."

"Our men?" I couldn't keep from laughing. I visualized a force of Evan clones, all in steel-plated armor.

"There are women here in the city, as well," Evan told her, not cracking a smile. "They're dedicated to the MacRae's safety."

"Do you communicate with them by phone or through a Vulcan mind meld?"

Hunter shook his head as he picked up his wine and sat down. "Zoe, ease up. We're in new territory here."

"You don't have to tell me about new territory," I said angrily. "I'm supposed to have this gift and yet I can't even use it correctly."

Evan offered reassurances that made me want to slap him. "You have to give it time. You have to cultivate your gift and refine it."

"How do you know that?" I demanded.

"Because all this has been a part of my family for generations."

"How special for you, but it hasn't been that way for me, and I'm scared. What the hell are we going to do if th-that…animal decides he wants to come up here and rip us all apart. If I can't warn—"

"Let it go, Zoe," Hunter said quietly.

"We're well protected," Evan added.

"Then how did tabby here get out tonight?" I pointed at Hunter. Evan's face darkened, but I spoke over him when he tried to protest. "I have a right to be upset. Hunter could have been killed again tonight."

"This is why he isn't taking chances like that again." Evan darted a fierce look at Hunter. "Are you?"

Hunter nodded and took sip of wine.

I groaned and laid my head against the sofa's soft, upholstered cushion. "God, Hunter, as much as I hate agreeing with Evan, you have to—"

"I've had enough of this crap from him. I'm not listening to it from you too," Hunter said.

I was relieved that the doorman buzzed from downstairs. The pizza was here. Rather than stay and witness one of Evan's soldier buddies making the hand-off, I escaped to the kitchen to get plates and napkins.

"Let's sit at the dining room table and pretend to be civilized," I suggested as Evan brought in the pizza boxes.

The two men agreed, and they sat around the table with two extra large pies, one with anchovies and one without. They tried to stay off the hot button issues. Evan outlined the security plan for the memorial service and reception, and we made plans for the day.

It might have been okay. Except that Evan was sitting where I usually sat when I was here with Hunter. It was a small thing, and I was small for not liking it. But I couldn't help it. No matter what he knew about ancient family feuds or what skills he possessed, I didn't want him here. Hunter and I had been a team for more than half of my life. I wasn't sure about a third wheel.

I felt so disheartened I didn't even want a fourth piece of pizza.

"I'll clean up." Evan expertly stacked plates and pizza boxes and went into the kitchen.

I was grateful to be alone with Hunter.

"There's something I want to talk to you about," I said.

He grimaced. "Can we leave this all alone until after tomorrow? We'll talk after the services and reception for Grandda. You heard Evan. All of us are going to be well-protected. Nothing's going to happen.

You don't have to worry about being on guard, as well."

"I don't think I'll ever stop worrying about that again. But it was actually something else I wanted to ask you about. About Kinley's girls."

He sat forward. "Is something wrong? I exchanged emails with Brad today about the hearing next week. Eric doesn't seem to be pushing for custody, although his mother is having a fit. I'm a little worried, but I think Brad—"

"That's not it." I took a deep breath and told him about my conversation with Lydia and about Kelly whispering to her stuffed cat. I outlined the plan I'd been working on and chewed on my bottom lip while I waited for Hunter's response.

"I don't know," he said. "Are you sure about this? Could it hurt Kelly?"

"I think it's worth a try. We're talking about a little girl who may be holding on to a secret that could damage her for the rest of her life. I think we can find a way to reach her."

"I couldn't forgive myself if anything more happened to either one of those little girls."

"I feel very strongly that this could help Kelly."

Hunter straightened in his chair. "Have you had a vision or something?"

I was beginning to hate the "V" word. "Just one of those ordinary, run-of-the-mill hunches I used to have before your grandfather appeared to me."

He chewed his lower lip. "Give me some time to think."

I agreed but was disappointed he wasn't eager to help. So much had changed in a short time. Before his grandfather's death, Hunter was as impulsive as I was. Not now. There was a distance between us and I feared it was growing.

"I need to go home." I pushed away from the table. "Tomorrow's going to be a long day."

"You should stay here."

"I want to sleep in my own bed," I protested. "Chymera hasn't come after me. I don't think he will."

"You can't count on that," Evan said, stepping in from the kitchen.

I glared at him in resentment. Couldn't Hunter and I have a private conversation?

Surprisingly, however, Evan was my ally. "Zoe should go home and be comfortable. She's being protected."

"I figured as much," I grumbled. I hated, absolutely, positively hated that confident, knowing man. And I especially hated admitting to myself that I was relieved to know someone looked out for me as well.

He insisted on seeing me to my car, of course. I tried to argue, but Hunter got a stony, weary look on his face. So I decided to give it up. .

As I pulled out of the parking lot, I wasn't unhappy to see the long, sleek car that fell in behind me, just as Evan said it would.

"Help me through this, God," I prayed as I headed for home.

Chapter 19

More than a thousand people attended Fraser MacRae's memorial service at St. Patrick's Cathedral. Stirling delivered the eulogy with genuine emotion that surprised Hunter. The bishop had conducted the funeral mass.

Now, for the family reception, several hundred mourners were streaming in and out of the Grand Ballroom at the Waldorf Astoria. Hunter sipped club soda and surveyed the opulent room.

Elaborate floral displays lined the walls. An open bar and hors d'oeuvres buffet were set up. Waiters moved through the crowd serving his grandfather's favorites wines. A string quartet played quietly in the background. Hunter's father was at Nana's side. She was resplendent in a Chanel suit accented with a diamond brooch and earrings. Hunter could see her weariness, however, and he would be glad when she boarded the plane tomorrow for her return to Scotland. She needed to get away.

His mother was in her element, however, rubbing shoulders with "her" crowd of well-heeled New Yorkers. Meagan was mingling with long-time MacRae employees and sorority sisters. Zoe was talking with friends from their school days. Evan and his group of male and female guards patrolled, looking like Secret Agents in their dark suits and discreet wireless ear pieces.

Hunter wondered if any of the people here that he didn't recognize were relatives. Shifters perhaps? He found himself thinking often about those far-flung cousins he hadn't met. Being the only shifter left in his immediate family, he wanted to connect with others who shared his DNA burden.

Burden. The word made him sad. What he used to think of as a blessing seemed less so now.

He was happy, at least, that many of the attendees were people whose relationship with Fraser had sprung from philanthropic endeavors. Hunter had chatted with many people whose lives had been changed by Fraser's generosity—a doctor who now worked with "Doctors Without Borders" and had recently had built a new clinic in Haiti; a young law student who planned a career in the DA's office after escaping life in an inner-city gang; the mother of a mentally handicapped child who now had access to badly needed treatment.

Hunter realized anew what big shoes he had to fill since Grandda was gone. This fed into his anxiety about his future. What was he supposed to do with his life?

He walked to the front of the room and stood beside a life-sized portrait of his grandfather wearing the kilt of the MacRae hunting tartan. The painting, commissioned three years ago, was being sent to the family home in the Scottish Highlands.

A sudden murmur in the crowd made Hunter turn from his study. He followed the gazes of others to the main doors, where a group of men stood shoulder to shoulder. The noise of the crowd ceased. The musicians stopped playing.

Hunter growled when he recognized the man who

stood in the center of the doorway with a polite smile on his lips.

Before Hunter could move, Evan was beside him with a hand on his arm. And a low, terse command, "Stay where you are," into the small microphone of his headset, he murmured, "Get the music playing again. Now."

Hunter fought the rage that swept over him as music once more filled the room. Not that it deflected from the main item of interest—Stirling was striding toward the slick-haired, tall, and imposing Lion of Wall Street, Michael Killin. The murdering bastard had dared show his face at Fraser MacRae's funeral reception.

Fury simmering, Hunter shrugged Evan off and moved toward his father. Guards were fanned out on either side of Stirling. Hunter saw that others ranged themselves near his grandmother. No doubt the rest of his family was similarly protected.

Hunter and Evan reached his father's side just as Stirling faced Killin in the almost silent room.

"Hello, Michael," Stirling said, his tone mild. "I'm surprised to see you here."

"I've known Fraser all my life. It seemed inappropriate to stay away." The men behind Killin stood in a small semicircle with hands clasped in front of them. Killin smiled at Hunter. " I don't think we've formally met."

Killin extended his hand but Hunter didn't move. All he wanted to do was bite the hand and listen to Chymera scream in pain.

He heard a gasp. Zoe was beside him. Her brown eyes were wide as she touched his arm. She knew what he was thinking of doing to Michael Killin.

"You're the reason we're here," Hunter said to him through gritted teeth.

Killin gave him an innocent look. "I'm sorry?"

Stirling stepped between Killin and his son. "Perhaps you'd like to see my father's portrait."

Nodding calmly to the murmuring crowd, Stirling led Killin toward the front of the room. Killin's men remained in the doorway. But Hunter caught the faint but familiar scent of rot. Were they all chimeras?

Hunter spared one last look at their unflinching faces before following his father and Killin. Zoe and Evan flanked him.

"Would you like a drink?" Stirling asked Killin when they reached the portrait.

"Do you have some of Fraser's twenty-five-year-old Macallan's Scotch?" Killin asked smoothly.

"I'm sorry, no," Stirling replied. "But we do have some nice Bella Vida wines from Dundee. Shall I get you a glass? Red, of course."

Killin chuckled and nodded as he looked up at Fraser's portrait.

Stirling signaled to a nearby waiter while Killin continued, "Fraser was quite a man. I feel honored to have known him."

A warning look from Stirling silenced the angry words that rose to his lips.

"My father was a calculating and intuitive businessman who taught me the value of honesty and integrity," Stirling said.

The server returned with two glasses and each of the men took one.

"To Fraser." Killin raised his glass to the portrait.

Hunter noted that Evan's people had formed a

barrier between the crowd and the two men.

Stirling turned and looked directly at Killin. "Why are you here?"

"Paying my respects, of course." Killin sipped his wine. "Excellent."

Hunter couldn't take the bullshit any longer. As he stepped forward, however, he saw his grandmother heading their way.

Isobel walked up to Stirling and took his arm, keeping her gaze on Killin. "Michael, I'm surprised to see you here."

"My condolences, Isobel," Killin said with cold politeness.

Her eyes flared with anger but she spoke quietly, "How's Bethia?"

Killin looked into his drink, his face stiff, the muscles in his jaw clenched. "Mother is not well. She took to her bed after my brother was murdered."

"I'm sorry to hear that. Please give her my condolences and thank you for stopping by today," Isobel said.

She signaled to Evan. "Could you escort Mr. Killin to the door? He's leaving now."

He stepped forward, moving as if to place a hand on Killin's elbow.

Smiling, Killin kept his arm out of the guard's grasp. He gave his glass to a hovering server, nodded to Isobel and Stirling, and hesitated slightly in front of Hunter.

Hunter met the man's gaze, his nostrils flaring as the creature's wild scent increased. There was something flat, cold, and inhuman in the other man's eyes as Killin made his way to the door. Nervous conversation echoed through the crowd once more.

Isobel patted Stirling's arm. "I hope you don't mind, dear, I just couldn't stand him being in the same room with people who care for Fraser."

Stirling kissed her cheek. "Not at all, Mother, I think you handled that quite well. But you look tired. Can I get you anything?"

"I'd love a double scotch on the rocks if you can find one," Isobel said with a smile.

"For you, of course," Stirling replied and walked toward the bar himself instead of summoning a server.

Hunter escorted his grandmother to a seating area near the portrait. "Nana, please admit you're tired and sit here for a while. Let everyone come to you."

"Don't you dare treat me like an old woman," she said, although she sank heavily on a settee.

Zoe took a seat in the chair beside her. "This kind of thing is always exhausting," she said. "You should rest for a moment."

Stirling brought his mother's drink. She took it and had a healthy sip. Hunter noted that color again bloomed in her cheeks.

"Nothing like Macallan's." She patted Zoe's arm. "You're right, these kinds of gatherings are exhausting. I'll greet guests from my little throne for a while."

When the last guest was gone, the family gathered in a suite to discuss the next steps. Stirling and Margaret sat on the overstuffed sofa and Meagan with her grandmother across from them. Hunter and Zoe occupied chairs nearby.

Isobel had invited Zoe despite raised eyebrows from Hunter's parents. Evan, of course, didn't need an invitation. He was rarely more than an arm's length away, always confident about where he belonged. Three armed guards stood outside the doors.

Isobel clasped her hands in front of her and took a deep breath, "I don't think any of us were surprised to see Michael Killin show up today. Frankly, I would have been surprised if he hadn't."

"Mother—" Stirling interrupted and stood.

"You know we need to talk about this. It's not going to go away if we don't." She turned to Hunter. "What are you going to do?"

"What are you talking about, Nana?" Meagan asked.

"Really, Isobel, do we need to do this now?" Margaret asked, smoothing nonexistent wrinkles in her black Ralph Lauren dress.

"There's a very serious clan feud going on, and we're right in the middle of it," Isobel said. "We've got to decide how to respond."

She walked to Hunter and laid a hand on his arm. "As if we didn't already know he was intent on murdering all of our kind, Killin's appearance here today made a bold statement."

"Nana." Meagan faced her grandmother. "He can't just kill Hunter."

"Yes, he can, Meagan. That's exactly what he can do," Isobel said calmly. "Just like he killed your Grandda."

Though she now knew about the feud with the Killins, Hunter's practical-minded, accountant sister was still skeptical. "Well, if you know he did it, why not go to the police and let them handle it?"

"What proof do we have?" Isobel retorted, not unkindly. "Michael Killin is a feared but highly respected businessman. His name has never been associated with a public scandal. There's nothing to indicate he's the murderous animal that he is."

"Look, Nana," Hunter said. "We've done everything we can to prepare for this. You need to go Scotland and leave it to us."

"He's right," Stirling said, standing. "We're fighting him on all fronts."

Isobel pursed her lips. "Stirling, your father wanted you to stay as far from Killin's business as you could. He didn't want you to take him on."

"Father's no longer here," Stirling replied evenly. "He made all the decisions for us about how I did business and about how Hunter was prepared for his life. But now he's gone, and I will follow my own instincts. When it comes to business, they're damned good."

"He made mistakes," Isobel admitted. "But he loved you."

"And now we have to make our own way," Hunter said.

Isobel hesitated a moment. "Fraser would want you all to feel free to do as you wanted." She looked at Stirling, then at Hunter. "He tried to protect you both."

"Dear God," Meagan said. "How do you protect yourself from something like Killin? He's untouchable. He could kill us all and get away with it."

"Not on my watch." Hunter stood. "I'm not letting this family down."

Evan stepped forward. "I think I can offer some measure of comfort here. Craig is sending more guards. We'll be keeping an eye on all of you. We know everyone is in danger, and we're not just sitting around waiting for it."

"That's good." Isobel nodded. "I know that all of the extended MacRae family has a stake in this. Shamus was murdered, too, as well as that poor man from the clan in North Carolina."

"I'd like to talk to our North Carolina kin," Hunter said. "We need to be working together."

"Someone will be calling you soon." Evan exchanged a look with Stirling. Hunter frowned, wondering what the two of them were hiding from him.

His mother interrupted as she got up. "Oh, it will be so nice to get acquainted with the rest of the shifters in our family."

"Margaret," Stirling said in warning.

"No, I mean it, Stirling." Her laughter was thin. She stopped at the room's ornately carved bar and poured whiskey into a glass. "All I've wanted since the day you filled me in on your family's proclivities was to have more monsters in my life."

"We are not monsters," Isobel protested.

"Mother, please," Meagan implored.

Margaret took a long drink of the whiskey, her expression openly hostile as she studied her husband.

Hunter expected his father's usual stoic acceptance of his wife's bitterness. Instead, there was so much hurt in Stirling's expression that Hunter looked away. He felt like a kid, peeking around the door during an adult moment he'd rather not seen. It was easier to think of his parents as willing partners in a business arrangement than as human with fears and disappointments of their own.

"Margaret, please steady yourself," Stirling said. He looked at the others in the room. "It's obvious we're all tired. This has been a long day, and we have many more in front of us."

Evan called for a security detail to escort Stirling, Margaret, Isobel, and Meagan to the front of the hotel and the limousines that were waiting to take them to their apartments. Another would take Isobel to the airport tomorrow.

Hunter hugged his sister and said cordial goodbyes to his parents before Nana enveloped him in one of her patented, rose-scented embraces.

"You're Fraser's brave boy," she whispered, the lilt of her Scottish heritage in her musical voice. Then she let him go and reached out to Evan and Zoe, clasping hands with both of them. "You've been entrusted with his life."

The room was still after she had exited.

Zoe let out a breath. "Nothing like a little pressure."

To diffuse the situation, Hunter turned to Evan. "I need to go for a walk and breathe some air that's not full of chimera stink or funeral flowers."

"No problem." Evan spoke to someone who was holding a car for them and then followed Hunter and Zoe into the hallway.

Outside the hotel, the trio headed down Park Avenue toward Times Square. They took a turn at 47th Street and ended up at the club Denim and Diamonds, with country music pounding and girls in tight jeans everywhere. Hunter soon grew restless and bored, so they left, again heading toward the bright lights of 42nd Street.

He was crossing 44th Street when a movement caught his eye. He did a double take, sure he'd seen a huge cat standing in a doorway down an alley. But when he looked back, the doorway was empty and people were walking by undisturbed.

"I saw it too," Evan said. "Killin is playing with us."

Hunter stopped, staring down the alley and trying to see what wasn't there.

"That seems risky," Zoe said. "What if someone saw him and screamed?"

"Michael Killin is very old and very skillful. He can switch forms faster than you can blink."

"I'm still working on keeping my clothes on as I change," Hunter grumbled.

Evan sighed. "For lack of a better word, Killin's movements are often…magical."

"Magic," Zoe breathed her eyes somber. "I'm feeling a little like Meagan. There's not much we can do against him."

Evan disagreed. "We have magic of our own."

"Nana told me to believe in magic," Hunter said.

"What else would you call what you can do?" Evan asked.

At his question the busy city sounds around dimmed. Hunter had a sense of de ja vu, as if he and Evan and Zoe were standing with their backs against edge a wide, deep precipice.

"Whoa," Zoe said and jerked Hunter back to the present. He knew by her expression that once again, she had seen what he pictured in his head.

Evan darted a look around them. "I think we should go home."

For once, Hunter agreed without protest.

Chapter 20

I was at the office before eight the next morning. I had a couple of busy days coming up.

If Hunter agreed to cooperate in regard to Kelly, I had a plan that might help draw the little girl out of her mute shell. Yesterday, I had gone out on a limb to clear the plan with Lydia.

The truth was that I had shared as much as I could tell Lydia about a plan involving a shapeshifter. Now all I needed was a cat named Hunter.

First, however, I had to call Lizzie Howerton. Even though I hit a wall with Elaine Hayden Richards and didn't have any other promising leads, it was time for an update.

She didn't accept my news with grace.

"Well, I'll just go talk to her," Lizzie said. "I know her somewhat. She and her husband were on the board of the children's hospital with Mommy for a couple of years. I've talked to her at various events."

"I'm not sure she'll budge."

"Maybe if she knows who is asking for the information she'll be a little more forthcoming," Lizzie replied. No wasn't an option. In this case, however, I had a feeling that Lizzie's identity might slam the door for good. If there was something to hide, Mrs. Richards wouldn't want the Howertons to know. "Let me take another run at her before you do anything."

"Well, make it soon," Lizzie said. "I have to go to court next week with my dad about Mommy's will. Apparently she was very clear with her lawyer that Dad wasn't to get anything, and I have no idea why. Dad wants to contest it even though my lawyer says it's useless to try."

"I'll find a way to get the information from Mrs. Hayden. It's what I do."

I hung up hoping I sounded more confident than I felt. Elaine Richards had the upper hand right now. Medical records were sacred these days.

It just seemed logical to me that Lizzie be able to see her mother's file. Camilla was dead, the clinic was closed, and the doctor was dead. What was the harm in just reading a few records?

I was still stewing about it when Darla came in at eight-thirty. We did the usual morning small talk while she got her computer powered up and got some coffee. Only a few moments had passed before she came around the corner to my desk.

"What's up with Hunter?" she asked.

I evaded her gaze as I entered notes in Lizzie's file. How do you discuss the fact that a supernatural creature was stalking Hunter and his entire family? Or that Hunter was a shapeshifter himself?

Being a good Jersey girl, Darla had a fondness for animal print—she was wearing a cheetah print sweater over a tight black leather skirt today.

I couldn't ask Darla such a question, of course, so I said, "I haven't talked to Hunter this morning. Is something wrong?"

Her pretty face was lined with worry. "It's not just this morning. Something's not right with him. I know it.

He was upset about his grandfather's death, but he barely called in on his cases at all last week. He dumped a bunch of stuff on Brad. We have a meeting this morning. There's another with Brad this afternoon."

I frowned as I clicked onto my email. Sure enough, Hunter had sent out meeting invitations. At four this morning.

"Do you think he's finally going to join his father's firm?" Darla pressed.

"He'd rather have a root canal every day than work there."

"I'm worried," Darla said. "I had a boyfriend whose grandfather left him a lot of money and he quit working. Do you think there's a chance Hunter would decide that?"

"He's never wanted to do anything but practice family law," I said.

"Yeah, that's what I thought, but he's transferring everything to Brad."

"You don't like Brad?"

"He's not Hunter." Darla's words were simple and to the point. "Brad's fine. I think clients like him. I mean, he's good-looking and young like Hunter, which is what some of these cougars like, but—"

I struggled not to smile. Darla had no way of knowing how appropriate her feline characterization of Hunter's typical client was.

She continued, "With Brad there's just no..." She hesitated, as if searching for words. "He just doesn't make things sizzle and pop around here like Hunter has. What if Hunter's bored and wants out?"

It hadn't occurred to me that Hunter would stop

practicing law. Together we made a great team for our clients. Besides, Hunter would have told me if he was considering something big.

Wouldn't he? I wasn't happy with the doubt creeping into my thoughts. I tried not to let my anxiety show as I thought about this weekend and how distant Hunter had been.

Hunter was dealing with a lot. I could sense him trying to block me. I'd had a couple of links with him yesterday at the reception—images straight from his brain to mine. I hated what I had read in his mind— violence and desperation. I was unnerved by the image of Hunter, me, and Evan with our backs against a deadly fall.

But what bothered me more? Fear of falling into the abyss or that Evan was standing there with us?

"Well?" Darla prompted, interrupting my reverie.

I had to be positive. "Just Friday, I heard Hunter tell his father he didn't want to join the family firm. He's going through a rough patch. Let's see how it shakes out and try not to project what might happen."

Darla and I both looked up as the front door opened and Hunter's voice called. "Hey, ladies, anyone interested in breakfast?"

"Welcome back," Darla said.

Hunter passed through the office, calling, "Doughnuts available in the break room."

Darla whirled back to me and whispered, "Who is that hunk with Hunter?"

Of course Evan was with Hunter. The man was his freaking shadow.

I stood. "Come on. Let's have you meet the new eye candy."

In the break room, Hunter performed the necessary introductions. Darla was practically salivating as she shook hands with Evan.

I couldn't blame her. If I could overcome my dislike for his calm demeanor, I might be able to appreciate the way his jeans clung to his butt.

True to his stoic style, he smiled and said very little, focusing on making fresh coffee. "What brings you to Wayne?" Darla asked Evan.

"Evan's my..." Hunter hesitated, his brows drawing together. "He's joining the firm," he finally said.

Startled, my gaze flew to Hunter's. What did that mean?

Even Darla stopped her perusal of Evan's manly form to say, "Really?"

"He specializes in security." Hunter avoided looking at me.

I wondered if everyone could hear my blood pressure rising like the tick-tick of a bomb.

"That's great news," Darla said with a nervous laugh. She knew Hunter and me well enough to know when there was trouble. I had never felt this level of anger at my partner and supposed best friend.

"Let's sit and eat," Evan said.

"How about in the conference room?" Hunter suggested. "I wanted to have a staff meeting at nine. Is that okay? We could go ahead and get started."

"Sure," I muttered. Rather ungraciously, I pushed around Darla and scooped up two doughnuts—a chocolate-iced and a jelly-filled—and a handful of napkins.

"I got you those low-fat egg white breakfast

sandwiches you like," Hunter said.

"Like that's going to happen," I said, went to conference room and took a seat at the head of the table.

The smoke coming out of my ears practically became flames when Evan placed a steaming mug of coffee beside me. "You take it black, don't you?"

I couldn't stand that he remembered how I liked my coffee, but I forced myself to give him a stiff nod.

Hunter looked wary as he sat opposite Evan. Darla appeared with a notepad and a half of a doughnut. I knew she'd go back later for the chocolate-iced donut with sprinkles. The guys just wouldn't see it. It made me want to smack her, the way she was acting all girly while I was sucking down sugar and carbs like a truck driver.

I watched in disgust as she turned to Hunter and said, "Where should I set up Evan's office?"

Hunter cleared his throat. "That, uh…well—"

"I don't need an office," Evan explained with his usual smoothness.

I cut to the chase. "Hunter, why don't you tell us what's going on?"

"I never could keep a secret from you, Zoe. That's why we never play poker."

"We don't play poker because I'm a better player than you and it pisses you off." I took my last bite of jelly-filled delight and started on the chocolate iced.

Hunter rewarded me with a glare, and I felt better.

"Am I about to lose my job?" Darla blurted out.

"Of course not," Hunter reassured her.

Relief flooded her face as she let out a breath. "Thank God. I have bills, you know? The economy's not so good."

"You're not going anywhere if I can help it," Hunter replied. "But there are going to be changes."

I raised an eyebrow. Changes in the firm should have been run by me, his partner, before he announced them to our staff.

"I'm letting Brad take over most of the active cases." Hunter's eyes were on me. "I'm taking some time away from everyday stuff here to consider…things."

"Oh." Darla darted an uncertain look between me and Hunter.

"It's family stuff," Hunter continued.

The silence in the room stretched to an uncomfortable level.

Again, Evan saved the day. "Darla, can you kind of show me ropes? Tell me where I can plug in my laptop, where the printer is, that kind of stuff."

She practically popped out of her chair. "Just follow me."

Evan was courteous enough to shut the door of the conference room as he exited behind her.

I struggled to control my fury as I faced Hunter. "Did you think not telling me about changes would make me more compliant?"

"I didn't want to give you a chance to talk me out of it."

"Partners usually talk things like this over. You and I usually talk everything over."

"Jesus, Zoe. Do you really think I need to be handling cases right now? I can't arrange my own thoughts in a straight line, much less do my best for a client in court."

I had to give him credit. That made a lot of sense.

"I understand." I squeezed my eyes shut and trying to shove down my resentment. "I know all of this is a nightmare. But if you had just told me instead of springing it at me. And in front of him, especially—"

"You're going to have to get over this shit with Evan."

My eyes snapped open. "Excuse me?"

"He's not trying to take your place, Zoe. He's doing his fucking job, something he's been hardwired for from conception."

Though I wanted to remind him that he had been having plenty of problems with Evan himself not more than 48 hours ago, I held back. "So what are you going to do with yourself if you're not working?" I said instead. "Screw around with Mandy? Go into the city to lunch with your father and play financial tug of war with Michael Killin? Prowl the streets and try to draw him out?"

Hunter sat back. "For starters, I thought I might try the housecat trick to see if we can help Kelly."

That took the wind out of my sails.

"I don't know why I hesitated to say yes to your plan with Kelly the other night," he continued. "It's just that shifting has always been something I did for me, because I could. It's new to think about my abilities having another purpose, of using my talent, so to speak, to help someone."

I touched his arm. "I've felt so odd since I started having these visions, Hunter. Instead of making things clearer, they've made me unsure of myself and of you. I thought you might be turning your back on our practice."

"Even if I weren't a divorce attorney any longer, I wouldn't turn my back on you."

I was only partially reassured, and Hunter saw that in my face.

"I'm not saying I'm cutting out of here." He grinned. "You know how much I've enjoyed the fringe benefits of my work."

Thinking of the parade of women through this office in the past three years, I nodded. "Unfortunately, yes, I know that."

"But the situation we're in has me messed up." He frowned. "I'm questioning a lot of assumptions I had made."

"About what?"

"For starters, about my father and his feelings for Grandda."

"It was kind of hard for me to hold onto the belief that your father is a cold, heartless bastard after listening to his eulogy yesterday."

"Exactly," Hunter murmured. "I'm also realizing that being a shifter isn't just…extra."

I cocked my head at him, puzzled.

"It's who I am." He looked at her intently. "Before I was Hunter and a shifter. I thought Grandda was a big shot attorney and environmentalist and businessman and a shifter. Now I realize that we're—I'm—a shifter. We're the MacRaes first. Do you know what I'm saying?"

I wasn't entirely sure.

"I don't know that I've ever thought about my true nature, about who I really am or what I want to do when I grow up."

"I thought that's what we were doing with this

business."

Hunter paused and took a sip of coffee. He was struggling. "I'm not sure, Zoe."

I swallowed hard. What I did day-in and day-out was vitally important to me. No, I didn't really like chasing cheating wives or insurance scammers, but I enjoyed helping people like Kinley and Lizzie find answers they needed. Unlike Hunter, who seemed to be searching for his identity, I'd known for a long time I was meant to solve puzzles.

What if I couldn't do that with Hunter?

"I wish everything could be the way it was just a week ago."

"I'm glad I know everything now. I want to meet the rest of the shifters in the family, too. I want to know what I'm supposed to do since everyone expects me to take Grandda's place."

"You don't have to make any decisions right this minute. Let's take everything day to day."

"You're right about that. Other family members will be contacting me soon. Evan told me last night that I should wait on them, as a show of respect."

"So there are shifter protocols to follow?" I asked, bemused.

"Hundreds and hundreds of years of tradition," he replied, then brightened. "But right now I want to work with you on some of your cases."

"Like the Lizzie Howerton case?"

"I know to trust your gut. You believe she has a sister, so let's find her."

"I was just going to start searching for former employees of the hospital where Lizzie was born." I told him what Bernie said about Dr. Hayden.

"Send me your files," Hunter said. "I've got some detail work to do before we meet with Brad this afternoon. But after that, I'll look for Lizzie's twin. Maybe Evan would have some ideas, too."

I tried but failed to stop my grimace of dismay. I cut Hunter off before he could berate me. "I know, I know, I have to accept him."

"You could bill Lizzie for the time he spends on the case," Hunter suggested.

I laughed. "Here you are, a newly minted gazillionaire, and you're thinking about billable hours."

"Old habits die hard. Maybe Grandda knew what he was doing when he set me free for a few years."

"Yes, you were free to build a business while living in a luxury condo and drawing the interest off a trust fund," I retorted dryly.

Hunter laughed, and just like that, we were back on familiar footing with each other.

I took his hand. "We're going to be okay, aren't we?"

He got up and kissed me on the forehead. "Better than that."

"I'll call Lydia to set up a visit with Kelly. Maybe tonight or tomorrow?"

He agreed and walked out of the room, whistling.

I tried, but I couldn't quite match his cheeriness as I went to my desk. I was uneasy and worried. Change wasn't easy for me. Change regarding Hunter was unthinkable.

The thought brought me up short. My deep connection to Hunter was truly my life's one constant. My father was my only family, and we rarely even spoke. Hunter was my center—friend, family, business partner—everything.

I remembered when one of my many stepmothers decided the way to stay married to my father was to try to get to know me. Yeah, she wasn't too bright. But I was about twenty and devastated after my break up with the latest in a string of young men that I claimed wouldn't allow me to be myself. As I recalled the problem was the amount of time I spent with Hunter. Stepmother Alice told me, on the pretext of giving me advice, that I used my relationship Hunter as an excuse not to develop intimacy with others.

I didn't like admitting that Alice had been on target. But if I were truthful, I had pretty much ruined every romantic relationship I had ever had because of something with Hunter.

The episode with Mike last week was a scalding reminder of that.

Alice had also said that Hunter used me in the same way. As long as he had me for emotional support, why did he need anyone else?

But if Hunter and I were so bad for each other, why were we bound together so deeply? Why had his grandfather come to me, in death, to tell me to develop my second sense to help him? Why had his grandmother told me she was entrusting me with Hunter's life?

Sighing, I buried my head in my hands for a moment. Then I put my troubled thoughts aside and turned to the computer. I was going to email Lizzie's file to both Hunter and Evan. While I was waiting for Hunter to find himself and for my own future to come into focus, I would focus on the solvable puzzles in my life—Lizzie's sister and Kelly's silence.

Chapter 21

"I need to be a cat," Hunter said to Evan as they walked into the apartment Monday night.

"Feel free." Evan shrugged out of his coat.

"I mean I need to change and run and do the stuff that will work the bloody kinks out of my brain."

"Is that typically how you unwind from a day at work?"

"Unwinding also often includes a hot blonde or brunette or redhead." Unbidden, Cyn's face popped into his head.

Evan gave him that peculiar look that meant he was reading Hunter's mind. "I'm not sure who Cyn is. I've put out some feelers about her, but until we know—"

"Yeah, yeah." Hunter glanced down at the cell in his hand. He didn't have to follow Evan's suggestion. He had saved Cyn's phone number the afternoon they met. He wasn't sure why he was reluctant to contact her.

If he needed sex, he should call Mandy. She had texted that Charlie was out of town and she hoped for a visit.

That wasn't what he wanted. Soon, restlessness had him prowling from one room to another. Evan was busy on his phone and laptop gathering reports from the teams. Today had been very, very quiet. Hunter wondered what the Killins were waiting for.

He, Zoe, and Darla spent the better part of the afternoon with Brad, going over cases. The meeting had extended into the dinner hour, but had paid off. Brad was ready to handle the current caseload. Zoe was finished with all outstanding investigations on their divorce cases and her insurance business. She was free to devote herself to Lizzie Howerton.

It turned out that getting Evan involved in the research for that case had been a good idea. He had found a number of former employees of the Hayden Clinic who were still in the area. After several phone calls, he'd talked to Carl Kowalski, a radiologic technician, who now worked at East Orange General Hospital. He had no qualms about discussing the clinic or its doctors.

Evan said Kowalski had laughed and said, "what an asshole" in reference to Dr. Hayden and "raving ambitious bitch" about Mrs. Hayden. While he couldn't remember anything specific about the babies born at the clinic during the months surrounding Lizzie's birth, he had been there and supplied names of some other staff, including doctors.

Much of Kowalski's information confirmed what Bernie said.

Dr. Hayden liked having young doctors on staff. He picked male doctors most of the time, but Hayden was old school. He enjoyed dominating nurses and browbeating young doctors.

According to Kowalski, most people thought Hayden was generous in giving these OB/GYNs a start, but none of the doctors lasted long. Kowalski speculated that the lack of stability in staff was one of the reasons the facilities didn't survive Hayden's passing.

"Apparently, Hayden was the clinic," Evan reported. "His widow took the money they made and bought a new life."

So Zoe had names of several staff members she was going to track down tomorrow. Hunter would help, but he also had plans to check some of the properties his grandfather had left him, a few in Jersey City. According to a list emailed to him this morning from the attorney, there were several more than he'd expected.

Tomorrow afternoon, he and Zoe were going to see Kelly.

Hunter rolled his shoulders. If he was going to be a tame kitty tomorrow, he needed to be a bit more ferocious tonight. He went back to Evan, who was patiently inputting information into his laptop.

"I'm going to break through a door if I can't get out of here," Hunter told him. "Let's go to the park."

"It's too dangerous."

"I'm the one who will be dangerous soon," Hunter snapped.

Evan studied him then stood. "The city makes me a little claustrophobic, too. You'll be careful? I need to stick close by. I'll call in some others to meet us there."

"Sure, sure," Hunter agreed, heading to his room to change into running attire. "Tell them to meet us at the parking lot at High Mountain Park Preserve."

Though signs were posted warning against being there after dark that had never stopped Hunter.

"You have to stay in my sight," Evan warned him as they walked to the head of the trail. The moon was a sliver in the sky. Hunter breathed in the scent of fir, damp earth, and wildness. He sensed rather than saw a small animal scurry through the underbrush. But he didn't smell or feel the chimera here.

"It's safe," Evan said, echoing the shifter's thoughts.

Hunter removed his shoes and stuffed his socks inside. Then he plunged forward. Not breaking his promise about getting out of sight, he stuck to the path, but picked up speed. He had been thinking about what Nana told him about changing while he was still in his clothes. It was magic, she had told him. It was in him.

So Hunter focused hard. He pictured himself as a bobcat. He felt his muscles tighten, his bones change. Something ripped. Then he was a cat. He cried out in freedom and excitement as he leapt down the path bordered by sparse winter foliage.

"Hold up," Evan warned. Hunter wanted to resist, to stretch out his legs as he could only in feline form. But he had to set a leisurely run, so the human could keep up with him.

Evan kept a short distance behind, his flashlight bobbing over the forested landscape, but Hunter didn't need the light to see. He was hyper-aware of the air around him. This was what he needed after a few days of being human. It wasn't enough, he thought, understanding why his grandfather needed the estate in the Adirondacks. It was true that a shifter could change anywhere, but in order to be free, he needed to be able to run wild occasionally.

Finally, Evan called to him, and Hunter knew his freedom was at an end. He was okay with going home, but still, he couldn't resist turning on the guard and growling in protest.

Evan showed no fear as he faced Hunter. "I'm not scared of The MacRae, even when he's a beast."

With that, Hunter pictured himself as a human again, fully dressed. His thermal hoodie and pants were ripped in several spots, and he was barefoot, of course, but he wasn't naked. His grandmother had been right.

"I see you're mastering the art of clothes," Evan said mildly as he handed Hunter his socks and shoes. "Your grandfather had a hard time with it."

"So you're used to seeing naked MacRaes after they shift."

"It's not a high point of my job."

"Thank God for that. I'm enlightened, but that would be a little weird for me." His shoes on again, he took off back down the path. He had five miles or more.

"Now I'm hungry," he told Evan. The guard didn't protest, so Hunter headed to the doughnut shop not far from the park.

And there was Cyn. She had her laptop open and looked up at him with liquid brown eyes that drew him in. She was sitting at the same table as if she'd expected him.

Hunter decided this meeting was not an accident. "Give me a minute with her."

Evan went to the counter to order.

"What are you?" Hunter asked as he took the chair opposite Cyn's.

She didn't even pretend to not understand what he was asking. "I'm human."

"You're not part of a plot to assassinate me?"

Her eyes flashed. "Of course not."

"My buddy there," he nodded toward Evan, "is human, too, although he also knows about people like you, and he feels you're safe. But we're not used to anyone outside knowing about us."

"The veil between the human world and the other world is invisible, which is why most humans choose not to look through it. I never had a choice. I've known about the others since I was a baby." Her expression was direct.

Hunter frowned. "Others?"

"Not human," she said. "My first memory—other than my mother's touch and my father's wonderful, deep voice—is of the faeries who danced in the moonlight to entertain me while my parents slept."

"You saw them while you were in the crib?"

She wrinkled her nose. "Technically, I think I was still in a bassinet when the faeries came. You see, I liked to stay up all night, and my poor parents had to work every day. I think the faeries took pity on them and took over."

"Did your parents see the faeries?" Hunter asked.

"Of course not." She laughed out loud. "My father is a Methodist minister in a small Southern town, and my mother was raised by two maiden aunts. I know now that one of those aunts was a practicing witch, but my mother didn't. She's a simple, straightforward person. Neither she or my dad have ever seen through the veil."

Hunter blew out a deep breath. "I imagine raising you was quite a trip for them."

Cyn laughed. "You have no idea."

Evan approached their table. He nodded to Cyn and handed Hunter a cup and box of doughnuts. "A dozen, glazed. Coffee with two sugars and a cream." He looked back at Cyn. "Can I get you anything?"

"I'm fine," she answered with the smile that all the ladies, except Zoe, gave Evan.

"Then I'll be over here," Evan took sentry duty at a table near the door.

"You're well protected," Cyn said.

"I need it."

"I know."

Now he was intrigued. What could this woman, a stranger to him a little more than a week ago, know about his life?

"It's complicated," she said. "You know I write about the paranormal."

"You know that world, I guess."

"I know a lot about it. I know the MacRaes are special, and under attack."

"How did you find out all of this?"

"Years of research," she explained.

"For a book?"

She bit her lip, then took a deep breath. "It's for my son. He just turned fifteen."

"You're kidding. Fifteen? You don't look old enough—"

"I was fourteen when I got pregnant. Fifteen when he was born."

Hunter was surprised but not shocked. "Does your son see the other world, too?"

"Sometimes. But mostly he's a nice, normal teenage boy who lives with his grandparents and wishes his mother would live there with him, too. Next year, however, I don't know what he'll be."

Hunter frowned.

"If all my research is true, when John turns sixteen, I'll know for sure about him," she said. "About what he is."

Only then did Hunter realize what she was saying. "Does he know?"

"Did you?"

Hunter closed his eyes, remembering that confusing summer. They couldn't be sure until he was sixteen. There, in the forest, where it was safe, he had imagined himself a tiger. And he was.

"What do you need?" Hunter reached out a hand to her. "How can I help?"

She blinked back tears. "John will probably be chimera."

Hunter stiffened. "You were with a chimera?"

Her smile was thin and brief. "It's a long story I don't really want to share now. But what I want you to know is that Chymera, The Killin, the Lion of Wall Street, is very dangerous. I've been tracking him and his kind for years. I wanted to know, so that when John changes, if John changes, I'll know what to expect."

Thinking of half-man, half-beast creature he'd seen in the woods, Hunter shuddered. It was difficult to imagine a monster like that being part of the beautiful woman in front of him.

"I don't like what they are," she added. "I don't want John anywhere near them."

There was more Hunter didn't understand. "Why have you come to me?"

"Because you're strong. I saw that from the start. The chimeras are strong, too, but they can be beaten. You could do it." She nodded toward Evan and the other guards. "You and those who stand with you."

"Are you offering to join the fight?"

"I guess I am. I have a lot of connections. I know

261

others who are ready for war. I could provide information."

"I appreciate that."

"We shouldn't be seen together often. I don't know what they know about John, but I know they're watching you."

"Of course," Hunter agreed. "For what it's worth, if your son does become chimera, maybe he won't be like them. He hasn't been schooled in hatred, murder, and vengeance."

"He's a good boy," she said, reminding Hunter of his Nana's last words to him. "But even in the other world, there's not a sure answer about nature versus nurture. All I know is John can't be with them. Ever. That's why I prefer they were destroyed."

Her sudden fierceness sparked something in Hunter. Not desire, exactly. That had been simmering below the surface since the moment he had scented her. No, his feelings now were more…appreciation. He had respect for her fiery protectiveness toward her son. And the two of them were added to the list of those Hunter wanted to protect.

"You need to go." He glanced around the shop. The only other patrons were Evan and the two guards. "You have my cell number. Call with any information you think can help me, but don't take any chances."

Nodding, Cyn closed her computer and got to her feet. "Thank you for trusting me."

Hunter wasn't sure why he did, but he knew she was telling him the truth. And they had the same goal: destroying the Killin dynasty.

Cyn put on her coat, gathered her things, and he followed her to the door. "Watch her," he said to the

Evan. "Make sure she gets safely out of here." He turned back to Cyn. "Two guards in the parking lot are going to follow you home."

"No, I need to stay under the radar. I'm used to looking after myself. Don't follow." Her eyes locked with Hunter's, and he reluctantly agreed. Then she was gone into the dark, cold night.

"She's human," Hunter said in a low voice, anticipating Evan's question. "And you were right. She's a friend."

Chapter 22

Lydia's house looked peaceful as I parked in front of it Wednesday afternoon for our second visit with Kelly.

While Kelly hadn't talked to us yesterday, she had stroked Hunter in his gray cat form and snuggled with him briefly on the couch. She had been excited when I told her we'd be back. Lydia called last night, reporting Kelly had drawn pictures of herself with the gray cat. These were the first pictures without the angry red and black.

I didn't know if it was woman's intuition or my newfound psychic power, but I felt success was imminent. Whatever that success might be. No matter what Kelly had locked in her mind, Kinley was dead. I hoped I wasn't giving her child more pain.

As I walked up to the door, I turned the pet carrier around so that Hunter faced me. "You okay in there?"

He meowed softly and rubbed his nose against the cage door. I rang the doorbell.

Hunter had been remarkably patient yesterday as a lively gray tabby, doing as much as he could in his animal form to provoke a response from Kelly. His intention was to distract her so she talked without thinking, sharing secrets without realizing she was doing so. I looked over my shoulder and saw Evan park Hunter's car behind mine. He would go to the kitchen and listen through a baby monitor while Hunter and I were alone with Kelly. Evan would record whatever she said for the police.

As usual, my fear became an uneasy roil in my stomach.

Lydia opened the door. "Kelly's really excited about seeing her cat friend again today."

I smiled at Kelly who leaned around Lydia's hips to sneak a peek. "Here's Tiger, and he's excited about seeing you again too."

Hunter purred as Kelly stroked his forehead through the wire cage. He'd forced me to use the ridiculous name to keep me from calling him Kitty or Fluffy.

I gave Lydia my coat and gloves and while she put them away, I opened the carrier. Kelly sat on the arm of her uncle's recliner, adorable in embroidered blue jeans, a Tinker Bell shirt, and tiny UGG boots.

"Come on, Tiger," I said. "You can come out now. It's your friend, Kelly."

Hunter meowed and stuck his head out. He looked around and sniffed before slowly creeping out. He scanned the room and licked his paws. With a graceful leap, he was in the chair with Kelly and bumped his head against her arm. She immediately pulled him into a hug and placed little kisses on top of his head.

Hunter never had a problem getting females to adore him.

"How long have you had him?" Lydia asked.

"He has been a part of my life a long time," I said. "Sometimes he's an aggravation but mostly I love having him around."

Hunter meowed and Kelly laughed.

"He didn't like you saying that," the little girl whispered with a giggle.

Lydia and I froze. Lydia put her hand across her mouth to stem her emotions and brushed her other hand down Kelly's hair.

Kelly laughed as Hunter's purr vibrated against her belly. He snuggled closer and she made long strokes down his back to the end of his tail. As she petted him, I asked her questions about her day, about school, about anything that would keep her talking.

But it didn't work. She nodded and kept rubbing Hunter and snickering at his antics.

When Kelly relaxed, I pulled out the pictures I brought from Kinley's refrigerator. Kelly had always expressed herself with art. We needed to understand what she was trying to tell us. When I showed the first drawing to Kelly, she stiffened.

I moved over to sit on the sofa and laid the two drawings on the coffee table. "I really like these drawings, Kelly, especially the flowers in the yard and the blue dress you drew on Claire."

"It's her favorite," she whispered, never stopping the motion of her hand on Hunter's fur.

I asked Kelly if she wanted to hang the pictures in her room. The baby monitor transmitter was also there, as it had been since the girls moved in.

"I like being here with the cat," she mumbled.

"He'll go wherever I go." I stood. "Let's go put these on your bulletin board."

Kelly didn't move until Hunter jumped down, stretching and yawning. He looked up at me and meowed.

"Come on, Tiger, let's go upstairs with Kelly." I

headed for the stairs.

Hunter raised his tail in the air and followed me. Kelly trailed after us.

I put the pictures along the bottom edge of the bulletin board with tacks. "There. That looks nice."

Kelly sat on her bed with Hunter curled up beside her. The quilt she'd helped her mother make looked sweet on her bed.

"He really likes this." I scratched under the cat's chin. Hunter purred louder and Kelly giggled, copying my actions.

I rambled on about things in the room. Lydia and her husband had made it homey, filling it with stuffed animals and dolls. A Barbie dollhouse was in the corner with Barbie's dream car parked beside it. When I asked about her favorite Barbie doll, Kelly showed me Teacher Barbie.

"I want to be a teacher," she whispered.

When she laid the doll on the bed, Hunter stretched and walked to it. He sniffed, rubbed his face on the doll's hair, and then laid a paw on Teacher Barbie's chest. I pulled the doll away. "Let's put this over here. I don't want Tiger to scratch it."

I laid the doll on the table beside Kelly's latest drawings. I saw she was still drawing the dark pictures. "These are very different from what you used to do." I turned back to Kelly. I pointed to what was obviously a bed in the picture. "What is this?"

Kelly kept stroking Hunter and watching him. She glanced up briefly and then went back to the cat. "My bed."

I held the picture up to compare it to the bed where she and Hunter sat. "It doesn't look like this bed."

"It's at my Nonna's house. Me and Claire have our own bedroom over there."

While I scrambled for the right questions, my anxiety grew. My palms were sweaty and I felt a moment of pure panic.

Hunter rubbed against my calf. His comfort eased my distress, and I went to sit beside Kelly. Hunter jumped up and lay across Kelly's lap.

"Tell me more about your room at Nonna's. Do you have dolls there too?"

She kept petting Hunter. Finally she said, "Nonna doesn't like Barbie dolls. I only have baby dolls over there. She says little girls should play mommy and take care of their babies."

"Well, that's fun too," I glanced back at the picture and asked about the lamp and struggled not to laugh when Kelly identified the square box beside the bed as a "chester drawers."

"This looks like a person," I pointed to the red figure outside a door. "Is this a person?"

She nodded her head and didn't look up as she ran her fingers through Hunter's soft fur.

My heart rate increased as I pondered my next question. I wanted this precious little girl to tell me something horrible about her father. I watched her and Hunter. He licked his paw. When he finished, she ran a finger over the damp fur as if testing it.

Hunter stretched and yawned and bumped his head into the paper I'd let lie across my lap. He knew I was stalling. I picked up the picture and pointed to the person covered with red.

I kept my tone as even as possible. "Who is this, Kelly? Who is the person by the door?"

Kelly stroked Hunter and kept her eyes down. Her single word response made me gasp aloud.

****

Hunter, Evan, and I stood beside Hunter's SUV and watched the police activity at the home of Eric Russo's mother. Eric was corralled in the front yard by two uniformed officers. Other officers were moving in and out, carrying boxes to a waiting van.

It was Thursday morning and already near 45 degrees, perfect weather for an arrest.

We had taken the audio tape to Mike last night. He worked half the night to get the search warrant.

"That's the fourth box they've brought out," Hunter said.

"I can't believe a little girl held that knowledge inside her and didn't just shatter," Evan said quietly.

"She sure as hell shocked me." I was still wrestling with guilt over what I'd put Kelly through. But we knew Eric's mother had killed her daughter-in-law.

"Once Kelly started talking about it," I added, "she couldn't stop. She'd actually watched her grandmother wash blood off her face and arms. She said Nonna left the bathroom door open while she washed and changed clothes. She had no idea Kelly saw her."

We all jerked as a woman's shrill scream filled the air. Eric tried to get free, but hefty arms across his chest kept him in place.

"Mama!" Eric screamed. "Let me go. She needs help." He couldn't move. "Let me go, you assholes, that's my mother!"

Eric was pushed to his knees.

The front door opened and two female officers came out with Eric's mother. I knew now that Nonna meant grandmother in Italian, but the screeching woman we were watching didn't have the soft face and warm smile of a typical grandmother.

Mike told us Antonia Russo was a second-generation Italian American. Her parents came through Ellis Island after World War II and she was born a year later. She didn't learn English until she went to school. She still spoke with a heavy accent. Despite the Old World background, however, she was fashionable. Her black hair was short and stylish and a single silver streak ran from her temple to the nape. She looked like most women her age. Except she was raving at two police officers.

"Let me go!" she screamed and then went off into a stream of Italian. "You cannot do this. I have done nothing wrong in the sight of God."

Neighbors gathered on the sidewalk, watching and whispering.

"I did what I had to do," Antonia yelled. "She was killing my son and destroying his family. Divorce is not an option, and I told her that. She didn't believe I'd do anything about it. Death was the only answer. I had to kill her."

She pulled against her captors, but the women holding her were strong and tenacious.

"Eric! Eric!" she screamed. "You know why I killed your wife. I helped her out of the marriage she didn't want. Now you can raise your children in a godly household. Go and get your daughters. We can raise them together."

Though Antonia fought, she was shoved into the backseat of the patrol car. The door slammed on her screams. Eric collapsed, falling on his face in the yard and sobbing as his mother was driven away.

A few minutes later, Mike came out and talked quietly with the stricken man and got a nod. The two officers helped Eric to his feet and escorted him inside.

It had done me good to see Antonia taken away.

Mike took off latex gloves as he walked toward us. "We've officially got the secondary crime scene. Kelly was right on the money. We found bloody clothes in the hatbox her grandmother kept in the bathroom closet. Everything was there, down to her underwear and bloody gloves."

He glanced over at the officers dispersing the crowd of neighbors before continuing. "What Kelly didn't know about was the baseball bat wrapped in old newspapers in the garage. We've already had officers talk to the neighbors. They said Antonia had been noisy and violent for years, humiliating her late husband whenever she could. When they had an argument, the whole neighborhood knew, and she threw whatever she could get her hands on at him. One neighbor thought the poor guy died just to get away from her."

"But no one suspected her when Kinley died?" Hunter asked.

"Could anyone expect this kind of thing out of a 63-year-old woman?" I asked.

"We sure didn't." Mike shook his head. "We talked to Mrs. Russo the day after the murder and she was cool as a cucumber, saying they'd spent the evening playing games with the girls. She said they went to bed early. I had no reason or evidence that pointed in her direction."

"I'm just glad it's over," I said mentally exhausted. "Did Eric know what his mother did?"

"When we showed him the warrant, he let us in

without question," Mike replied. "But his mother came tearing down the hall, screaming. They had to restrain her while we searched. I saw the hatbox as soon as I opened the bathroom closet. When Eric saw the bloody clothes inside, he threw up in the sink. I don't think he was acting."

"How was Kelly able to see her grandmother so well?" I asked.

"The girls' bedroom is diagonal to the bathroom door, a direct line of sight to the bed. I figure Mrs. Russo thought she was safe. We believe she may have given Eric and the girls something in the cocoa they had before bed."

"But Kelly woke up," I murmured.

"Thank God," Mike said. "If it's any comfort, I don't believe she understood what she saw. Then police were at the house, and her mother was dead. Instinctively, she may have known her grandmother was involved. Maybe that's why she couldn't talk. She didn't want to put the pieces together in her head. Without Kelly's revelation, we had nothing on Mrs. Russo and no reason to suspect her."

"How is it you couldn't get a search warrant before?" Hunter asked.

"Eric was here, in his pajamas and apparently dead asleep when we arrived," Mike said. "The engine of his car was cool. There was nothing to indicate he had been out. We were on scene just after the murder."

"What about the mother's car?" I asked.

"She doesn't have one," Mike explained with an exasperated grunt. "But she sometimes drives a car belonging to her sister, who lives just over there." He pointed down the block. "Mrs. Russo had her own set of keys. We didn't know that until this morning.

"Everything came together after Kelly talked. We asked the right questions, and the DA got a warrant." Mike put his hands on his hips and looked back at the Russo house. "We found everything we need for an indictment. Kelly shouldn't have to testify."

"I hope not," I said.

"Half the neighborhood heard Mrs. Russo's screamed confession a few minutes ago. With the physical evidence, it's a slam dunk."

Mike turned to me. "Thanks for everything, Zoe. You were smart to do what you did. Bringing your cat in was a stroke of genius."

"It was actually a loaner from a friend," I said. Here I went again—lying to Mike because of Hunter. "I'm just glad I could help. I wanted justice for Kinley and her girls. I thought Eric was guilty."

"For his daughters' sakes, I'm glad we were wrong," Mike replied. "This will be tough enough on them."

We stood there for an awkward moment. I couldn't help but wonder how it would be if our intimate debacle hadn't occurred. I had rushed into something that had ended in disaster. So typical.

Mike shook hands with the men beside me, his eyes meeting Hunter's for a brief second. Then he turned and walked away without a backward glance.

Hunter looked at me. "He still doesn't believe you about our relationship, does he?"

I glared at him. Sometimes he had the sensitivity of a spoiled child.

"Let's get out of here," he said. "Go to my place and have some brunch."

"I need to get back to the list of Hayden Clinic staff," I said. "So far I'm striking out, but there is a long list of employees, just like the radiology tech told Evan. Quite a few people I've called gave me other names."

"You can access your files and search the Internet at my place as well as at the office," Hunter protested. "Please. Evan will fix us a great meal."

Evan, who had been very quiet, nodded. "You should listen to Hunter. You've not been sleeping well."

I had barely slept last night, worried we put Kelly through a fruitless emotional wringer.

"Come on," Hunter said. "Evan will drive Master PI Zoe Buchanan to my place for a celebratory feast."

"You're getting bossy," Evan said. "Ordering me to make brunch and drive you around. I am a highly trained soldier, not a chef or chauffeur."

"Home, Jeeves," Hunter said.

I smiled despite myself at the slight tightening of Evan's usually calm features.

Chapter 23

Hunter was feeling pretty good. Maybe it was the half dozen Belgian waffles he had enjoyed with fruit and bacon. Or perhaps it was knowing Kinley's murderer was behind bars. His part in Antonia's arrest helped to make up for his failing to protect someone who had depended on him.

He stretched and looked out on the unseasonably beautiful Jersey City day. The view through the French doors in his dining room showed blue skies and the Manhattan skyline sparkling on the opposite shore.

"You should put that stuff down for a while," he told Zoe, who had barely waited for the brunch dishes to be cleared before she opened her laptop. She was studiously conducting Internet searches of former employees from the Hayden Clinic. "It's a beautiful day. Let's go somewhere."

She shook her head. "Lizzie's breathing down my neck. She's convinced her missing sister is connected to the reason why her mother cut her father out of the will. She wants some ammunition to take to the hearing."

"She could just give her father money and be done with him."

"This isn't about money," Zoe said. "It's about her sister."

"You're just as obsessed as she is," Hunter claimed with a laugh.

"I can't help it. I like finding answers."

Reflecting on his own feelings of satisfaction about the morning's events, Hunter agreed. "Helping someone resolve a big issue is a pretty damn good feeling." In truth, that's what he had always enjoyed about his law practice.

Evan brought in a fresh pot of coffee and topped off all three mugs. He nodded toward the window. "Hard to believe it's supposed to snow tomorrow."

Hunter grimaced. "All the more reason to get out of here today. Let's go run by the river."

Evan was silent, no doubt thinking of all the ways the chimera might snatch Hunter.

"Nana scared Michael Killin off at the memorial service," Hunter said with pride. "Haven't the troops reported that he and his minions have been hunkered down in his apartment fortress all week?"

"We'd be fools to think it will stay that way," Evan retorted.

Hunter sighed. He hated sitting around and waiting for something to happen. He was almost disappointed the Killins hadn't made a move on him. He was ready to take them on.

He was getting back to normal. He'd spent an extremely pleasant two hours with Mandy yesterday at her house. Charlie was on the west coast, and she dismissed the servants.

Evan's disapproval had been plain, but he and the others guarded the perimeter of the Morris property while Hunter lost himself in Mandy's voluptuous body.

He'd also shifted and gone running Tuesday and Wednesday nights with no sign of his mutant enemy. On a more disappointing note, there had been no sign of

Cyn when they had stopped for coffee.

He knew she needed to keep her distance from him, but he worried about her. Though she claimed knowledge and connections with the supernatural world, Hunter suspected she spent most of her time alone. Zoe and Evan now knew about Cyn's son and her desire to ensure the chimera never found him.

Hunter felt more comfortable with his new role. In the past two days, while he and Evan toured new properties, a plan had formed in his mind. He needed to discuss it with Zoe.

"Leave that for a minute." He pointed at the computer. When she didn't react, he pushed down the top.

"Hey! I may be on to someone interesting. A young doctor who worked with Hayden for longer than most of them now practices in Manhattan. He's a big-time OB-GYN to the beautiful people. He might know something."

"Groovy," Hunter said. "But I need to talk about something else." He got his laptop and pulled up some photographs he had taken yesterday at a warehouse complex in Riverdale. "Look at this place. Isn't it cool?"

Zoe clicked through the photographs for a few moments, a frown creasing her smooth forehead. "All I see is a big glass and brick building—with most of the glass broken. It's surrounded by broken concrete and weeds and a bunch of warehouses."

"It offers great protection and can easily be renovated and secured."

"And?"

"It would be a great place to live."

She squinted at the photographs again, blinked, then looked back at Hunter. "I think the stress has finally gotten to you."

"The location is perfect and it's in better shape than it looks. We could live in apartments on the upper floors. The ground floor would be the office—"

"Office?" Zoe interrupted. "What office?"

"We could move the office there and live on the upper floors."

"We?" Zoe just stared him. "You mean all of us?"

"You'd have your own floor and lots of privacy."

"Living in the same building as you should enhance my romantic life," she commented dryly. "Working with you has caused me enough problems."

"Not everyone is like Detective Scala," Evan said. "There are men who would be secure enough in themselves not to be threatened by what you and Hunter share."

Zoe darted him a harsh look, but as usual Evan was oblivious to her resentment. She returned her focus to Hunter. "You're serious, aren't you?"

"Dead serious. I want to make some changes."

"I thought you weren't going to make any quick decisions."

"I have to be realistic. The chimera won't just go away. I have to find a way to live with the threat. Grandda moved to the mountains, but that's not my style. I need a home and an office that offer protection. I've got to think like a predator. I must be alert at all times for danger and ready to fight for my life on a moment's notice. This warehouse property includes a couple of acres and lots of trees. It's a place where I could be myself when I wanted."

"Be a cat, in other words," Zoe said.

"Be a shifter," he corrected.

She spoke slowly. "I understand that you need to live some place more private. But it's hard to imagine clients coming to a bunker."

"It won't look like bunker," Hunter protested. "And perhaps new clients might need our fortifications as well as our special talents for investigation and protection."

Sitting back in her chair, Zoe gave him a steady look. "I don't understand."

"What we're doing now is great," Hunter said. "But helping Kelly, working to find Lizzie's sister...that's the kind of stuff we should be doing all the time. Maybe we can help Cyn and others like her."

Zoe said nothing, but Hunter could see the hurt in her eyes.

He took a deep breath. "Here it is in a nutshell...we'll all be investigators, in a firm that promises to find whatever you're searching for—whether it's a relative, a family inheritance, someone who has been missing for years, or the murderer in an unsolved case. Whatever you seek, we'll find."

Evan nodded, but Zoe hesitated. "You're talking about a new partnership with the three of us?"

"There are forces at work here that dictate we're all stuck together," Hunter said. "Isn't it practical to use our skills as a team? Evan is a security expert. While he's working to protect me, he could consult on other cases, help us plan strategy."

"Where would we advertise our services?" Zoe asked with acid in her tone. "In the weird classifieds of *Out There*?"

Hunter decided that was a good idea. "Why not?"

He had the latest issue of *Out There*. Since he now knew more about Cyn, he believed the publication was more than a tabloid full of alien abduction stories and Big Foot sightings.

"I'd like to be a part of something like this," Evan spoke up. "It was great to help Kelly, and I'm enjoying searching for leads for Lizzie."

"Come on, Zoe," Hunter said. "You know you hate the other stuff we do. That's why you're putting so much effort into finding a sister that most people say never existed. That's why you kept pushing to find a way to help Kelly. You love cases like this."

"But we don't get enough of these kinds of cases to pay the bills."

"Fortunately, thanks to Grandda, that's not something we have to worry about."

That set Zoe off. She stood. "I'm not living off your family's fortune. I make my own way in the world."

"I think we'd get plenty of cases to make a living." Evan looked at Zoe. "Besides, your primary job is the same as mine—protecting Hunter."

"Oh, and I'm so good at that," she returned. "I'm able to predict what's going to happen, but not in time to help him."

"You will," Evan said.

She brushed him off with a flip of her hand. "So what if I agree that we change the focus of the practice and move the office? That doesn't mean I need to live in an armed compound."

"It would be easier to protect you," Evan pointed out.

"And that should be the point of my life—making things easier for you?" she demanded.

"It would make me feel better if you were closer," Hunter said.

Zoe rubbed at her face, looking exhausted. "But there's my home and Bernie next door…"

"You'd see Bernie all the time. There's more to this, Zoe. I want to search for other shapeshifters. According to Evan and my father, the rest of the MacRae clan will be contacting me soon. But there must be more of them out there that we don't know about. Cyn said there are many who guard against the Killins. I don't know who they are, but I'd like to meet them. Maybe we could connect and take on Michael Killin as a structured group."

"Is that all we're going to do?" Zoe argued. "Just spend our time as vigilantes looking for cat people and werewolves?"

Hunter swallowed his impatience. "I don't want to dedicate my life finding other shapeshifters. Nor do I want us working only jobs with supernatural connections. We'll do it between other cases. I thought this would mean more freedom for you to pursue work you love."

Zoe sighed as she sat down again. "It's a lot to think about."

"But you will think about it?"

Before she could reply, Evan added, "I want to work with you, Zoe. I can help you refine your gift."

Zoe sucked in a breath, and Hunter feared an explosion.

He was grateful when his phone went off. "It's Cyn," he said.

"I need to see you," she said without preamble.

"You can come to my place."

"That's too risky. Meet me in a public place. Come to the mall closest to the coffee shop where we met."

Hunter calculated. She sounded fearful that someone was listening. "But where—"

"Think about it and you'll know where. Second level, near the middle, as soon as you can. I'll find you."

The phone clicked off. "I think she's in trouble."

Evan mobilized his forces to provide eyes and ears against chimera.

An hour later, Hunter walked into the mall. Evan and Zoe trailed him at a discreet distance. The mall was crowded with shoppers. Valentine's Day decorations were displayed in every corner.

Hunter scented Cyn not long after he exited the escalator on the second floor. She wore a bulky coat and had covered her flame-colored hair with a knit cap. He spotted her at a jewelry kiosk near the center of the mall. She tipped her chin at him and walked away. He fell in step beside her.

"What's up?"

In answer, she handed him a small box, an innocuous looking silver foil package. Hunter lifted the lid and saw a square school photograph of a dark-haired young boy.

"My son," Cyn said. "Look under."

Hunter picked up the photo. Beneath it lay a claw. Though small, it was curved and sharp and lethal.

Cyn took the package back from Hunter and slipped it in her pocket.

"Someone sent you this?" he demanded.

Cyn paused at a glass railing that overlooked the first floor. Only then did Hunter notice she was limping. "Are you hurt?"

She shook her head and darted glances all around. "I'm fine. They found my apartment last night. They were waiting when I got home from teaching a late class."

Hunter knew who "they" were.

"I ran after I walked in on them," Cyn continued. "They chased me, caught me in the hall, and pulled me down the stairwell to the parking garage. I got away once, but tripped and fell. I hurt my knee, and they jumped me."

Hunter wanted to pepper her with questions.

She drew a deep breath. "Two of them held me while the other delivered this package. They said you couldn't help me."

"Me?"

"They called you The MacRae."

"You're sure they're chimera? Did they shift?"

"No, but I smelled them. They left me at the bottom of the stairs." She shook her head, as if to erase the memory. "I didn't go back to my apartment. I left my car in the garage. I called a friend from a pay phone, and he came for me."

"We'll protect you."

"I have to get to my boy. A colleague at school who understands is taking my classes for the semester. I'm going to John. He and my parents may have to move."

"The chimera could trail you," Hunter said. "It's not safe for any of you. Let me help—"

'He's my son, and my parents and I will protect

him the same way we always have." Cyn walked away.

Hunter caught her by the elbow. "You can't just leave like this."

"I wanted you to know. You're not safe. They know everything you're doing."

"High-tech surveillance, maybe," he muttered.

"Or magic?" She arched her eyebrow. "There's a new wickedness in the air. Those of us who feel it are frightened. I have to be with my family. You should see to yours."

Cyn pulled away, tugging her hat down and threading her way through the shoppers.

This time Hunter let her go. His chest clenched with fury.

"What did she want?" Evan asked.

Hunter shrugged him off. "Where's Zoe?" He looked around, relieved when he spotted her conservative gray raincoat moving toward them. His hands shook as he pulled out his cell and punched in a number.

"What is it?" Evan demanded.

Not answering, Hunter spoke as soon as he heard Marie's voice on the line. "I need my father."

As he knew she would, Marie put him through to Stirling's private line immediately.

"Hunter?" his father asked. "Is something wrong?"

"Are you okay? What about Meagan and Mother?"

"Your sister is sitting here in my office, going over some company reports," Stirling replied. "It's Thursday, so your Mother is no doubt at Elizabeth Arden. What's wrong?"

"Chymera threatened a friend of mine. My first thought was for the three of you."

"We're fine, but are you?"

"Yes," Hunter replied.

As he clicked off the phone a metallic gleam caught his eye. On the walkway directly across from them, a little girl in a pink sweater chased a cluster of heart-shaped balloons that had escaped her grasp. Apparently caught by a current of air, the balloons soared straight to the skylight above them and burst with three tiny little pops.

Hunter realized he was just as vulnerable.

Chapter 24

I was exhausted, but didn't sleep well. Even staying at Hunter's, where I knew I was well guarded, I couldn't relax. How could I rest after what Cyn had said?

Early the next morning, I gave up and went back to work on Lizzie's case at Hunter's dining room table.

One of the contacts that Carl Kowalski had given Evan had led to a list of young doctors practicing at the Hayden Clinic near the date of Lizzie's birth. Yesterday, before Cyn called, I had been exploring a Dr. Blake Taylor.

I clicked back to a photograph taken as few years back that I found of a doctor by that name with a very pregnant Lady Punk. The picture had been taken at a benefit, and he was listed as the rap star's OB GYN, "a very important man in my life," according to the quote from the star.

The man in the photograph was the right age— early 50's. He was blond and handsome, had kept himself in great shape and perhaps had a nip or tuck made to his face. As I followed more links to his name, I found a variety of newspaper articles, photos, and information. Blake was a man who made an effort to get into the news. He attended everything from the New Jersey Symphony Orchestra to the gala Oscar parties given by Vanity Fair.

His reputation as a fertility doctor was equally documented. He was in the forefront of the field and listed Dr. Hayden among his mentors. There were a number of articles from his patients, who adored the handsome doctor. As I moved from photograph to photograph, something nagged at me. He was familiar. Had I met him at party with my father or at Hunter's parents?

I paused on a headshot of Dr. Taylor on his practice's website. His features were vaguely Nordic, and his eyes a deep blue. Vivid blue.

I recalled another pair of blue eyes, equally as crystalline, and just as memorable.

Almost holding my breath, I checked the information on Dr. Taylor again. He was a graduate of Princeton, class of 1978. Several more clicks of the mouse and I had a photo from Dr. Taylor's university days. His hair had been darker then, more of a light brown than blond, but those blue eyes were undeniable.

I downloaded the photo and put it in Photoshop to enlarge it.

"What are you doing?"

I jumped at the sound of Evan's voice. Though it was barely six in the morning, he was dressed for the day, looking as if he had slept deeply and well.

"Let me show you something." I sorted through other files until I found what I was looking for. I pulled up a photo of Lizzie Howerton taken at her debutante ball, then enlarged Dr. Taylor's college photograph and placed them side by side on the monitor.

"What do you think?" I tapped the screen.

"They could be brother and sister," he said.

"Or father and daughter." I let out a sigh. "Oh my

God, I think I've just found out how Dr. Hayden made all of those women pregnant. It was the young doctors."

"What?"

"They must have given him their sperm."

"Christ," Evan said. "Are you sure?"

"No, but there's someone who can tell us. It's time to let Lizzie call Dr. Hayden's wife and demand some explanations."

****

The San Remos, where Elaine Hayden Richards lived, was beautiful, even on this cloudy, cold day. Watching the limos and well-dressed, well-coifed residents come and go, I could almost smell the money in the air.

Lizzie asked us to wait for her outside so we could go up together. Earlier today, I met with the younger woman to show her Dr. Taylor's photographs and tell her my suspicions.

She took the news well. In fact, she wasn't even that surprised. "I always wondered why I was nothing like Daddy," she said with a sniff. "It's kind of a relief to know we're not related."

She called Mrs. Richards to tell the older woman what we'd discovered. Mrs. Richards had said nothing except that Lizzie should come to her apartment at two p.m.

Evan and Hunter joined me. Lizzie needed an attorney present, and of course, Evan went wherever Hunter did.

My trepidation grew as my gut told me it wasn't going to go well with Mrs. Richards. I tried to focus my second sense, but all I felt was a fuzzy aura of danger.

Lizzie was sure it would be her happy ending.

Hunter carried the Italian leather briefcase he used to impress clients. I knew there were a stack of legal pads inside, but hopefully Mrs. Richards would think it was full of papers meant to cause her many problems if she made things difficult for Lizzie. I wondered if the older woman would have her own lawyer present.

Another black limo pulled up on the street and before the driver could get to the door, Lizzie popped out and ran over to embrace me so hard I stumbled back. Evan easily caught my weight and steadied me. As usual, that annoyed me.

"I'm so excited," Lizzie said. "I feel like we're going to learn the truth today."

I tried to calm her down. "Don't get your hopes up. She may stonewall us again. I'm afraid you're in for a big letdown if your expectations are too high."

Her face became serious. "I understand what you're trying to say, Zoe, but I refuse to believe the woman can get out of this. In fact, she called me back after you left and we talked for a while."

I was dismayed. What was the older woman trying to pull?

The doorman found us on his list and sent us on our way after calling the apartment. Lizzie chattered nervously, causing Hunter to keep looking at me over her head and rolling his eyes.

When the maid answered, her face was pale and drawn and her voice edgy as she said in heavily-accented English, "Come in, please."

I automatically put my hand in front of Lizzie before she crossed the threshold. "Are you all right, ma'am?" I asked.

She looked over her shoulder, dark eyes wide.

Douglas Howerton stepped into the foyer. "We've been waiting for you."

He held a small handgun with a silencer. It was pointed at the maid's head. "Why don't all of you come inside so I don't have to splatter this little woman's blood all over the wallpaper," Howerton said.

I didn't think it was possible for the maid to get any paler, but her skin lost all color.

We moved en masse, including Evan, whom I could see in my peripheral vision. We were both armed. If we could get an opening, maybe we could take down Howerton.

"Now, Miss Buchanan, please put that nasty gun that you so proudly keep with you on the floor," Howerton said.

Guess I shouldn't have been so eager to show it off.

I took my gun out, holding it with two fingers and laid it at my feet.

"Uh-huh," Howerton said with a smirk. "Let's put it inside the vase. Out of sight, out of mind."

He pointed to a large cloisonné vase in the corner of the foyer. I took a step and deposited my gun on the bottom, noting there was no dust. I hoped Howerton didn't hurt the maid; she was obviously good at her job.

"Gentlemen, I'm sure you're carrying too. Let's have them." His hand on the gun was steady.

"Not me." Hunter raised his hands so his jacket would open. "I'm always afraid I'll shoot myself."

Howerton moved to cover Evan, who undid his ankle holster and put his gun in the vase with mine.

We went further into the room as Howerton backed up. An elderly woman I assumed was Mrs. Richards sat in a French Chippendale chair with her arms duct-taped to its arms.

"Will you please remove this tape from this chair?" she snapped. "I'm sure it's ruining the fabric and this is a priceless antique!"

I felt better. She was doing fine, more concerned about her antique chair than herself. Lizzie ran forward. Evan grabbed her when she got close to Howerton's gun.

"Daddy, what are you doing? Put that stupid gun away. How did you get one anyway? Aren't guns illegal in New York City?"

Howerton frowned at her. "My chauffeur has connections. You can get whatever you need in the city."

"Look," Lizzie tried again. "We came to talk with Mrs. Richards about something important. I don't understand why you're here. Please, Daddy, don't do this."

Her eyes were filled with tears as he indicated she should sit on the sofa;

I pushed Lizzie ahead of me and took a seat beside her. Evan and Hunter opted for chairs, spreading the group so Howerton had to keep his gaze moving. The maid stood behind Mrs. Richards. Her loyalty was admirable if not stupid.

"I must insist you remove this tape," Mrs. Richards said. "Douglas, I never would have called if I had thought you'd do something like this."

"You called him?" Lizzie said, shocked. "Why in the world would you do such a thing?"

"I thought between us we could talk sense into you and keep this nonsense private." Mrs. Richard huffed.

"Please, Douglas, it's obvious I'm frail and not able to hurt you. I don't want my furniture ruined."

"Please, Daddy," Lizzie said. "Let me take the tape off."

"Oh, all right. If it'll shut the old hag up."

He pointed the gun at Hunter. "You get the tape off and then sit in the chair beside her."

Hunter did as asked, though it took a while to remove the tape without damaging the older woman's delicate skin. She rubbed her wrists and winced in pain as Hunter tossed the tape to the floor.

I was watching Hunter and Evan. If there was a chance to take the fat, sweating Howerton down, they would do it. It was obvious the older man was agitated. He wasn't holding the gun as steady now. Of course, with this many people in a room he was bound to hit one or more of us if he started firing.

Holding Lizzie in place with my arm across her waist I decided to draw first blood and get this showdown on the road. "Have you always known Lizzie wasn't your daughter?" I asked him.

"Of course," he retorted.

"What do you know about my sister?" Lizzie demanded.

"Good God in heaven. Why couldn't you let this drivel about your sister go?" He waved the gun from Lizzie to me. "Then you got involved, Miss Buchanan. That just made it worse because Lizzie had someone to listen to her ravings. I offered you a hundred thousand dollars, and all you did was show me your gun and spout some garbage about Lizzie being your client. Isn't it obvious the girl's not all there?"

"You're being awful," Lizzie said. "The truth was

bound to come out."

"No, it wasn't, little girl. All I needed to do was keep this old bat from ruining what chance I had of getting back on my feet. If you all had come five minutes later, I'd have shut her up for good and been gone. I would have destroyed the proof of your sister, and got my share of that foolish will of your mother's."

Hunter and Evan were on the edges of their seats. I pulled Howerton's attention back to me. "I don't know why you thought killing Mrs. Richards would make any difference. Lizzie knows the truth."

"Shut up!" he yelled and poked the cold barrel against my cheek. "Now I'm showing you my gun." He jabbed it roughly against my skin. "And I'm going to use it if things don't go my way."

Evan stood. Howerton flipped the gun around and fired. Though there was no sound, a small figurine shattered on a shelf above Evan's head.

"My God, that was a hand-painted, nineteenth-century Meissen!" Ms. Richards exclaimed.

Howerton kept the gun on Evan and backed up to a small table beside Mrs. Richards' chair. He picked up the roll of duct tape and tossed it to me. "Tape their hands together."

I guess I didn't move quickly enough because he fired the gun at the wall behind me. Plaster flew through the air. "Do it now or the next one goes into somebody's knee."

I went to Evan first. He held his hands out and I began wrapping them with the silver tape.

"What are you doing?" I asked Howerton as I pulled the tape loosely around Evan's wrists. "Are you going to kill all of us? You know you can't—"

"I can do whatever I like," Howerton screamed. "I'm in charge here. Now finish what you're doing and sit back down."

I moved across the room to Hunter, who watched Howerton like a cat stalking prey. He didn't move as I bound his wrists with plenty of room to spare. His eyes never left the older man.

"Please don't do this," Lizzie said. "I'll give you all the money you want. Just stop this. Mother always told me you were crazy, but I never saw it."

"Shut up!" He fired once again though his shot went wide and to the left. "You insignificant little bitch. I put up with you and your stupid cow of a mother for all these years. She finally died but still found a way to screw me. All I needed was a few million to get back on my feet and now I've got to beg you for that."

I looked at Hunter, hoping he'd interject something, but he was still focused on Howerton and looked ready to pounce. Evan was working with the tape on his wrists. I needed to keep Howerton distracted.

"There's no way you'll get away with this," I said.

He gave a shrill laugh. "It's just a little secret. It's not even important. It was a tiny deception to keep things happy for her majesty Camilla. She had her babies and everything was okay."

"Babies?" Lizzie said, her face going paler.

"Ah, goddammit." He rubbed his face. "You've upset me and I'm not even thinking straight."

"Why don't you put down the gun and we'll—" I said.

"Keep your stupid, bitchy mouth shut and let me think." He fired the gun into the wall above my head.

White flakes rained down on Lizzie and me.

Mrs. Richards shrieked and I pushed Lizzie down to protect her. The maid crumpled to the floor. If Howerton kept this up, at least he might run out of ammunition.

Evan stood and Hunter jumped, but Howerton was ready. He held his gun with both hands, aimed at Hunter's chest. "Sit down."

Lizzie started to move toward the maid, but Howerton stopped her. "Stay where you are. She'll be fine. At least that's one I don't have to worry about."

Everyone was quiet. Howerton jerked the gun on Mrs. Richards. "You're the one I need to get rid of."

I had to give it to the old girl; she didn't even flinch. "Why kill me now? She already knows most of it."

"Stupid little cunt." Howerton swung the gun back to Lizzie.

She jerked like he'd slapped her.

"What difference does it make now, Douglas?" Mrs. Richards asked. "It's over. There's nothing we can do about it."

"Yes, there is!" Howerton screamed.

I looked at Hunter and was surprised to see his hand was covered with fur and claws. In a second the tape was ripped and his hand was human again.

Then Hunter lunged at the older man. The two of them landed on the fragile table, which broke apart like matchsticks. The gun fired and Mrs. Richards fell forward, blood seeping through the fingers of the hand she put on her shoulder. Evan went to her, pressing his bound hands against her wound.

I pushed Lizzie down. Hunter was on top of

Howerton, who pressed the gun into Hunter's face. I looked across the room, wondering if I had time to get to my gun.

Lizzie was sobbing now. Evan was shielding Mrs. Richards. Her blood was dripping to the floor.

Hunter held the older man down with his knees. He looked at me with questioning eyes and I knew what he wanted to do. I nodded and pulled my arms tighter around Lizzie. Evan covered Mrs. Richards.

The air crackled as Hunter changed into a cougar, his lethal teeth shining in the older man's face. Then Hunter quickly changed back to human.

Howerton froze. Hunter snatched the gun and cracked it against the side of Howerton's head. The beefy man grunted and fell unconscious.

I let Lizzie up and stood. She walked across the room and looked down at the unconscious older man. When I turned back, Mrs. Richards was sitting up with Evan's white handkerchief pressed against her collarbone.

The maid was rousing as I yanked the tape off Evan's wrists. As soon as I freed him, Evan went back to Mrs. Richards. I hurried to the maid as Evan laid the elderly woman on the couch. When the maid saw her mistress, she pushed me aside and rushed to help.

"They've destroyed my New York Stand, Constanza," Mrs. Richards wailed, looking at the rubble of the table underneath Howerton's wide back.

"They saved your life," Constanza chastised the woman as she would a child. "Mr. Richards will find you another table."

The old woman laughed, a faintly hysterical sound that brought us back to reality. Evan called 911 while

Hunter bound Howerton's hands and ankles with the duct tape.

The maid hurried to get a blanket while I retrieved the guns from the vase. I holstered mine and handed Evan his. Lizzie still stared down at Howerton. .

"Miss Howerton," Mrs. Richards said. "Please come here so I can talk to you before the police get here. I'm sure they'll take me to the hospital, and you need the truth."

Constanza came in and tucked the blanket around her mistress and then hurried to the kitchen muttering about tea. I suspected she needed something to do.

The story wasn't complicated. Douglas Howerton paid Charles Hayden to guarantee Camilla became pregnant. Howerton's sperm count was too low, a little fact he neglected to tell the very rich Camilla before they married. Hayden used sperm from a young doctor who worked at the clinic.

"Dr. Blake Taylor," I said.

Mrs. Richards didn't flinch. She turned to Lizzie. "You may pursue the question of your paternity if you want. I can tell you that the doctors thought they were participating in fertility studies when they donated their sperm. Charles had them believing everything they were told in exchange for the chance to practice with him. They had a great mentor. And lots of women had babies."

She groaned and clutched at her shoulder. "Good heavens, when someone as rich as Doug and Camilla Howerton said they wanted a baby, Charles did everything he could to make it happen."

"But what about my sister?" Lizzie said.

"I don't know what happened to her." Mrs.

Richards paused, her lips thinning with pain but she continued, "She was much smaller than you but when you left our clinic, you had a baby sister, younger than you by two minutes. That's all I know."

Lizzie said nothing for a minute. She looked from Mrs. Richards to the man she'd always thought was her father. She picked up a vase of fresh flowers from a nearby table, turned it over, and dumped the water and flowers onto Howerton's face.

He revived, sputtering and trying to bat away the blooms and water with his bound hands. Lizzie turned to Hunter and held out her hand. He looked at her dumbly.

"She wants her father's gun," I told him.

"I don't think—" he said slowly.

"Give it to her." I walked over beside Lizzie.

She put her feet on either side of the man's fat neck and pointed the gun at his mouth. "Where is my sister?"

"I don't know what the hell—"

Lizzie fired at the floor above his head and Howerton screamed like a hysterical woman.

"Where is my sister?" She dropped to her knees on his chest.

"You don't have a sister," he said weakly.

"Wrong answer," she said and stuck the gun with its hot barrel under his chin.

"You've got one more chance," she said through gritted teeth. "Where is my sister?"

Chapter 25

Secrets and lies.

They never did a family any good.

As I sat in front of my computer on Sunday afternoon, I reflected on why family members so often hid important truths from one another. Lizzie's parents lied to her about her sister. Hunter's grandfather neglected to give Hunter all the facts he needed to assume his position in life. And there was my own family, of course, with my father who seldom mentioned my mother since her brutal murder.

But that was beside the point, of course. This wasn't about my family. It was about Lizzie's.

I was hoping for a happy ending. Hunter, Evan, and I were at the office, waiting to Skype with Lizzie. After she coerced the truth out of Howerton, she dealt with the aftermath of his rampage. Now she was in Dublin meeting Elise, the sister taken from her almost 25 years ago.

The truth was vastly different than I expected. Lizzie's sister was diagnosed as autistic at a time when the disease was almost unknown. Elise didn't talk. She was prone to outbursts of physical violence toward herself and others, including Lizzie. Camilla had been distraught over the child's condition. According to Howerton, she took Elise from specialist to specialist, fully expecting her wealth to guarantee a cure. When that didn't happen, Camilla collapsed.

While she was in the hospital, Howerton suggested they send Elise away. To his credit, he had his attorneys find a good home with a family who adopted a number of children with mental disabilities. But it said everything about Howerton's character that he persuaded Camilla they should tell everyone Elise was dead.

What did it say about Camilla that she agreed? Or that they'd been able to convince families, friends, business associates it was true? Howerton said Camilla said it was too painful to speak of her deceased daughter. She moved her family to New York and pretended Elise never existed.

Lizzie protested her mother's complicity when Howerton first presented the story, saying, "Mommy would never do that. Never."

But I saw the doubt in her face. I watched it grow during the long hours after her discovery.

Howerton was arrested for assault and attempted murder. An investigation was opened into the practices of the former Hayden Clinic. Elaine Richards was in the hospital and her husband and attorneys were doing the talking for her now.

Dr. Blake Taylor, who was probably Lizzie and Elise's biological father, had also been brought in for questioning. My sources in the D.A.'s office said what Elaine told us was the truth—he had no idea his semen had been used for anything other than a study conducted by Dr. Hayden on sperm motility.

On Saturday morning, when Hunter, Evan, and I returned to Manhattan to help Lizzie begin the search for her sister, she was no longer composed. She confessed she thought everything Howerton said about her mother was true. She believed Camilla sent Elise away.

Lizzie experienced firsthand the long, slow death of her parents' marriage. She believed Howerton's charge that Camilla came to regret her decision about Elise and allowed that resentment to grow like a poison inside her.

"Mommy came to hate Daddy," Lizzie said. "I never knew why. In the end, when she lay dying, I believe she struck out at him in the only effective way she could—by taking away the money. He'd lost everything of his own so she knew what that would do to him."

"Why didn't your mother tell you the truth?" I asked Lizzie.

"I believe she was ashamed," Lizzie said. "I have to believe that."

As well she should have been I thought, understanding Lizzie's pain.

The good news was the O'Neills of Dublin had said Elise was well and happy. They loved her dearly, and wanted Lizzie to meet her. They knew Elise had a twin and had spoken to Camilla several times through the years.

Moira O'Neill, who was Elise's mother in every way that counted, helped Lizzie. "Don't judge your mother too harshly. Having special needs children isn't an easy path."

Lizzie, being who she was, chartered a plane. It was evening there now, and she had undoubtedly met her sister.

"I wish she would call," Evan complained, looking

uncharacteristically impatient.

I couldn't help but grin. I liked it when he lost some of his robotic perfection.

The computer signaled. I greeted her with a tentative, "How are you?"

"I'm wonderful," Lizzie said, her usual ebullience tripled. "I'm very happy to introduce you to my twin sister, Elise Brianna O'Neil."

The young woman beside Lizzie bore a strong resemblance though they weren't identical. An older woman stood behind them with a hand on their shoulders.

"This is Moira, her mother," Lizzie said. "She has something very special to show you."

There were some jerky movements as Lizzie adjusted the monitor. Moira held up a small framed photo of two little girls in white dresses standing on a huge stairway.

"Just as you remembered," I said. "You were right all along."

We all spoke with Lizzie. Her sister was quiet and tentative, but after all, we were strangers to her. I was pleased she kept smiling at Lizzie.

"Elise has a wonderful family," Lizzie said. "I'm going to stay and get to know all of them." Before we signed off, she said she looked forward to seeing us all when she returned to New York.

"It wouldn't surprise me if Lizzie ended up staying there for good." I pushed back from the computer. "All she has here is a father in-name-only who is going to prison and a biological father who was a sperm donor."

Hunter's cell rang. It was Mandy Morris. He walked away to answer, and I frowned. Now more than ever, I wanted Hunter to stay away from Mandy. He had enough trouble without continuing to flirt with disaster with a mob wife.

"Do you believe Lizzie will want a relationship with Dr. Taylor?" Evan said.

"It's hard to say. I'm not sure what I would do."

"If I were him, I'd want to know about her."

"Seriously?"

"Family's everything," he said. "Even an accidental family. It's your heritage. Your identity. Your fight for family."

"Hunter's not really your family. Yet you've killed for him."

Before Evan could reply, Hunter came back around the corner, frowning. "That was Mandy. She wants me to come over."

"Where's hubby?"

"On a business trip."

"Why don't you look happy?" I asked. "Hot woman. Husband out of town. That would normally be a perfect Sunday afternoon for you."

"She just sounded kind of weird," Hunter said. "Charlie doesn't travel much on weekends."

"I'll take you there." Evan pulled the keys out of his pocket.

It said something about how far Hunter had come in the past two weeks that he didn't protest.

"I'll come, too."

"Now that would be strange," Hunter protested. "I don't need both of you waiting outside for me to meet with my lady friend."

"Grow up." I took my coat from the back of my chair. "I think I know what you and Miss Mandy are up to when you meet while her old man is away. Evan and I will make sure there are no unwanted interruptions."

Hunter continued to protest, but Evan and I hustled him out the door. I pulled on gloves and a hat. Winter had turned fierce again. There'd been snow every day since Friday, and the forecast was for more of the white stuff tonight.

We headed toward the affluent side of Montclair and "the house that dirty clothes built" as Hunter liked to say about Mandy's elegant residence. Hunter asked Evan to park a block away. "I'm just going to check on her." He got out of the car.

"Yeah, right," I said. "We'll be here."

"Call if you need me," Evan added with a sly grin that surprised me.

Hunter stepped into the bushes that rimmed the road. He emerged a minute later as Tiger, the sleek gray Tabby who had visited Kelly. He streaked through the bushes behind the houses to Mandy's back door.

Evan alerted the MacRae guards who trailed us from the office.

He loves this. He would be comfortable in armor with a sword at his side on a white steed. He was content with the role of the gallant knight.

"Did you ever want to do something else?" I asked him.

"Did you?" he returned.

My laughter was rueful. "Let's face it. We've both been chosen. We have no control." For the first time since meeting him, I felt comfortable with Evan.

The snow began while we sat in the car, a flurry of tiny flakes blown sideways by the wind. The afternoon became like twilight.

"When did you learn being a protector was your destiny?" I asked.

Evan smiled. "It sounds a bit dramatic, but it was when I was sixteen."

"Sixteen is a big year in the supernatural world." I thought of Hunter's first change. "Did you have to pull Excalibur out of the stone or something?"

"Nothing so dramatic. My brother, Craig, and my father took me to the MacRae ancestral home in the Highlands of Scotland and told me the legend."

"What if you had chosen your own path? Maybe you'd be a rocket scientist or a CPA in Pittsburg?"

He peered toward Mandy's home through the snow. "It never occurred to me. I felt all along there was something waiting for me. When my father told me the legend, I thought, there it is.

"I began training in high school. I finished college while in the military and served two tours in Iraq and Afghanistan. Then I came home to apply my training to protecting The MacRae."

"So you went to a lot of special warrior schools."

"I did. I'm skilled in a number of weapons and martial arts. I've also had endurance training." He reached across the seat to gently take my fingers in his hand. "Trust me, little girl, you're safe with me."

I found I didn't want to pull my hand away even after he called me "little girl."

"You're happy doing this?" I was skeptical. "You're satisfied following Hunter around and watching for bad guys?"

"I'm satisfied I'm doing what I should be doing. Not many people can say that."

Panic danced on the edges of my psyche. I turned

to scan the road as an ache began in my temples. "I wish I knew more about my destiny where Hunter is concerned."

"You got the gift. You're the right person for the job you've been asked to do."

"Then how come I always know what's happening too late?"

He took my hand again and ran his thumb across the top of it. "Maybe you need some training, like I did. I have family in Scotland who have the true sight and had to work to develop their gift."

"Aren't you psychic? Can't you teach me?"

"Everyone in my family has some degree of sight, but mainly, I know how to read people. I can help, but not like someone who is truly gifted. There are others who could train you."

I was intrigued by the concept. Was there a University of ESP or a Psychic Camp somewhere?

"All you need is a little guidance."

"Right now I need ibuprofen," I said.

"What is it?"

"Sad," I mumbled, frowning as the world blurred. "So sad. Hunter's heart is breaking."

Evan took both my hands. "Focus, Zoe, concentrate on Hunter. What's happening?"

"He thinks it's his fault." My heart grew heavy with Hunter's grief.

"Why is Hunter sad? Concentrate!"

I pushed past the pain in my head and struggled to find the vision. I saw Hunter lying helpless on the floor. "He can't move."

Evan was yelling and I thought my head would burst.

"Mandy's dead. They cut her throat. He had to watch her die." I moaned. "He couldn't move. His body wouldn't move."

While barking into his cell for backup, Evan started the car and ripped a U-turn, heading toward Mandy's house. He screeched to a stop in the driveway. A roaring motor and squealing tires filled the air. Evan leaped out of the car and leaned across the hood to fire at a black SUV with his Sig Sauer. The SUV bounced across the smooth front yard and skidded onto the street. Evan's shot hit a hubcap, but the vehicle sped away.

Jumping back into the car, he yelled, "Get your seatbelt on!" and took off with the tires spinning. We quickly gained traction in the snow and were careening through the neighborhood.

Struggling not to black out, I gasped, "They've got Hunter. They're going to kill him."

Chapter 26

I struggled to buckle the seatbelt while Evan sped after the SUV. Forcing myself to concentrate, I brought the vision into focus. What I saw chilled me to the bone.

"Mandy bled to death," I said. "Hunter's wrapped in ropes and can't move."

I held on to the handle above the door. Evan guided the speeding car skillfully, but I was terrified of the horror that filled my mind. Evan brought me back to reality. "Get the iPad out of the backseat, we have service anywhere. I've got a program connected to Hunter's cell phone. All you need to do is click on the icon to activate it. We can locate him with that." He swerved around the car in front of him.

I undid my seatbelt and got the computer case from the backseat before strapping back in. Evan drove with great precision, kept the speed high and steady as he moved through the residential streets. The wipers fought with pelting snow that was now whitening the landscape. It was dark as night outside.

Evan punched a speed-dial number on his cell and waited, then began to speak in Gaelic. I recognized the language Hunter had often used with his grandmother.

The iPad responded as Evan clicked off his call. "Which is the tracking program?" I asked him.

He pointed to an icon. In seconds, I was watching

the progress of Hunter's cell phone moving through the road ahead of us as a blinking dot. We held back a bit but kept up.

I fought against the pain in my head as I yelled turns to Evan. My headache was agony. How could I possibly help Hunter if I couldn't function? I had to concentrate on the dot on the computer screen. We were following a circuitous route of side streets.

Evan spoke in English on his cell now, but it sounded like a shorthand code.

The blinking dot veered onto another side street. Recognizing the landscape around us, I knew where we were going. "They're headed to Totowa. It's near Wayne in an area filled with warehouses and manufacturing plants." I gasped. "The dot has disappeared."

"They found his cell phone." Evan slammed his palm against the steering wheel. "I tried to get him to let me put wireless devices in his clothing but he refused. Shit! Now we'll have to look building by building."

He grabbed the phone again. "Get to that area as quickly as possible and look for a black Escalade. That's the best I can tell you. Right. Call me with anything."

Evan drove slowly, his eyes fierce with determination. He would rescue Hunter. Still, there were a group of men like Evan in the mountains with Fraser MacRae, and he was dead.

Evan turned as if he'd read my thoughts. "Have faith in me, Zoe. I will get to Hunter. I need you to believe that."

Warmth rushed into my chilled bones as he held

my gaze, and I did believe him. He looked unstoppable. "I trust you." I glanced back at the road. "You'll need to turn right just ahead. That will take us to the warehouses."

The snow was thicker and the wipers had ice on them. We moved through the field of manufacturing facilities as Evan's phone rang.

"Any luck?"

No car yet. I could tell by Evan's dour face. He took my hand again and held it loosely in his. "Do me a favor."

"Sure."

"Close your eyes, relax and listen to what I say. Focus on my voice."

I leaned against the headrest, closing my eyes.

"Relax."

I didn't realize I was clutching the seatbelt like a lifeline. "Bring Hunter's face to your mind. He trusts you. He believes in you. Slowly back up. We know he's restrained and unable to move. Where is he?"

As he spoke, my world became Hunter. I almost spoke when I saw him. His face was contorted with pain. There were little tremors throughout his body. His thoughts were a jumble.

"I think they've drugged him." I forced all my energies on describing the scene. "He's tied to a pole, like a support beam. Lots of rope wrapped around his body and the pole. They've got his head duct-taped to the pole." I jumped. "There's a young boy taunting him, spitting at him. He's very young but he looks absolutely vicious."

"Is the boy dark haired and blue eyed?"

I nodded as the boy kicked Hunter.

"I think he wants to kill Hunter."

"I'm sure he does. That's Michael Killin's youngest son, Garth. No doubt he's pumped with hatred and rage to keep the family's quest going."

I winced as Hunter jerked from the pummeling by the boy.

Evan kept stroking the tops of my fingers with his thumb. "Slowly back away from Hunter. I know it's hard, but we need to find where he is."

Hunter groaned as the boy kicked him in the groin. I raised my eyes to the area above Hunter and saw a huge ceiling lined with ducts and machinery.

"It must be a manufacturing plant." Anxiety made my voice rise and my body tense.

"We're on the right track. Don't worry. Describe what you're seeing."

Hunter pressed against the big pole, anger was slowly replacing pain. As his thoughts cleared, I saw more of his surroundings.

Fluorescent lights hung from a tall, open ceiling. Two men watched the scene with Hunter and the boy. They both held guns.

"Two men guarding with rifles."

"That's good. Keep looking."

"Another putting things from a black case on a table."

Though Evan's touch on my hand never wavered, I sensed his fear. "No problems, Zoe. Just keep telling me what you see. You're doing great."

I squeezed my eyes shut to lock onto Hunter as my vision moved outside the building. I was flying above the industrial park and I could see our vehicle below.

"Stop! He's over there." I pointed to a dark hulk of

a building not too far away.

The walls were solid concrete. No light showed through windows. A row of empty cargo bays faced us. There was no way to discern any activity inside, but I knew Hunter was there. "Cut the lights."

He did and was immediately back on his cell, giving coordinates for others to meet us. I felt like I'd awoken from a deep sleep. I got out of the car while Evan removed extra ammunition and body armor. I wasn't surprised when two men in full cammo gear walked out of the darkness.

"There's a single door on the back side in the middle of the cargo bays," the taller man said, his accent Scottish. "That should be our point of entry."

"Zoe, meet Paul and David. They're going to help us get Hunter. You can trust them like you can trust me."

Evan reached inside the SUV again and pulled out a savage-looking crossbow. He checked it, slung a tube of arrows over his shoulder, and shut the door.

Seeing my face, he said, "Arrows make less noise and do more damage."

Paul and David had their own bows in hand, and rifles slung over their shoulders.

The snow was thicker, providing a buffer for our footsteps as we moved across the parking lot into the cargo bay and up concrete steps to a door. David worked on the lock for what seemed a long time, then he and Paul entered the building. They came back shortly.

Paul signaled to go left so David went right, meaning Evan headed in at the center of the building through the machinery. He signaled for me to go between the machines to the left.

The machinery was covered with grime and dust, and the floor was filthy. In the dim light Black grease was all around the green machines. Motor oil and the lingering stench of something I couldn't identify filled the air.

I stayed close to the equipment so I could scurry into an opening if someone came. The light increased inside the building. I slowed my pace. All it would take for discovery was one unexpected noise. I squatted beside a conveyor belt.

My adrenalin kicked in when I saw one of the guards. I took measured breaths to calm down. We were in the right place. Hunter was nearby.

The guy with the gun leaned against a metal desk and stared across the room. I hoped he was looking at Hunter.

I needed to get out of the shadows. My goal was to free Hunter.

Using another huge machine as a shield, I went to my right and saw the pole where Hunter was bound.

I glimpsed Evan to the side. With a motion filled with grace and speed, he loaded his bow and fired. I jumped at the thump and watched the guy at the desk fall forward. There was a shout and a scuffle of feet. Seeing no obvious threat, I headed for the area near Hunter.

A shot was fired to my left, but I didn't stop. I came up against huge stacks of bales of soft white material. Moving slowly, with my gun in front of me, I leaned around the edge of a bale in front of Hunter.

He looked unconscious, his head down, his body completely still. To my left, Evan and his men had overpowered the other guards and were disarming them. One of them opened his mouth to shout and got a pistol to the side of his head. That meant there were others nearby. I hurried, crouching, to Hunter.

He opened his eyes and managed a weak grin. The heavy, thick rope was wrapped many times around his body, all the way to his knees.

"Anybody got a knife?" I muttered.

Paul pulled a hunting knife out of his pack and slid it across the floor. He and David were putting plastic ties on the wrists and ankles of their captives. The third guard lay in front the desk, his blood pooling.

"Are you okay?" I asked Hunter.

"My body feels like it's been slammed with a truck. They drugged me. I can't shift. My hands and feet are tingling, but that's probably because the rope is so tight."

"We're going to fix that." I sawed through the rope around his feet.

The knife was extremely sharp, but it was slow going. My hands shook from the effort. I freed his knees and was moving to his waist when a yell came out of the darkness. Something slammed me onto the concrete, and the knife skidded across the floor.

Before I could get my breath and turn over, blows rained down on my back. I struggled to breathe but couldn't get in any air. I pushed with all my strength to get to my knees and shake off my attacker.

In the next instant he was gone, and I was gasping for breath. I turned to find Evan holding a wriggling boy—Killin's son. "Let me go," he said through gritted teeth. "My father will kill you if you hurt me."

Evan clamped his arms tightly around the boy until

he was still. "I'm not going to hurt you, but I'm not going to let you hurt Zoe either."

I was still prone but pulling in huge gasps of air.

Paul and David were fighting with more guards.

"Zoe, get the knife!" Hunter yelled.

I stumbled to my feet and finally found the knife in a pile of dust and grime. I rushed back to Hunter.

I don't know what Evan did, but the boy was out cold. Evan restrained him and was helping Paul and David take the other men.

I worked on the rope again. The knife was cutting the rope, but I was tired. I thought I would pass out at any moment.

"Slow down." Evan brushed debris from my hair and put palm against my cheek. "Relax. Take slow, even breaths. You're okay now. All you need to do is breathe normally."

I didn't realize Evan was there until he touched my face. He took the knife from me.

We both jerked as a roar echoed through the building. It was like no sound I'd ever heard before. I thought of all the people I'd seen through the years, numb with shock as they said, "It sounded like a train was coming through our house," to describe a tornado.

Still, that was exactly what it sounded like—a huge train barreling through the building.

But it wasn't a train, it was a man…and it wasn't a man. He stood beside the desk where the boy lay and changed.

I had seen Hunter shift, and it was a fascinating, exciting experience. This change was extraordinary.

Evan said Killin could shift in the twinkling of an eye. He didn't exaggerate.

When his metamorphosis was complete, Killin raised arms that were now huge lion's paws with every claw extended. The shaggy mane covered his upper body. His face was pure enraged lion. Killin's clothes were in shreds. His thighs were twice their normal size, though his legs and ankles had remained human. He leaned into a pouncing stance, his body aimed at Hunter as he bared teeth that were long, yellow, and sharp. All this happened in seconds. No one moved.

I wanted to run, but I was mesmerized by the sight of him.

Evan frantically sawed at the rope. Hunter was moving, struggling to free his arms. I could tell from his red face and his heightened breathing he was beginning his own change. He sprang free of the ropes and let out a feral roar as he became a Bengal tiger.

Evan dragged me away from the open area where Hunter and Killin faced each other. Paul and David were standing with their bows ready, but they made no move to help Hunter.

I struggled to get free. "Why aren't they shooting?"

"There's nothing we can do," Evan said.

"You can shoot Killin. I can."

I wrenched away, grabbing for my gun, but Evan was too fast and strong. He took my gun away and held me back. "This is to avenge Fraser. We can only watch."

I muttered, "Stupid machismo," and struggled against arms like bands of steel.

Lions and tigers are seldom in the same territory. So it's almost geographically impossible for them to fight.

What would happen here? The two beasts faced off

like heavyweight champions. How much of their human tendencies remained when they were using their second nature. Did they think like humans or cats?

Killin was sure of himself, waiting. Hunter fidgeted, moving from side to side with teeth bared, his growl rumbling low in his chest. Killin pounced first, and the two big cats grabbed each other around their necks. They hung on, claws digging, as they rolled around the floor. Then, as quickly as they had moved together, they separated and growled. Blood splattered the floor, and I groaned. Hunter was going to die and I had to watch.

What could I do to stop two wild animals determined to kill each other?

They circled one another. Crimson ran in streaks as their claws slashed and they pounced again and again. Cats were known for prolonging the kill. This went on for several minutes.

Hunter walked away and Killin buried his claws into Hunter's flank. Hunter howled and used all his strength to shake the other cat loose.

Rising up on his back feet, Hunter roared and lunged, his entire body slamming Killin back. While Killin was sprawled, Hunter bit into his groin.

Killin pushed and howled. Hunter didn't let go. Killin's human legs failed him. For the first time, I thought Hunter might survive.

Another half-human flashed into view behind Hunter. I screamed a warning, but the new chimera latched onto Hunter's back. I expected Killin to move in for an immediate kill, but instead, he abruptly turned and raced toward the door.

I turned back to the fight in time to see Hunter

pounce and throw the chimera to the floor. He clamped his teeth onto the cat's neck. Blood gushed. There was another howl. And then silence.

The chimera was dead.

Hunter dropped the body, stepped up on it, and gave a roar that ricocheted off the walls like sonic boom.

While I stood horrified, he pulled the carcass around, as if displaying a magnificent prize. Traditionally it's believed the lion is the victor most often in these battles. Not today.

I slumped to the floor. This animal was my best friend and I had just watched him fight to the death. There was nothing remotely human about him.

How did we arrive at this special place in hell? I wondered.

And where did we go from here?

Chapter 27

The blood tasted sweet.

That was all Hunter could think as he roared his triumph toward Zoe and Evan. His heart pounded in his chest, and the exhilaration of victory flowed through him like a raging river. In all the years since he had learned what he was, he had never gotten used to killing. He had enjoyed hunting other animals and had killed by instinct, but he had never felt this sort of thrill.

He had won.

So why wouldn't Zoe look at him?

Slowly, he backed off from his kill. Weariness seeped around the edges of his excitement. The wounds on his flanks and the bruises on his ribs pulsed.

With a low growl, he rested on his haunches. The sound brought Zoe's head up. Hunter smelled her hesitation, her fear. The emotion startled him. In all these years, he had never frightened Zoe.

He had to change now. He had never been so reluctant to become human again. But he had to become a man again—for Zoe.

Through a veil of pain, he focused his gaze on her. Finally, she looked him in the eye. And he crossed over. A roar tore from his throat as his limbs melded into his first nature. He slumped to the floor, and the blood in his mouth turned bitter. His voice weakened to a moan. He could barely lift his head, but he forced himself to do so, to look once again at Zoe.

Biting back a cry, she pulled away from Evan and ran to Hunter's side. She dropped to the dirty, bloody floor and cradled his head in her lap. He could still sense her wariness, but above all, he felt her familiar, loving touch on his torn and throbbing flesh.

"Oh, my God, Hunter. Oh my God," she murmured.

An odd sense of disappointment swept over him. Didn't she realize he had won?

After that, the pain almost knocked him out. Aside from his wounds, he was hungry. Starving. Vaguely, he heard Evan snapping orders. There were shouts and a sense of movement. The world turned black, and then became a swirling vision of white as he was carried into the night. Hunter was mostly aware of Zoe's soothing voice and the empty, aching void in his gut.

Maybe he passed out. He didn't know where he was when hands pushed meat at him. He ate like a man who had never seen food before. He gulped water. Then he ate again.

Gradually, the agony melted away. The gashes on his flanks stung as they began to tighten and heal. The pain that had knifed through his midsection ebbed.

Wrapped in a blanket, he was able to able to hold himself upright as Evan and another man hustled him unnoticed from a car to the freight elevator in the parking garage of his apartment.

Zoe was beside him as he was lowered to a bed. His bed. She brought warm, damp cloths to wash the worst of the blood and gore away. He slept.

But in the deepest part of the night, Hunter awakened and knew Zoe wasn't there. She had left his side. Most importantly, she was absent from his mind in a way that he could never remember before. She had not been so far from him since before that day back in middle school when they had outsmarted the bullies and had become partners. Even when he was taken away to the mountains to change for the first time, she had not felt so lost to him as she did now.

He winced, raising a hand to his throbbing forehead. "But I won," he muttered.

A now familiar voice answered him. "You have to give her time." Evan stepped up to his bedside and snapped on a lamp.

Hunter blinked in the sudden light. He didn't bother to pretend that Evan hadn't read his mind.

"Time for what?"

"You killed a man in front of her," Evan said.

The truth of the matter rushed in. The memories were fresh. Hunter could feel how his teeth had cut through flesh. He smelled the stink of the chimera's blood on his body. He sat up, and the room spun for a moment. But he couldn't stop the surge of satisfaction that pushed aside his momentary horror at what he had done just hours ago.

He looked at Evan. "I killed a monster."

"But some will say you are the same," Evan replied. "What is your path? That's the question your kind has always had to answer, each in his own time."

"My grandfather was not a monster."

"Aye." Evan nodded. "But what will you be, Hunter MacRae? Especially if you have to do it without her?"

Do without Zoe? The question shocked Hunter into silence.

Chapter 28

I rolled over again and flipped my pillow to the cool side for probably the fiftieth time. I couldn't sleep because every time I closed my eyes the scene of Hunter laying the bloody body in front of me came to mind. That was followed closely by the thought of Mandy's gaping throat as she fell over like a rag doll in a careless heap. Blood, every time I closed my eyes all I saw was blood. I was afraid I might never sleep again.

The clock said it was three in the morning, five minutes later than the last time I'd looked at it. I got out of bed and padded through the silent apartment to the living room. I wore one of Hunter's T-shirts and a pair of huge sweat pants tied at the waist. I still felt chilled and grabbed a throw off the couch to wrap around my shoulders.

The blinds had been left open. The magnificent lights of the Manhattan skyline lit the room. Another time I might have enjoyed it. Tonight it did nothing to ease my misery. There were no "normal" days anymore. I had been constantly tense and afraid ever since the night we had found the body behind the office.

Rubbing my face, I heaved a great sigh. I looked at the familiar surroundings and wondered how everything could be the same and still be different. I went to the kitchen and gazed in the refrigerator for a few seconds but found nothing to rouse my interest. In the cabinet, I discovered Hunter's stash of Nutter Butter cookies, a weakness we both shared. Pouring myself a glass of milk, I took the cookies to the living room and sat in Hunter's chair, staring out at the night.

But my misery wasn't going anywhere. I was at a crossroads. I needed to decide which way to go but I'd left my directions at home. Depression settled back on my shoulders and the cookie lost its flavor.

I slipped to floor and took the lotus position in front of the floor-to-ceiling windows. The rug was soft against my feet. Probably worth as much as my house, I thought as I worked my muscles to hold my pose. I had never really been very good at yoga. So I relaxed and sat, Indian style, thinking.

Hunter was an animal, capable of horrific acts I couldn't fathom. I had always known that. But from now on, violence could be a part of his life at any time. Killing his enemy was his ultimate goal. Could I share that?

As hard as I tried, however, I couldn't picture the rest of my life without Hunter.

"Something wrong, Zoe?"

Evan didn't startle me. I realized I'd been waiting for him. He stretched, his back popping loudly, and then joined me on the floor, one knee bumping against mine. For a second I considered just leaning over to lay my head on his shoulder.

"Trouble sleeping?"

"Every time I close my eyes I see Hunter placing his prize in front of me."

Evan looked at me with searching eyes. "You've known what he is for many years."

As usual, I bristled at his echo of my own thoughts. "I've never had a corpse given to me before. Pardon me if I'm not following the proper shifter etiquette for a death fight," I said angrily. "What should I have done? An end-zone victory dance? He killed a man, for God's sake."

Evan's tone was irritatingly reasonable. "That beast that would have killed him without hesitation, and then started in on you. Hunter fought to save his life, as well as yours."

"I know that." I stood and stomped to the sofa, where I sat. "That doesn't mean I have to like to it."

"But you have to accept it." He stayed where he was but turned to face me.

I gnawed on my bottom lip for a moment. "What if I can't?"

"That's something you'll have to decide for yourself." Evan got to his feet. "And the sooner the better. Change is the only sure thing in life, and you're headed for some big changes. You'll either accept that or choose to stay where you are—without Hunter."

"Who are you to tell me how I need to live my life?" I barked. "Until a couple of weeks ago neither of us had ever heard of you. Now you're running Hunter's life and trying to run mine."

"You asked me to help you with your gift. I'm trying to help you accept your fate."

It irked me that he could goad me without even raising his voice. He got up, came over and held out a hand. "Come on, you'll think more clearly if you get some rest."

Well, isn't he Mr. Wonderful?

"I can't sleep," I said with a childish whine I

instantly regretted.

"I think you'll do better now." He took hold of my hands and pulled me to my feet. "You're more tired than you realize."

He touched my cheek and a wave of warmth moved through me. I didn't protest as he led me back to the bed. I lay down and he pulled the covers up. He rested his hand on my head and I smiled as I closed my eyes.

When I opened them again the sun was bright outside and I could hear the murmur of voices in the other room. I stretched and realized I felt rested. Glancing at the clock I knew why. It was almost two o'clock.

I had to face Hunter. And the rest of our lives.

After washing my face and brushing my teeth, I walked into the living room to find him and Evan poring over something spread out on the coffee table. The TV was on, with News 12 New Jersey mumbling in the background.

I eyed Hunter warily. In a worn pair of sweats and an ancient T-shirt that stretched tight across his shoulders, he looked remarkably well. No visible sign of last night's battle. Evan was in a crisply pressed shirt and jeans, also looking almost supernaturally well.

"Good afternoon," I said. They nodded, openly cautious. Like I was the one who was dangerous.

I went looking for coffee. The inky liquid smelled like it had been there for a while, so I fixed a fresh pot. I poured a mug. I went back to the living room.

A news crawler moved across the bottom of the giant TV screen. It said Mandy Morris, wife of prominent New Jersey citizen Charlie Morris, had been murdered in what was being described as a home invasion.

I turned to Hunter, who said, "Evan's men took care of making Mandy's death seem random."

"Random?" I repeated. "Are you okay with that?"

"What do you suggest we do? Tell them about Chymera? About me?"

"No, but…" I didn't know what I wanted.

"We have to move on, Zoe," Evan said.

Move on to what?

The moment became awkward. I didn't know what to say. Evan was calm, and Hunter was acting as if the savage actions of yesterday were removed from today's reality.

In an obvious attempt to change the subject, Hunter turned what appeared to be blueprints on the table to face me. "These are plans for the empty building in Riverdale that I showed you."

I barely glanced at the drawings.

"What do you think?" he asked, his eyes glowing with excitement. They were so green they actually sparkled.

"I think you've decided what you want. What does it matter what I think?"

Both men looked at me with questions in their eyes but said nothing. They seemed wary, as if they didn't know what I was going to do next.

Welcome to the club, I'm not sure myself.

"So all of this is decided and you're ready to go?" I asked.

"These plans were delivered this morning. The building is already mine, so there's no hold up there."

I took a sip of coffee and burned the tip of my

tongue, which didn't help my temper. "I didn't know you were this far along with this. It was just last week that you told me about the building."

"I thought we could talk—"

"What we need to talk about is your old family feud. You grandfather, Shamus, the guard from North Carolina—they're all dead because of this. Cyn's out there somewhere running to keep these monsters from her son. And Mandy, who was completely innocent, had her throat brutally slit. They made her call you, Hunter. She got you over there, and they still killed her. All she was guilty of was jumping in the sack with you. Is she just collateral damage that you just move past?"

"That was cruel, Zoe," Evan said. "You of all people know how upset Hunter was about Mandy's death."

"Yeah, but he seems to be doing fine today."

"I never thought she was in danger," Hunter protested. "These are ruthless animals that kill without thought."

"From what I saw last night, so do you," I blurted.

The light dimmed in Hunter's eyes.

"That was low," Evan said. "Think about what you're saying, Zoe."

"I thought about it all night. This isn't my fight." I looked back at Hunter, trying to make him understand. "I never thought I'd be involved in anything like this."

"Then why do you carry a gun?" Evan asked calmly.

Surprise made me jerk my head around. I couldn't think of a proper snarky remark. He was right, of course. You only carry a gun when you want to be prepared for unforeseen threats and danger. I leaned my head back and sighed. God, what am I doing?

Hunter rubbed his forehead as if he had a headache and then gestured toward the couch. "Sit down a minute and talk about this," he said.

I looked at him, feeling helpless, something I hated. I covered my face with my hands. Releasing another big sigh, I looked directly at Hunter and decided honesty was the best response. "I don't know if I can be part of this. What happened last night changed everything."

Hunter's eyes darkened with emotion as his gaze held mine. "I defeated my enemy."

"Evan could have shot him. I could have shot him. You didn't have to fight him like that—"

"So it was the fighting, rather than the killing that bothered you?" Hunter challenged. "You were much more cold-blooded when it was Lizzie holding a gun to her father's head the other day."

"It's not the same—"

"Isn't it?" Evan asked. "You allowed her to fight for the truth. Why shouldn't Hunter be allowed the same?"

"But that wasn't the truth. It was barbaric, it was—"

"Part of who I am," Hunter replied. "I know last night was terrible for you, but from the very first time I showed you who I was, you accepted me. Why not this?"

"I don't understand it. Explain to me what happened. Why did you have to fight him?"

"It was The MacRae against Chymera," Evan replied. "That's how it is."

I groaned. "But why did Killin run away?"

"Because he was beaten. I won. A substitute stepped in and sacrificed himself so Killin can fight on. He isn't ready to cede his legacy to a new generation."

"Speaking of which," I said. "What happened to Killin's son? The last I saw of him, he was passed out cold and tied up."

"We left him for the chimera to rescue," Evan explained. "I expect he was back in his grandmother's loving arms soon after we cleared out of the warehouse."

I looked back at Hunter. "You'll probably fight him one day, won't you?"

"If the bloody little bastard comes after me and what's mine, I will kill him."

I looked from Evan to Hunter, stunned by their blind acceptance of these uncivilized traditions. I made choices about life, between right and wrong, good and evil. Now the lines were blurry. It was the same reason I had hated chasing cheating wives and husbands and dealing with broken families and helping insurance companies decide not to pay disability claims. I liked clean cuts and reasonable explanations. None of that was very likely if I fell in step with Hunter as he was now. Hell, I didn't even know the rules of the supernatural world, and he was proposing we plunge into it headfirst.

Evan spoke up again. "What is it you want, Zoe?"

"I don't know that I can just go along with all this."

"What about the vision of my grandfather telling you to be my first defense?" Hunter said.

"The connection you established with Hunter last night," Evan added. "You found him."

"You saw through my eyes," Hunter said. "I could

feel that. I knew you were coming."

I made a sound of frustration. "It didn't feel like I did much more than watch you be tortured by that horrible little boy."

"Do you think what I do just came to me one day?" Evan's normally even voice held an edge of anger. "I had to learn everything I could from centuries of my family's history. Nobody feels called to a destiny like this and immediately knows how to fulfill it. You've got to work at it, Zoe. I told you I would help you. We'll get you more help."

I wanted to be out there in front of Hunter, looking better than Wonder Woman in my cape, tights, and sexy super-hero outfit, telling him how to avoid the big bad Lion of Wall Street. A big, bad lion that wanted Hunter's blood in his throat. More than anything, I didn't want to feel useless and frightened. I had felt that way years ago, when my mother was killed and my father wouldn't talk about it. I knew I had been searching for control ever since that awful day. I wanted the safe, the predictable.

So what was I doing with a shapeshifter?

Hunter took my hand in his. "You left me last night. It was awful. I couldn't figure out what I'd done wrong, why you'd run away. What happened?"

I stood, unable to contain my anger any longer. "What happened? What happened? You killed a man and laid him at my feet, but you were prancing around and licking your paws like a fucking house cat that just killed a mouse!"

Hunter was quiet, his expression wounded.

I tried to explain. "You weren't my Hunter. You were a killer, someone I'd never met."

Hunter's pain at my comment was obvious. His mouth opened but he couldn't find the words. He walked to the window, his head bowed.

Evan stood now, drawing my attention. "This is who he is." His gaze was level and darkly serious. "Make your choice. Don't drag it out so he suffers. If you can't handle it, just say so now."

My resentment toward this man bubbled over. "Who are you to be telling me what I have to do?"

"This is part of me, too," he replied with that damned certainty that made me want to claw at him.

"But—" I sputtered.

"There's no buts, no what ifs, and only one choice—yes or no," Evan said.

I whirled toward Hunter, but he still had his back to me, his hands on his hips.

What did he expect me to do? For Hunter, decisions are impulsive and immediate. If he bought a new car, he went to the car lot, haggled a little, and drove it home within a few hours. When I bought a new car, I did Internet research, checked all the facts and figures, and went to at least three dealers before making a decision.

What more could I speculate about? The facts were right in front of me. Hunter was a shapeshifter, a man with two distinct bodies. But he had one heart and what I knew to be a good soul. He was my family in every way that counted.

Buck up, Zoe, you're a strong woman and you can do this.

I walked to Hunter. "Last night shook me to my core," I said to his back. "I've never seen anything like that." He turned to face me, and I put my hands on his cheeks. "Much as I hate to admit it, Evan is right. I know who you are and I know what you have to do."

He leaned forward until his forehead touched mine. "You know I couldn't make it without you," he whispered fiercely. "Thank you for not making me choose."

"So you're in?" Evan asked.

Still not sure why I needed to answer to him, I glared his way, then turned back to Hunter. "I'm in. But I can't promise that I'm going to like everything about you being The MacRae."

"Understood."

"I'm not living in that factory building with the two of you."

A look passed between the men that I didn't care for at all. A smug, male, we'll-handle-her-later look. Suddenly I wished Darla were here to stir a little more estrogen into this mix.

"I even have a name for our new firm," Hunter said. "We'll call it 'Seekers'."

"Because we find answers," I murmured.

"Among other things," Hunter said.

We talked for hours, poring over the blueprints and discussing options for the new business. I still wasn't happy about Evan being a full partner, but this was apparently a long, family tradition. How could my fourteen years with Hunter stack up against centuries?

Evan wasn't going anywhere.

Neither was I.

So here we were—a shapeshifter, a dysfunctional psychic, and a man descended from an ancient line of warriors. What could possibly go wrong?

A word about the author...

Neely Powell is the pseudonym for co-writers and friends Leigh Neely and Jan Hamilton Powell.

Writing as Celeste Hamilton, Jan published 24 romance novels before leaving fiction for corporate communications. Leigh became a successful nonfiction writer and editor, though she was still interested in fiction.

Something clicked when Leigh focused her talents on the paranormal. Her short story "A Vampire in Brooklyn" was published in the anthology, *Murder New York Style: Fresh Slices*, in 2011.

Around that time, the friends started a novel together. The result was *True Nature*, and Neely Powell is contracted for several more novels about shifters, witches, weres, faeries and ghosts, mixing in shades of romance, mystery and thrillers.

Find Neely Powell online at:

http://www.neelypowell.com

Thank you for purchasing
this publication of The Wild Rose Press, Inc.
For other wonderful stories of romance,
please visit our on-line bookstore at
www.thewildrosepress.com.

For questions or more information
contact us at
info@thewildrosepress.com.

The Wild Rose Press, Inc.
www.thewildrosepress.com

To visit with authors of
The Wild Rose Press, Inc.
join our yahoo loop at
http://groups.yahoo.com/group/thewildrosepress/